Also by Anthony McGowan

Stag Hunt

ANTHONY McGOWAN

Mortal Coil

HODDER &
STOUGHTON

Copyright © 2005 by Anthony McGowan

First published in Great Britain in 2005 by Hodder and Stoughton
A division of Hodder Headline

The right of Anthony McGowan to be identified as the Author of the Work has been
asserted by him in accordance with the Copyright, Designs and Patents Act 1988.

A Hodder and Stoughton Book

I

A CIP catalogue record for this title is
available from the British Library

Hardback ISBN 0 340 83047 6
Trade Paperback ISBN 0 340 83048 4

Typeset in Plantin Light by Palimpsest Book Production Limited
Polmont, Stirlingshire

Printed and bound by
Clays Ltd, St Ives plc

Hodder Headline's policy is to use papers that are natural, renewable and
recyclable products and made from wood grown in sustainable forests.
The logging and manufacturing processes are expected to conform to the
environmental regulations of the country of origin.

Hodder and Stoughton Ltd
A division of Hodder Headline
338 Euston Road
London NW1 3BH

This book is dedicated to all my old friends at Corpus Christi High School in Leeds, and especially, John, Phil, Johnny, John, Ian, Patrick, Neil, Benny, Peter, and Chris. And also to one of the teachers, Margaret Freeman, an inspiration and a delight.

Lully lullay, lully lullay,
The faucon hath born my lover away.

'The Corpus Christi Carol'

PART ONE

The Melancholy Doorman

I

Power's Bar

As soon as I stepped in out of the rain I knew that someone was looking at me. He must have seen me through the window shrugging off water. I suppose I'd taken in the dark, feral eyes subliminally, without fixing on a bearing, and I felt the tension thrum across my back like the hard rain I'd walked through.

I'd arranged to meet Jonah Whale in Power's Bar, the least scary pub in Kilburn. That's not to say you won't find yourself talking to a man with ragged stumps instead of fingers, who throws his arm around your shoulders while he murmurs a scheme into your ear that will make both of you rich if only you can stake him fifty, no, OK, *ten* pounds, his bristles and his breath on you like a plague. And if the man without fingers isn't there, then of course you might meet Jonah Whale himself, six foot four of philosophical psychopath, the outline of his trademark hammer as clear against the sharp jacket of his suit as a vacuum-packed chicken leg. Catch his eye and he'll prowl over, an Easter Island monolith on the move, and ask you: 'Are yez familiar with the works of Friedrich Nietzsche?' in a voice deep and resonating enough to be heard back in the Gorbals.

But Knuckles and Nietzsche aren't typical of Power's Bar. You're more likely to meet students, wide eyed, or easy; couples passing an hour before a film; office workers caught by the blue light on the way back from the Tube station; middle-aged men in jeans, fooling themselves into thinking that working on the coding for an oil company website or subbing the unread text in a fashion magazine makes them creative. And sometimes those were the people that you wanted.

I looked around, partly to see whether Jonah was here yet, partly to find the source of my unease. Jonah wasn't there, and nor could I see anyone staring at me. I smiled at my own paranoia and put my hand in my trouser pocket to scoop out change for a pint.

That's when he made his move. I saw a blur as he came towards me, crouched like a sprinter coming out of the blocks.

I didn't go to pubs to fight. I went to pubs to sit quietly, to talk, to mull over old times. But that didn't mean that I didn't know what to do when some drunk comes flying at you with a glass or an ashtray or just the slabs of bone and meat at the ends of his arms. And what you do is to throw a feint. Forget subtlety. Forget the beautiful things that a body can do when it moves. A simple lurch one way, and then a step back. They'll still catch you. An arm will flail out and scuff you round the ear, but the fucker won't put you down. And he'll be off balance, his centre of gravity a thing he can't get his head around. That's when you drive him down, and then you take your opportunity, and you only get one, to nail the fucker, and to let his friends know that there's no point sticking with their pal, loser that he is.

That was the theory, and with both hands free I might have been able to put it into practice; but with one in my pocket I didn't have a chance. He took me from the side, low, and we went over together. My shoulder hit the ground hard, and my head bounced off the tiles. He rolled me over and got his knees on to my chest. He was light and, dazed as I was, I nearly managed to twist him off, but he took hold of my ears and clung on tenaciously. He shook my head, screaming, and spittle hit my face.

Screaming – screaming what?

'Fucker! *Fucker!*' he yelled as we writhed together. His breath smelt bitter, like dark chocolate. He banged the back of my head on the floor again, but almost gently, as if he wanted to keep me conscious. '*Sting*,' he screamed, with each bang. '*Sting, Sting, Sting!*'

I tried to talk, to ask him what he was saying, what it meant, and then, looking into his eyes, seeing for the first time that narrow face, the spiky yellow hair, I knew that I was doomed, and I ceased to speak, ceased to struggle.

'It's fucking Sting, isn't it? I can tell by looking at you. I knew it would be. I knew it was in you.'

He stopped banging my head, and let go of my ears, and then he kissed me on the lips, through my smile.

'He's not so bad,' I said, finally. 'I don't mind that one with the Moroccan guy. The yodelling.'

'Yeah,' said Jude Lovell Malcolm Flaherty, known as Ju when I'd last seen him seventeen years before, on the day he'd finally been expelled from school. His face now, as it did then, carried a Billy Idol sneer. 'And it's OK to send your kids to private school and read the fucking *Telegraph*.'

Before I had the chance to answer a shadow loomed over the two of us, and Ju was lifted from me like a kitten, by the scruff of his neck.

'It's OK, Jonah,' I said, before something grievous happened to Ju. 'He's a friend of mine.'

'Friend, you say?' Jonah held him up, looked for a second

into the startled face, and then set him softly down on his feet. He shook his head and began walking slowly over to his habitual corner, lost in the gloom. Then he stopped, turned, and said to me: 'I'll need to be talking to you, and soon.'

'Jesus,' said Ju, 'I didn't realise you came with your own personal fucking bodyguard. What are you, a dealer or a pimp?'

When I'd known Ju, his hair had taken many forms, but the default setting was a random bristling of blond spikes. He now had a more cultivated version of that, and he dabbed at it to make sure it still conformed to whatever master plan he had in mind for it.

'It's good to see you, Ju,' I said, and I meant it.

The smile had stayed on my face ever since I'd realised it was him. I'd heard years before that he was doing well, that he had a job as a session musician in Manchester, although as it all came through his mother and my mother, Christ only knew what the reality was.

'What brings you down here?' I asked, smiling, stammering, trying to get some normality back into things. My hand was on his shoulder.

For a moment I thought I must have said the wrong thing. His face hardened, the line of his jaw materialising like ice in freezing water. And it came to me what it was. Why, said the hard line of his jaw, why shouldn't *I* be in London? Are you saying I don't belong here, that I couldn't make it in the city? But that face was gone before it had settled, before the ice had become the only truth.

'Lived here for years, old love,' he said.

I grinned at the endearment, surely deliberately chosen to take us back. In our part of Leeds, by some quirk of microlinguistics, men used the term in place of 'pal' or 'mate'. Sometimes it would be part of the subtle escalation in courtesy that let you know that something violent was about to happen, but usually it was nothing but friendly air.

'Jesus, me too. Funny I haven't run into you before.'

'Well, I don't hang out much in Kilburn. I use it more as a way to scare the shit out of the execs.'

'Execs?'

'Yeah.' Ju gestured back and over his shoulder. Two guys, one in dress-down-Friday casuals, the other in leather trousers and a white shirt, were sitting at a table, watching us with equal parts apprehension and uncertain amusement. God knew what they'd made of Ju's comical assault on me. 'Come and say hello. They're OK. No, they're cunts. But they're OK cunts.'

I didn't really want to meet Ju's friends. I wanted to talk to him, to chew over the old times, to find out where he'd been for the past couple of decades. But I thought there'd be time for that later.

As we approached, one of the men stood up.

'Hi. I'm Jack Coen.' He was American – you could tell from his teeth before he spoke. He was tanned and handsome and out of place. I shook his hand.

'Jack's the money,' said Ju. 'But don't hold that against him.'

'No, I won't. Anyway, I can tell he's one of the good guys,' I said.

Coen looked puzzled, and glanced towards Ju and the other man.

'Am I? I mean, can you? I mean, sure, why not?'

'Because you're a Jack,' I said. 'Come on, you must have noticed. In American films, the good guys are always called

Jack, it's like some kind of law. OK, you get the occasional Harry, but usually it's Jack.'

Coen smiled, but you could see that he still wasn't sure whether he was being ridiculed. He wasn't – not by me, at least.

Then Ju joined in.

'Same with the computers, the goodies always use Macs – have you noticed that? – and the baddies use Windows PCs. It's a big corporations versus the maverick individual thing.'

'Ah,' said Coen, 'then there's a flaw. I use a PC. So does that make me a good guy or a bad guy?'

'Ever heard of a split fucking personality?' That came from the man in the leather trousers. I got the impression he didn't like being left out of things.

'And this,' said Ju, giving me a meaningful look, the meaning of which I couldn't begin to fathom, 'is Billy Adams, and I *know* you've heard of him.'

Suddenly things became a little clearer. Yes, I'd heard of Billy Adams. His record company – what was it . . . Hell something . . . *Hellbent* – was one of the shooting stars of the early nineties. The critics all loved the bands he signed, and he was photogenic enough to garner a lot of the attention for himself. You couldn't walk through a newsagent's without seeing his sardonic grimace on the front of *Mojo* or *Q*. He was photographed at a reception with an arm around the Prime Minister, a slopping pint glass of champagne in his free hand. He *was* Cool Britannia. But the Hellbent world-view didn't work in the USA, and none of his bands ever made it to the point where the sales income beat the A&R spend. The last thing I heard was that a multinational had bought a stake, prepared to put up with the cash haemorrhage for the sake of the credibility.

Adams looked rounder than the old pictures. There was too much neck happening in the trademark white silk shirt, and his pants held a feminine little bulge of fat under the waistband. At least his smirk hadn't changed.

We exchanged nods.

'This is my old mate, Matty. We were at school together. I taught him everything he knows about everything.'

'Not everything about everything. Mainly, as I remember it, about stealing records.'

Coen and Adams coughed out some laughter.

'Sit the fuck down, then,' said Ju. I pulled over a chair. 'I'll get you a drink. You still on the crème de menthe, you poof?'

'That's me. A pint.'

'Go and get the man a Guinness, will you, Billy?' Adams didn't look especially pleased, but he went to the bar.

'And what do you do, Matty?' the American asked in a friendly way. 'It's OK for me to call you Matty?'

'Yeah, sure.'

I had to think for a moment before I could answer the first part of the question. Just what did I do? I could have said that I spent a couple of nights a week tutoring Open University students. After all, it was true. But then I thought about why I was here on this night, and I said, enigmatically: 'I work in security.'

I thought they'd laugh, that Ju, at least, would take the piss and then try to find out what I meant. But instead the conversation moved on to other things. Soon a mixture of Coen and Adams, along with randomly shy or boastful elaborations from Ju filled me in on the past twenty years of his life. Yes, he'd made it as a top session musician in Manchester. From there his musical ideas filtered into the

Manchester scene. Listening to them, you'd have thought it was Ju who taught indie how to dance.

'I'm telling you, I fucking invented the indie shuffle. Taught it to the Roses, gave it to the Mondays,' said Ju, leaning close, so again I could smell the dark chocolate on his breath.

I looked sceptical.

Billy Adams said: 'Look, none of those cunts could play bass for shit, more than just *dum dum dum* on the beat. Now Ju, as you know, plays lead, but he also plays bass, and when he plays bass he plays it like lead, so you've suddenly got a new world opening up. Nothing they haven't been doing in jazz for two hundred fucking years, mind, but for those Mancunian skag-heads it was St Paul on the road to fucking Damascus time. So any track from then that you hear and the bass isn't like a tortoise having a shit, that's Ju. Hey, that's due to Ju.'

'Funny guy,' said Coen, irony either absent or artfully disguised.

'So what are you doing now?' I asked, still not quite taking it in.

Adams spoke before Ju had the chance.

'The Sistine chapel. *Mona Lisa*. His fucking masterpiece.'

'What is it, Ju?' I tried to focus on him, to cut the others out.

'Just a record. It's taking me a while.'

'We've got faith, Ju,' said Billy Adams, and he drained the beer out of his bottle.

'You bet,' said Coen, nodding fiercely.

Their enthusiasm seemed to suck something living out of Ju. There were tensions here that I couldn't understand. I studied their faces. Adams and Coen had started to pay attention to the carpet. Ju was looking grey and hollow: the fake chemical fizz was leaving him. I should have realised it was time to go, but I wanted to talk to Ju alone, to see whether there was anything of the old spark between us. After a pause he said, 'Look, Matthew, I've got some shit to talk through with the guys here. Maybe we can meet up another time to chew the fat – although by the look of your gut you maybe ought to make that a rice cake.'

'OK. Let me get a round in before I go. What you having?'

I went to the bar, squeezing between the big coats, but before I was served I sensed a movement behind me. I waited for a couple of seconds and looked around. The table was empty.

2

A Modest Proposal

I took my drink and went to sit beside Jonah Whale. Living where I lived I got to meet all kinds of people – weasel-faced burglars, madwomen pushing prams full of bloated bin-liners, slumming intellectuals, even a few normal types, sucked into the inferno by Kilburn's 'affordable' houses. But there was no one like Jonah Whale.

I'd met Jonah one morning on the first-floor landing, one down from my flat. There had been three or four tenants since I'd moved there, none of whom had shown much of an interest in getting to know me. Jonah was opening the door with one hand, while he held a sideboard under his other arm, much in the way a Viking might carry off a virgin for the ravishing of. The load looked awkward, and I asked whether I could help, without taking stock of the man or his burden.

He turned and looked up at me. His face was like some unworked slab of rock cracked out of a quarry, but his suit was sharp. He nodded slowly, and I could have sworn I heard the grind of granite on granite.

'Sure you can.'

From his intonation it was impossible to work out whether that was a statement or a question.

I took hold of the sideboard. It was six feet long, 1950s. Probably cool in ways I couldn't understand. Anyway, I guessed it was made of tissue and balsa wood.

'Got it?'

'Think so.'

He let go. My legs buckled and I let out a curse. The damn thing weighed as much as a steam engine; I felt as though my internal organs were about to burst with the pressure.

He opened the door, and I staggered in.

'Let me get this end,' he said.

'No need,' I groaned, like a man using up the last of his resolve before he finally confesses to the torturer.

I put it down in the first empty space I could find.

He held out his hand.

'Jonah Whale.'

I saw that he had the dull blue of a homemade tattoo across his knuckles.

'Matthew Moriarty. You just moving in?'

'No, no,' he said, and I shunted his accent from generic Scots to definite Glasgow. 'I'm, ah, an *agent*, you might say. I'm getting the place sorted for the young lady who'll be staying here. Can I, ah, offer you a cup of tea, to thank you for the helping hand? Unless, that is, you're on your way to work . . .' He looked uncertainly at my jeans and sweat-shirt. There was a small round grease-spot in the middle of my chest – hey, it was morning, and I wasn't exactly headed for a high-powered business meeting.

'No. I'm . . . looking for something at the moment. Tea, yeah, tea would be good.'

It was an unexpectedly dainty offer from the stone giant, and I'd been startled into an uncharacteristic acceptance. So Jonah made tea and I looked around the flat. It was neat, almost bare. But there was a bookshelf full of Penguin classics. Jonah came back with the mugs as I was looking through them.

'I use this here as an . . . ah . . . *overflow*. And you never know when one of the tenants might take something in. And you, are you a reading man?'

'Yeah, I guess so. I used to . . . well, it used to be part of my job.' Time to deflect: 'You seem to be into philosophy.'

There was a lot of Nietzsche up there, which I supposed you got with most self-educated psychos, but other stuff too, from the pre-Socratics down to Russell. Funny how madmen and mass murderers always seem drawn to philosophy, as opposed to literature. I suppose it's because you can find a justification for anything if you spend any time looking in Plato or Bentham or Schopenhauer. But novels show you people in all their helpless vulnerability, and like someone said, it's hard to kill a person when you've seen them sleeping.

And then Jonah put the mugs down on a coffee table and walked steadily towards me. He held out his clenched fist. I didn't know what the fuck he was about, and then I focused on the tattoo. 'HUME', it said. He held out the other fist. 'KANT' was written there.

'The great thinkers saved my life,' he said. 'Without philosophy we're no but beasts. Sugar in your tea?'

After that I was an official acquaintance of Jonah Whale. And soon I learnt that he was a useful person to know. When bar staff saw that I was on nodding terms with the great man, I'd find myself served a little quicker. The nutters, mutants and hustlers kept their distance. A man came unbidden to fix my blocked drain, and charged me no more than was reasonable. It was the plumber who told me about Jonah's catchphrase. When he had a job of work to do, a person to see, he'd introduce himself by asking, 'Are yez familiar with the works of Friedrich Nietzsche? *Philosophise with a hammer*, he said.'

And then that's exactly what he'd do.

There were other things I heard about Jonah. He was said to preach to the drinkers in the park, joining their raggedy little groups, adding a carrier bag of Special Brew to the stash, and then trying to get discussions going. Could he really be bringing Hegel and Schopenhauer to the bums? It didn't seem likely that it was Jesus. At the very least he seemed to be a friend to the weak, to the wretched. More than once I met him in the pub and he'd be talking to a hopeless case in a singed nylon jacket, or he'd be giving gentle advice to a drunk schizophrenic woman, known locally for the way she wore her hair in a vertical spike, like a Tellytubby. Maybe it was guilt about the fact that he earned his money by scaring people, and when scaring didn't do the trick, by hurting them.

There was one thing he said which stuck in my mind. He was lamenting the fact that our culture now judged everything by how funny or amusing it was, and that this frivolousness was a mark not just of our decadence, but also of our conservatism. 'Deflect the energy of the people into laughter,' he said, 'and there will be nothing left for revolution.' And then, portentously, 'No one sits down and laughs at the sea.'

At the time I had to fight my own strong urge to laugh, or at least to smile, but later, much later, when Jonah was just a memory to me, I was standing on a beach in Tunisia, wide and empty in the early morning, and the sea still white-flecked from a storm in the night, and as I looked to the east there was no land for a thousand miles, and I thought about what Jonah had said, and if it still made me want to smile, it also made me think that I should do something serious with my life.

A couple of months after our first meeting I was reading in the park. A shadow fell across the sun and a weight hit the bench next to me like the statue of a fallen dictator.

'Tacitus now, is it?' said Jonah.

I didn't know any small talk about Tacitus, so I just smiled.

'I'm glad you're a reading man. Not that there's much from the Romans I'd be keeping. No philosophy to call their own, just the dregs of the Greeks.' He lapsed into silence for a couple of minutes, clearly troubled by the paucity of Roman metaphysics. I wasn't going to interrupt his stillness by talking about the weather. Finally he said, 'I've a need of someone. A thinking man. How are you placed for work?'

It happened that I'd just been given the job teaching part-time in the evenings. Hence the Tacitus: I was scooting through all the stuff I'd forgotten. But the Open University paid three hundred and fifty pounds a month to its course tutors, and that didn't leave me with much when I'd spent what had to be spent.

'What kind of work?'

'Night work.'

'What do you mean?'

'I suppose you could say that it is in the, ah, security field.'

'I do a couple of nights a week at the moment. But only until nine.'

'Well, we might be able to help each other out. But I'm getting in between you and your Roman. Let's have a wee chat over a pint.'

And that was how I came to be meeting Jonah Whale in Power's Bar.

He didn't ask me anything about Ju. That was one of the things about Jonah – with him there was no periphery, just the centre ground.

'So,' he said, 'your teaching leaves you free from nine?'

I'd never told him that I taught, but then Jonah always knew what he needed to know.

'I only work Mondays and Thursdays. The other nights I'm free any time. And the days. What did you have in mind?'

'You know the Zip?'

The Zip was the nearest Kilburn came to a cool bar. A year before it was just another of Kilburn's old boozers, the stench of piss leaking out from the lavatories, not just into the bar but right out into the street, where it drew the drunks the way Chum draws sharks. Now it was like a seventies take on the twenty-third century, all weird pods and purple lights. The music was too loud if all you wanted was a quiet drink, but I'd been in once or twice, drawn by the tall girls on bar stools. But once you were in, the feeling that there was something wrong with the place discouraged lingering, no matter how pretty the girls. And a bottle of beer cost four pounds, which meant that getting drunk was going to cost you fifty quid.

'Yeah, I know the Zip.'

'But you're not a regular?'

'No.'

'Not your kind of a place?'

Jonah wanted to know what I thought of it, and didn't want to prejudice my response by signalling his own concern, but subtle interrogation wasn't really his gift.

I thought carefully before answering.

'The thing is, Jonah, outside the West End and the City, the relationship between how smart a place is and the kind of punter you get becomes all fucked up. In a place like Kilburn, if you create a cool modern bar, you're not going to get cool modern people, or at least not the ones you want. It isn't going to be TV producers and new media creatives popping out for a Japanese beer. It's going to be the top strata of the local thieves and drug dealers, along with whatever general-purpose young thugs can get past the door. That's why, with fancy suburban bars, underneath the shiny suits and the smiles you always get that edge of violence, the feeling that if you say the wrong thing you're in for a kicking. You never get that with a local boozer, full of pensioners nursing their light ales.'

Jonah was nodding. He was open to what I was saying. 'So what would you do about it?'

'About it? Why do anything? A pimp's money buys a pint, same as mine or yours.'

'And who wants to run a bar for pimps and pushers?'

'That's capitalism.'

Jonah smiled his slow, grim executioner's smile.

'A debate I'd enjoy. But another time. Look, let me tell you what I'm about. I've been asked to help with the security situation at the Zip. As you, ah, *diagnosed*, the quality of paying customer isn't quite what the owners expected when they spent three-quarters of a million pounds designing the place. A lot of that was on the kitchens, and nobody's eating. Kilburn's coming up. There *are* these . . . what did you call them? . . . TV producers and new media creatures living here now, and whatever you say, they must want to go out locally. And that sector has to have more

. . . ah . . . *stability* than the other sort. The problem, as I see it, is how to keep the wrong sort out. But the quality of door-control staff we have is . . .' Jonah shifted uncomfortably in his seat. '. . . *primitive*. I need a man, a thinking man, a man with some intelligence, to help me with this. I think that if we control the wrong sort, the right will come in, to fill the vacuum.'

And then, remembering Jonah's bookshelf of philosophy, I thought of a joke.

'And as we know, Nietzsche abhors a vacuum.'

It took Jonah a moment or two to respond, and then his shoulder began to shake, silently.

'"*abhors a vacuum*". Not *nature*, but *Nietzsche*. I like that, son, I like that. You'll do me. What do you say?'

'Let me get this straight, you want me as an *über-bouncer*?' I couldn't keep the laughter out of my voice.

'Ah, no, I don't see you standing with the big lads on the door. What I see is you walking the floor of the place, keeping a general eye, then wandering over to chat with the bouncers, giving a little guidance, a subtle nudge. You're my, ah, *thermostat*.'

'And you couldn't do that yourself? You're the philosopher, after all.'

Jonah smiled. His teeth were large and strong, but dull with age. I had a vision of him biting through chains.

'I have other, ah, *commitments*. But this job wants a younger man. What TV producer wants to see me standing next to him while he takes a piss at the nice new Philippe Stark urinal?'

I took his point. I was intrigued by the offer. It was so alien to everything I'd ever done. But there were some obvious objections.

'You say I wouldn't really be a bouncer, but if there's trouble on the door I'd have to get involved. And let me tell you, if we start filtering out the twats, there's gonna be trouble.'

'I wouldn't expect there to be anything the boys couldn't look after, in the line of, ah, *aggravation*. But Matthew, you're a big man. Have you not an eye for a challenge? Or are you . . . worried? If you have *concerns* about whether you could handle yourself in a spot of bother, then, well, maybe it's not . . .'

'I can handle myself.'

Yep. Sad. I fell for it.

Jonah smiled. '*I* never doubted you.'

There was one other issue.

'What's the money?'

'A hundred pounds a night. In your hand. Six nights a week, nine to twelve.'

Six hundred pounds a week. Eighteen hours' work. I liked the maths.

'Is there a dental plan?'

Jonah looked puzzled for a moment, and then said: 'If you've trouble with your teeth, I can fix it for you.'

The hammer.

'That's OK, Jonah. My teeth are fine.'

We both took sips from our pints of Guinness.

'When do I start?'

We had another drink, and then Jonah had to go. It was about ten, and I thought I might as well stay for a last one to celebrate my financial salvation. The truth was that things had been getting very tight. That's not to say that there's not a big difference between being broke as I was and living in poverty with children to support and no hope – I was a

single man, and I owned my flat, and there was always work
I could do. But that didn't change the fact I was wearing
the same clothes I'd bought three years before, or that I
always got my hair cut by an Albanian for five pounds, or
that sometimes I just plain ran out of drinking money.

But not tonight. On the way back from the bar I saw a
woman. The women in Power's Bar are generally a notch
up from the Kilburn norm of borderline bag ladies and
screaming lager swillers, their belly rings invisible beneath
the folds of flab. A notch, but only a notch. But this was
something different.

To begin with she was dressed with subtle elegance in a
neat, pale grey suit. At least it seemed subtle until you took
in that the skirt was about four inches long. She wore a
white silk shirt under the jacket and, under the white shirt,
to judge by the soft swelling of yet whiter flesh, nothing at
all. She was smoking a cigarette, holding it in long thin
fingers. She was leaning forward and her fine, golden hair
hung over her face.

When I found that I couldn't see her properly from my
original seat, I moved. She, in contrast, was as still as
Narcissus, frozen in some moment of contemplation. I
watched the cigarette burn down, watched the ash build
and fall, build and fall again. And then she raised her head,
put out the cigarette and sipped her drink. In that instant
the spell was broken. Not that this woman was anything
other than beautiful; but it was a beauty that had blossomed
first perhaps twenty-five years earlier. It was impossible,
through the murk of Power's Bar, to make out the tiny lines
around her eyes and mouth, but I knew that they must be
there, despite the tight look of the skin on her cheeks. I
could see that her lips were full, but that fullness suggested

the counterfeit pout of a syringe. And the gold of the hair was fool's gold.

So, the tension broke within me, and I began to watch her through curiosity, and not through desire. But still, I watched.

As I drank and watched the once beautiful woman, my mind turned back to Ju. I'd felt such exultation when I first saw him. He was from the time of my innocence – and if that time was imaginary it didn't mean it wasn't real to me. That alone was sufficient to make me love him. But there were other things, things from the past. Like the fact that he saved my life.

3

The Battle of Temple Newsome

I travelled back from Power's Bar to the Body. Twenty
years and two hundred miles. I didn't notice Ju Flaherty
for my first couple of years at the Body of Christ Roman
Catholic High School, although we usually called it the
Body, and ourselves Bodies. I had my own gang, mostly
nerds and geeks, but funny and clever, and Ju wasn't in it.
The Body was a tough school, mainly serving the sprawling
council estate that lay all around it like a red-brick womb.
It didn't have much of a record for academic achievement,
and the teachers kept control by a subtle mixture of violence
and brutality. Some of the kids were pretty scary, and life
at the bottom of the food chain could be, well, *difficult*. If
you looked small or weak or different, then you were going
to be subjected to terror, and that was all there was to it.
The only hope was to fight back, and fighting back is a
hard thing to do if you're puny and frightened and there's
a boy the size of a buffalo kneeling on your chest, spitting
in your face, his big fists daring you to flinch.

I was lucky. I was tall, and I was good at sport, and
between them those things take you out of the realm of the
bullied. And, because I was clever, that's where I should
have lived. I only ever had one fight, and that was how my
destiny first became entwined with Ju's.

There was a kid called Murdoch, a jackal who hung

around with the big carnivores. Standing in line out in the cold one day, I felt something hit my hair. I turned around to see Murdoch smirking. His eyes kept wandering off to seek the approval of Fat Gaz, the cock of the year. I put my hand to my hair, which was long then, and I was vain about it. I felt something sticky. I knew at once that Murdoch had thrown chewing gum in my hair. After that I didn't do much thinking. Murdoch said something to me, but I can't remember what. I was already taking a step towards him. His eyes widened when he realised what I was going to do. This wasn't supposed to happen. I was supposed to cringe and whimper. I hit him with all the weight in my lanky frame and he fell to the floor. He got half up and I hit him again, trying not to wince at the pain in my fist. Out of the corner of my eye I saw Fat Gaz begin to shift his bulk. He looked resigned: he didn't want to step in, but Murdoch was one of his. And then a small, slight figure came and stood in front of him.

'Fair fight, Gaz,' he said, in a reasonable tone. 'Murdo asked for it.'

Fat Gaz looked down at him. 'I don't even fucking know you,' he said. And then he looked at me, and down at Murdoch on the floor. Something went on in his head and he turned and walked away.

I found Ju's eyes, and said thanks.

'Hey, peace to the nerds,' he said. 'We need you as a reference point.' And then he was away, the light flashing and refracting off him like a tropical fish.

Well, it was a cool thing for Jude Lovell Malcolm Flaherty to have done, and it took guts, but it didn't count as saving my life.

From then on Ju and I began to nod as we passed in the

24

corridor. I don't know how I could have missed him for so long; no one else looked remotely like him. His hair was a classic blond punk spike – interesting, but hardly unusual – but everything else about him, from his silver-painted Doc Martens to the little pearls he wore in his ears, marked him out. And those huge black eyes of his, rimmed, even then, by pencil. Somehow he stayed in with the carnivores without ever really being one of them.

And then we started to talk. About music, to begin with. He knew everything. He talked as fluently about early Roxy Music as about late Sex Pistols. His favourite bands were the Buzzcocks and Joy Division. He ripped the piss out of my unformed taste, and I called him a short-arsed little fuckwit. We finally reached accommodation on the greatest record ever made: 'Another Girl, Another Planet' by the Only Ones. I'd still take some arguing out of it, despite the near fatal pub-rock nurdling that goes on with the lead guitar. It wasn't a friendship at that stage, but it was something close to it.

True friendship had to wait for the Battle of Temple Newsome. Temple Newsome was the name of a square Tudor mansion surrounded by scrubby parkland a mile or so north of the Body of Christ. The local comprehensive up there was called Temple Moor. Its reputation was almost as low as the Body's, and our rivalry was heightened by the fact that by some fluke both schools had purple blazers. There'd been skirmishes for years, and fabled single combats between the cocks of the schools, but at long last it seemed there was to be a final reckoning. News of the big event spread quickly. I had no intention of fighting, but there was no way me and my friends were going to miss the sport. This was the biggest event in the history of the Body of

Christ – it was to be our Thermopylae, our Stalingrad.

On the appointed day a good quarter of the school popu-
lation met outside the gates. The brutes of the fourth and
fifth years led the way up the hill to Temple Newsome.
Terry Jordan, the fucking mental Spencer brothers, plus
other shambling giants I knew by shape but not name. Fat
Gaz was up there, the one representative from our year
among the élite. It must have been a strange sight, this mass
of purple, curiously silent, rather than the usual post-school
straggling chaos. I don't think any of our lot carried
weapons. Those were innocent days, and we were expecting
fist against fist, arm against arm, Doc Marten against skull.

I didn't envy the Temple Moor kids; but nor did I feel
much for them: I was as intoxicated as the rest with the
expectation of violence. I was only a camp follower, an
outrider to the main phalanx, but its energy had touched
me too.

They met us in the Temple Newsome sports field. It was
the perfect venue: a natural arena with grassy banks rising
around the central space. Those of us not there to fight
found places at the edge. I'd saved my Tunnock's caramel
wafer biscuit ('four million made and sold every week', the
wrapper said) from my packed lunch; other kids had Wagon
Wheels, Marathons, packets of pickled-onion-flavour
Monster Munch.

I can't see, from here, which of my friends were with
me – their faces are blurred or blank – but there must have
been the O'Connells, Johnson, John Bray, perhaps Phil
Moody. Bray used to wear his wristwatch over the sleeve
of his school jumper, but hidden under the folded-back
cuff. I'm imagining him nervously peeling back the cuff
to check the time. And while I'm at it I'll fill in with Moody's

kicking about in the dirt, his shoulders hunched over, trying to think of a wisecrack, and Johnson with his finger up his nose as far as the second knuckle. We were excited and tense, but not afraid; after all, we were just watching, weren't we?

Down on the pitch, there was a stand-off for perhaps five minutes. At first it was eerily silent as hard eyes met across the twenty yards of no man's land. And then the calm was punctuated by the taunts and goads of each side trying to work itself up and slap the other down.

It was about then that I began to realise that this might all have been a big mistake. We had managed to put out a respectable force, but they were moments from their school gates and their line was both deeper and longer than ours, forming a semicircle lapping around our flanks. I also had the feeling that some of our adrenalin had been used up in that tense twenty-minute march to reach the battlefield.

Others had the same idea, and those of us not designated as combatants started to edge away, moving farther back from the trouble.

And then it began. Terry Jordan came charging out from our lot, bellowing, waving his fat fists above his head like an enraged chimp. I don't know whether this was intended as a solo display, or whether he thought that the rest of his troop would follow him, but none did. Instead, a swaying beanpole stepped out from the Temple ranks. I remember his face, long and melancholy like a concert pianist's. There were jeers, laughter from our side. This kid was six and a half feet tall, but so thin he was almost transparent. He looked like the sort of fishbone cartoon alley cats found in trash cans.

Jordan loped towards him, his arms still flailing away. We

all surged with him, thinking that the whole contest might be decided here, with the snapping of this insubstantial wand by our ape-like champion. But that's not quite how it worked out. The beanpole waited with serenity and patience, raised his arm high, and, as Jordan came into range, brought it down on his chin with a fearful crack that set the rooks up from the trees in the park.

Jordan was on the floor and he wasn't getting up. The Templers swarmed over him, kicking, stamping. Then they rushed on, and they were among us. It was carnage. Some of our boys tried to stand and fight, but they were soon isolated, surrounded and hacked down. And I saw then that some of the Temple kids had sticks or chains. Some were carrying half-bricks. I saw Fat Gaz running madly, his head flung back in panic. I also wanted to run, but already they were behind us, blocking the way out. We were trapped in the sports field.

'Shit me, Matty,' someone shouted, 'we're getting a pasting. Leg it.'

I've tried all the voices of my friends, and it works best in Moody's alternating cracked falsetto and rumbling bass.

Some puny kid whose name I can't even remember was holding on to my blazer. He was crying. I looked around again, trying to keep cool. No way back or forward, but it was possible to run up the sloping banks at the side of the field, and jump down the ten feet or so to freedom. I grabbed the kid by the sleeve – Fletcher, his name was Fletcher – and began to run. Two Temple kids were in our way. I shoved one aside, and let fly with a kick at the other, and they melted. But I lost my grip on Fletcher. Looking round for him I saw someone jogging towards me. There was nothing particularly hurried about his approach, and for a second I thought he was one of ours. And then I saw that he was carrying something, and I knew what it was and I knew where he had bought it.

There used to be a stall in Leeds market that sold old army kit – boots, combat pants, big leather cartridge belts; stuff you couldn't buy anywhere else back then. It was popular with the punks. The stall also sold other, slightly more esoteric objects aimed not at kids but at specialist collectors. There were Nazi insignia, caps, SS badges and buttons in a glass case. If he was in the right mood the old git who ran the stall would show you the emasculated Luger he kept below the counter. Best of all, however, was the assortment of bayonets hanging under the sloping roof of the stall. Some, the man claimed, were Boer War vintage, others from 1914–18. Some looked pretty new. All of them were long and sharp and evil, designed for one thing: messing up your insides. And now one of these was coming towards me, held outstretched in the hand of the jogging boy.

I can't say whether he really wanted to stick the damn thing in me, or whether he would have pulled away, content to see the terror in my eyes, the darkening pool of piss spreading over the front of my kecks. But either way he wasn't slowing down, and I felt pinned, as though already pierced by the steel.

The rest of the battlefield, with its Bosch scenes of punishing devils and quaking sinners, became mist, and just me and the jogging boy and the bayonet were solid. I looked again at the boy. He didn't strike me as one of the hard bastards: he was portly and wore glasses, and he had the tight mouth of someone desperately trying to make an impression. Perhaps he'd been bullied by the Temple toughs and saw this as his one hope of salvation, a redemption through blood. My blood.

I felt a pulling at my wrist, and I suppose it must have been little Fletcher trying to get me away. But I had other ideas. Telling the story afterwards, I spun it so that I was waiting to take him, I was going to do one of my famous football-field jinks, a feint and a swerve, and then take him down. But that was a lie. I was waiting for him to stick his bayonet in my stomach, and then I was going to fold over and cry for my mother while he stood over me and wondered what the fuck he was supposed to do next.

It didn't pan out like that. He was five or six feet from me, although it felt closer with the bayonet stretching out to meet me, when something heavy cracked down on his forearm. He dropped the bayonet and clutched his arm. His bemused expression was so comical I almost laughed. Then he looked to his left, and I followed his eyes. Ju was standing there with some kind of iron bar. It wasn't a crowbar, or any kind of tool, just a piece of iron, as thick and long as a cricket stump.

'Come on,' said Ju. 'Time we went some other fucking place.'

There was a bubble of calm around him. The fighting was still going on, but it couldn't touch us now he was here.

'Fletcher,' I said. 'We've got to get Fletcher.'

'He's right here.'

I saw that he was.

Ju set off towards the drop. We followed him. Then he stopped, walked back and picked up the bayonet. The fat kid with the glasses was still kneeling there, holding his broken arm, like it was something special he'd been told not to lose. His mouth was moving. I think he was praying, but he might just have been mumbling shit. Ju paused in front of him with the bayonet, admiring the sheen of it. Standing there with the big iron bar in one hand and the bayonet in the other, he looked like justice and vengeance and a mad punk on the rampage all in one. I thought he was going to kill the fat kid, slit his throat or open him up from belly to chin, and part of me wanted him to do that; but I didn't know Ju very well then.

'Nice,' he said.

And then he trotted back to us, and we ran away over the rim of the field and into the woods.

When I emerged again from the old memories into the dark beery warmth of Power's Bar, the woman had gone.

4

The Zip

The following Monday I taught my class at the college with at best half my mind on the job. The rest of me was already in the Zip. So I'm guessing it wasn't the greatest exposition of the different accounts given by Polybius and Livy of the wars fought by Rome against the Hellenistic kingdoms of the Near East. My group was made up of the usual mixture of retired middle-class professionals and sad-eyed waifs, with a couple of adequately medicated schizophrenics. On the whole the students were clever and committed, and I liked teaching them. But not tonight.

Afterwards most of the group loitered to chat. Quite often I'd take them to the pub to continue the talk.

'We not carrying on tonight, Prof?' asked one guy, a high-domed baldy, far more professorial in his manner than I'd ever be.

'Sorry, Colin, I've got something on. And I'm afraid it's a regular thing from now on.'

'What regular? And why looking so nice?'

I knew that tone, accusatory, hurt; tinged with the faint, unstated threat that you were responsible for whatever ills might befall the speaker. Dunyazad was an Egyptian post-graduate research student. She wasn't even doing my course, but she liked to sit in on the seminars, and nobody seemed to mind. Her field was the position of women in pre-Islamic Egypt. She was tiny and intense and, unfortunately, not very attractive. Her hair was thick and fibrous, and one of her eyes wandered around in a most disconcerting manner. One home, one away, as my dad would have put it. She'd been in love with me since the day we'd met, which happened to be my first day on the job.

'It's some work I've been offered.'

'More teaching?'

'No, other work. Look, everyone, I'm really sorry, but I've got to dash.'

It was a twenty-minute walk from Parsifal College back down to Kilburn, just long enough for me to beat myself up over Dunyazad. She'd been friendly and helpful on that first evening, showing me where the tutorial rooms were, and where to get coffee. Parsifal is the London outpost of the Open University, and acts as a kind of mini-campus. It attracts a lot of the London-based OU strays who have nothing better to do, and nowhere else to go, and I suppose that included Dunyazad. She was very bright and quick witted, and her knowledge of her period was astounding. In some ways that was her problem. Until she narrowed things down and got some focus into her work she was never going to get anywhere. Academic research is like sculpture: you advance by chipping away, not by addition.

Over the next few weeks we got to know each other pretty well. She asked whether she could sit in on the sessions, and I said it was fine by me. I had no idea that she was becoming obsessed. My first inkling came at the end of a post-seminar drink. The others had all left. Dunyazad obviously wasn't used to alcohol although, for a Coptic Christian like her, it was not forbidden. She'd had only two glasses of wine, but she was unsteady on her feet, and her stray eye was checking out the action somewhere over her left shoulder. I asked where she lived, and she began to giggle hysterically. I offered to put her in a taxi, but she found that even more hilarious. Finally she said that she would come back to my flat, and with a heavy heart I took her there.

We were barely through the door before I found her standing on tiptoe in front of me, her eyes closed, her lips offered up for a kiss. I noticed for the first time that she was wearing a low-cut top. With mild irritation I realised that I was just about turned on enough for there to be an element of risk.

'Sorry, Dunyazad,' I said, trying to concentrate on the coarse hair and the eye I could sense warbling beneath its heavy lid, and not at all on the swelling allure of the bosom, 'but nothing's going to happen.'

She opened her eyes. Even the bad one was fixed on me.

'What for? You just use me.'

'If anything happened, that would be using you. Let's have a cup of coffee and then I'll get that taxi.'

We sat in silence until the cab came. When the bell rang she flung herself on me and covered my face in kisses, heavy as bricks. I had to carry her down the stairs with her alternately kissing and beating me. The driver looked at me suspiciously, but was happy enough when I gave him thirty quid.

After that Dunyazad regarded me with concentrated disdain. But still she came to the seminars.

The Zip Bar glowed with cold seduction amid the grey sulk of the seedy high street. Through the big windows I could see that it was about a quarter full, but I didn't want to stare. There were two guys standing together on the door, filling it. One was a colossal black man, who looked to be about five feet across the chest. The other was skinnier, white, shaven headed. I noticed a smudge of blue spreading above his shirt collar. There was a narrow lobby beyond the doorway, leading to a second door that opened into the bar. I stepped into the doorway, expecting them to part to let me in.

The black man stared hard at me. After about four seconds of scrutiny he decided I was no threat to anyone and his face softened into neutrality and he stood aside.

The skinhead with the tattooed neck didn't move, and I had to brush against his hard frame as I entered.

I looked around. The place was clean and plush from its refit. Arcs of chrome, pools of red light. The back of the bar was one long, gold-tinged mirror, the kind that makes you look good, whatever your natural attributes. Jonah was sitting uncomfortably on one of the high bar stools, a sinister glass of tomato juice untouched before him. He looked like Samuel Beckett's monstrous brother.

'Up you get, son,' he said, gesturing towards the next stool. 'A drink while we talk?'

'A beer.'

'Pelly,' he said, and one of the two barmen spun to the cooler, took out a Budvar, cracked it, and set it down with a glass all in one movement.

'Cheers,' I said.

'Pelly, this is Matthew, he's working with Errol and Spider, keeping things, ah, relaxed.'

Spider. Yes, the spider's-web tattoo on his neck.

'Hi,' said Pelly, 'good to have you on board.' He was

Australian, dark skinned. I guessed Greek extraction, guessed Pellicarnos. 'Meet Simon,' he said, and the other barman, ginger, freckled, goofy, maybe eighteen years old, stuck out a hand.

'Hi, we're the "A" team,' he said, in a voice that modulated between cracked falsetto and deep bass.

'Is it just you two on the bar?'

'We can handle it,' said Simon, 'unless it gets mad, then Mercedes helps out. But she mainly does food. She's late.'

I tried to get a feel for the place, take its pulse. There were perhaps twenty people in. A cluster of men in suits, a group of girls, four couples, a dotting of single men and one woman, her face lost in a dark corner. So the joint wasn't dead, but nor was it exactly jumpin'. Still, it was just a Monday.

'First impressions, then?' asked Jonah, picking up on my thoughts.

'You could be busier. I can't see any trouble here. Makes the door guys seem a bit heavy handed.'

'Heavy. . . . ? What do you mean?'

'Not exactly the warmest reception I've ever received. Not so much hail fellow well met as what the fuck you lookin' at? And I've got to tell you, Jonah, I'm not the kind of person you should be discouraging.'

Jonah shook his head sadly. 'Jesus, I'm afraid it's all or nothing with those boys. You tell them to keep things tight and they end up throwing out librarians. No offence, son.'

'None taken. But the truth is they're not up to the job. The black guy seems all right, but the other's a bloodbath waiting to happen. In my opinion.'

The reality was more complex. It wasn't just that Spider,

36

the skinhead, had seemed brutal; I thought there was something cowardly in the way he'd waited until the black guy
had checked me out as harmless before he went through
with his hard-man-not-moving act. It was the kind of thing
I'd seen at school a million times.

'What are you saying?'

'I don't know . . . sack him? Or have words.'

'That's a bit, ah, *precipitate*. He's not let us down so far.'

'Maybe you're right. But you said you want to attract media
types, and they don't really want to be walking through a door
past a man with a spider's-web tattoo creeping up his neck.'

'Truly, my Satan,' he intoned, 'thou art but a dunce,
and cannot tell the garment from the man.'

I laughed. 'Yeah, maybe not.'

'I'll introduce you, and let's see how we go. Perhaps
words are the thing.'

Errol and Spider were friendly enough when they found
out who I was. If they didn't like the idea of having me
around they weren't showing it to Jonah. I supposed they
figured I wouldn't be there for long. Despite that, it
couldn't have been easy for them to accept that an amateur
like me was being brought in to tell them what to do.

'You know how it works,' Jonah was saying. 'You two
men are still the front line, but Matthew here is helping
out with deciding who comes in and who stays out.'

Errol nodded sagely, Spider looked blank, and then said:
'And if there's trouble?'

'I can't imagine anything you two can't handle, but if
you need him, he'll be there for you.' He looked at me
meaningfully.

After some more pleasantries Jonah announced that he
was leaving 'on his rounds'.

'I'll call in later on. It's a Monday. Nothing's going to be happening tonight.'

And then he took my arm and led me back from the doorway and the two bouncers. He slipped something into my pocket. I felt down after it. It was warm and heavy and strangely shaped. I was going to take it out, but Jonah again put his hand on my arm. He leant towards me and said softly, 'Just for peace of mind.' And then he was gone, slapping Spider solidly on the back as he went.

I stayed to chat for a few minutes. Once he got going, Spider talked quickly in searing cockney. He'd been a soldier. He said SAS, but they always say that, unless they actually were in the SAS, in which case they tend not to say anything. Errol said he was really a DJ, and did a quick DJ mime to prove it.

'So what about you, then?' Errol asked. 'What's your usual line of work?'

'How do you know this isn't my usual line of work?'

They both laughed.

'I teach.'

They looked at each other, and Spider shook his head.

'Softly softly, catchee fucking monkey,' he said, whatever that was supposed to mean.

I went and got another beer, and sat at the bar. Pelly was easier to talk to. He liked white-water rafting and girls with pierced labia. At ten Mercedes dashed in, taking her coat off. She was small and pretty with long, wildly curling black hair, and she looked like she knew no one was going to hassle her too much about being late.

'*Hola*,' she said to Pelly. Then she looked quizzically at me.

'This is the new muscle,' Pelly said. 'But there's supposed to be a brain attached too, so be nice to him.'

'I always nice to everybody. Anyway,' she added, smiling, her head cocked slightly to one side, 'you don't look like you going to kill nobody.'

'That's the idea,' I replied, and we shook hands. She had little red hearts painted on her nails.

After that I wasn't quite sure what to do. I went and sat at a couple of different tables, happy that I had a few cigarettes left from my weekly ration. I smiled at people, who either looked away or stared back, uncertain whether I was a serial sex offender or merely trying to sell them drugs. And then I moved again and I was able to see the face of the woman I had noticed earlier in the shadows. A shiver of recognition, and excitement, went through me when I realised who she was: it was the woman I'd seen the week before in Power's Bar. She had the same stillness that didn't seem to come from serenity, the same beauty desperately holding off the remorseless assault of time. There was a tall clear drink before her, and she drew on her cigarette with a languor that did much, but not everything, to conceal the hunger beneath. Her eyes were pointing towards the windows, but the focus was somewhere else entirely. If she recognised me she didn't show it.

'Not for looking at the guests, Mr Handsome Killer with brain attach. That's not why we pay you. Hey, sorry if I frighten.'

Mercedes was changing my ashtray. I think I might have jumped.

'But that's exactly why you pay me. I'm here to look at the customers, make sure they don't cause any trouble.'

'She no cause any . . .' Mercedes began, glancing up at the woman, but then she stopped herself.

And that was pretty well it. There was no bother, just a

trickle of customers. At 11.30 Jonah came back in, and I left at twelve, with little sense of having contributed anything. It was only as I was walking home that I remembered that Jonah had put something in my pocket. I took it out, and turned it under the orange glow of a street light. It was an oval of brass with four semicircular indentations on the inside. A knuckle-duster. Not one of the lethal spiked ones, nor one of those with an integral knife blade: just the plain, old-fashioned sort. Rather beautiful, in its simplicity and utility. I laughed, and put it back in my pocket.

And the rest of the week followed the pattern of that first night. I'd stand for a while with Errol and Spider, and then I'd wander round the bar, smoke a couple of cigarettes, listen to Pelly talk about the white water, and then go back to the guys on the door. I was trying to get the message across to them as subtly as possible. And the message? Look for class not money. Keep it friendly and informal. Errol began to call me 'Professor', but there was more affection in it than spite, and he was intelligent enough to pick up on what we were trying to do.

Spider was trickier. He was the kind of doorman who looks forward to the fights, or at least the kind that involve kicking the shit out of drunks, and we weren't supplying any. Sometimes I sensed him mouthing things to Errol behind my back, and sometimes Errol would smile briefly back over my shoulder, but I didn't get the feeling he took any pleasure from this.

One night I asked Spider, 'What came first, the name or the tattoo?'

I wasn't having a go, just trying to chat.

He stared at me with a kind of concentrated ferocity.

'Neither,' he said, unblinking, his skin expressionless,

stretched taut almost as if it had been burned, 'the attitude.' And then, unable to keep up the game, he burst into
his high-pitched cackle.

'Had you, fucking had you,' he said. Errol was laughing
too. And then so was I. Maybe things would be OK
between us.

In that time I never felt the need to reach for the security in my pocket; forgot most of the time that it was there.
Easy money.

And every night my woman was there, her attention
fixed on the spectres that danced for her in some other
world. By Wednesday I hardly noticed her any more. That
was partly because I was busy noticing Mercedes.

Then along came Friday night.

From the start it was busier. When I arrived at nine
there was already a good crowd in: local office workers
having an end-of-the-week drink, a smattering of our
target group of tapas-eating middle-class locals. For the
rest of the week you'd have been able to pick out any individual voice from among the drinkers, but now there was
just that general babble, cut by laughter, that you get when
things are going well.

Errol was on good form on the door, welcoming people
with a big laugh. Suddenly he was everyone's friend, and
everyone was a regular. Even Spider seemed happy. Perhaps
he knew what was coming. I walked the floor, asking the
customers whether everything was all right, whether there
was anything they needed. I even helped Mercedes with
some of the drinks. She was growing on me by the minute.
It wasn't just the way you suddenly start to see the attractiveness in people you work with for a while, and it wasn't

just that I was lonely. There was definitely something in her neat and compact prettiness, along with the sass and swagger, that lifted my heart, that gave my senses an extra awareness. I felt myself breathe her in as she flitted past me with a tray, savouring the smell of shampoo, of inexpensive perfume beneath the drink and the smoke. I found that I was making less of an effort to move out of her way as she went about her work, so that she would brush against me. Sometimes she'd smile; sometimes furrow her brow. I made a couple of tentative enquiries to Pelly about her status, but he wasn't taking the hint, or, if he knew what I wanted to know, he was keeping it to himself. At about ten she gave me a tray with a glass fizzing with tonic, oily with gin.

'Take please to your special lady,' she said.

'But you're my special lady, Mercedes,' I replied, over-weighting the sarcasm. But she was already pirouetting away on little feet.

My woman was in her usual place. She had an uncanny way of folding the darkness around herself. I put the tray down on her table, moved the drink from the tray and replaced it with the empty glass. I'd never been this close to her before. She leaned towards me and I had to force my eyes away from the shadow between her breasts. She looked up at me, and for the first time our eyes met.

Everything about this woman spoke of the struggle between beauty and corruption. It gave her a palpable allure, mixed with a visceral repulsion. She made me think of the story of the Lamia, the serpent-enchantress, who took on the form of a beautiful young woman. But that duality left no trace in her eyes. Whatever the struggle raging elsewhere, her eyes had achieved a transcendence. They were grey, and calm, and wondrous.

'Ashtray.'

Her lips had hardly moved. It was as if she spoke directly from soul to soul.

'What?'

'I said,' and now her lips were moving, and her words as clear and cutting as shards of glass, 'ashtray.'

Still I hesitated, dulled and stupefied by her presence.

'Change it.'

Her voice was clear and musical and inhuman, like a finger drawn around a wineglass.

I looked down. Her ashtray was full.

'OK,' I said, trying not to stammer. I found that I wasn't breathing, and I had to force air into my lungs on my way back to the bar.

I brought her a clean ashtray from another table, and I made sure my hand was steady as I put it down. I thought that the effort to keep my hand from shaking was going to mean that the rest of me went into a St Vitus's dance. The wondrous eyes looked at me and I thought she was going to smile, but she didn't.

'Thank you,' she said, but she was already somewhere else.

When I went back to the bar, Pelly and Mercedes gave each other knowing looks and then choreographed a collective smirk at me. Of course, they were just winding me up, but I thought I might have perceived a little flirtatiousness, perhaps even a suggestion of pique, in Mercedes' look. I was definitely going to have to ask her out.

It was then that things started to happen. The first thing was the arrival of Dunyazad. She'd made herself up, which I'd never seen before. Blue eyeshadow, heavily rouged cheeks. It didn't suit her. She marched up to me at the bar, tottering slightly in a pair of high heels. I hadn't before noticed her exceptionally large ankles.

'I heard this was where you were. Malcolm saw you. Said you were working as a doorman. I didn't believe him.'

'Let me introduce you,' I said. 'Pelly, Mercedes, this is Dunyazad, one of my students.'

'I am not one of your students.' She turned to Mercedes, and announced loudly, 'I am his lover.'

Pelly crouched down below the line of the bar to hide his laughter.

'Well, you . . .' I stopped, realising the futility of trying to explain who she was. 'Let me buy you a drink.'

'A big beer,' she said. I helped her up on to a bar stool.

'How's the work coming along?' I asked, trying to get a bit of normality into things.

'The work is laborious,' she said. 'But I must do it for the women of my country. I must give them their history. You know, things are very bad for women in Egypt, but the only opposition to the government is the Islamicists, and they would make things much worse.'

I nodded. I'd heard it a dozen times before. I began to explore other platitudinous lines of conversation, which would all come round to my need to get on with my job, but she interrupted me.

'I am not here to seduce you.'

'Oh.'

'I am here to say that it is to be all over between us.'

'OK.'

'I do not mean to give pain, but it is causing disruption to my studies.'

'And you got all dressed up just to tell me this?'

She smiled coquettishly.

'To show you what you are missing. And I am meeting Malcolm afterwards.' Malcolm was another of my students. He'd taken early retirement from an insurance company following some kind of mental collapse.

I felt a great wave of affection for Dunyazad at that moment. It may sound condescending to say it, but I found her indomitable will admirable, however distorted her vision of reality. Life had been cruel to her in almost any way you could imagine, but still she fought the good fight. Compared to her I felt like a fraud, a weakling, a man of straw, and I decided never again to notice her eye, her hair or the ankles like grapefruit. I leant towards her and kissed her on the forehead.

'You're a remarkable woman, Dunyazad,' I said. 'Perhaps you're right: it's best for both of us if we get our relationship back on a professional footing.'

'And you are not heartbroken?' She looked at me hopefully.

'Yes, a little heartbroken.' There was no lie – aren't we all a little heartbroken?

She looked quietly satisfied.

Her beer came. She took two little sips and then a big gulp, and then said that she must be going. We shook hands, and she was gone.

'On form tonight, mate,' said Pelly.

Before I had the chance to answer back, I heard a commotion at the doorway. For a second I thought that Dunyazad had picked a fight with Errol, and then I heard Spider's piercing cockney, 'You're not fucking coming in,' followed by an indistinct shout.

I suspected that the time had come for me to earn my wages.

When I got to the inner door, I saw a confused knot of bodies. I went into the lobby, and the shape of things became clear. Errol and Spider were grappling with a monster. A monster, that is, in an old suit of rough tweed, gone at the elbows. He had a frayed blue shirt and a dirty yellow tie, twisted tight at the collar, the way schoolboys wear their ties. His head was enormous, topped with patchy grey hair. His face was shining bright red, although I couldn't tell whether that was his normal complexion or whether it had something to do with the fact that Spider had his arm around his neck, while he punched ineffectually at the back of his head. He tried to grab or scratch at the man's face, but his hands just seemed to slide off the sweating, oily skin.

Errol had both of the man's arms bent back behind him, and he should have been completely immobilised. But somehow he kept coming forward. He looked up through his bristling eyebrows and saw me. His eyes were tiny bloodshot marbles set in his fleshy face. And he smiled at me. I don't know why. Maybe he realised that I was no doorman, that I'd be causing him no trouble, no trouble at all. But I don't think that was it. I think it was more that he was enjoying himself, having fun with one bouncer round his neck and another busy breaking his arms, and he couldn't help but let some of that joy spill over.

And then I saw him concentrate, and with a twist he wrenched an arm out of Errol's grip, and grabbed Spider and threw him on the floor, the way you'd throw down a jacket after work. Without Spider on his neck he was able to speak:

'I only want a fecken drink,' he said, his brogue still bog thick after God knew how many years on the building sites of Kilburn and Cricklewood.

Errol managed to grab his arm again, but now it was just him holding on. I didn't know what to do. Errol helped me out.

'Hit him,' he yelled through clenched teeth. 'Hit the bastard.'

I remembered the knuckle-duster, still unused in my pocket. I put my fingers through the loop of brass, and took out my hand. The dull gold of it caught the man's eye, and he stopped straining. Errol managed to get a better grip. Spider was still on the floor: he didn't look like he wanted to get back up.

'I said hit him,' Errol shouted again.

The man looked into my face. The smile had gone. There was now a look of resignation in his eyes. It was the look of the un-unionised working man, who's become accustomed to getting the shitty end of the stick, no matter how hard he strives, who knows that he'll never get the going rate, who knows that someone else is going to spend the profit he makes. Spend it in a place like this.

It was the face of my father. I put the knuckle-duster back in my pocket.

'Let him go,' I said to Errol.

'What?'

'I said let him go.'

'You're fucking mental.'

'On my head.'

'Too fucking right.'

That came from Spider, picking himself up from the floor, still keeping his distance.

'It's my call, this is what I'm for. Let him go.'

Errol sighed, and released the man's arms. He stood back against the outside door.

The man unbent himself. He was about the same height as Jonah, but far bulkier in build, with hard fat layered over his muscles. He was probably in his late fifties or early sixties. You see his kind in the park in Kilburn every day. They stand or sit in groups, drinking headfuck lager or Thunderbird wine. But somehow they always seem sprucely turned out. I always imagined little Irish wives making sure their ties were straight and their shoes polished before they set off for a day of self-annihilation.

My dad had never been quite like that. I suppose he had enough intelligence to know when to draw back from the void. And my mother kept him in line: not a woman you wanted clattering you round the head when you came in too pissed to even sit in a chair. And then perhaps it helped that he was from a village in Donegal, and not a Dublin slum or Cork tenement, and so there was still enough of the decent, God-fearing country boy in him to keep him out of hell.

Whatever; as drunks go, he was the best. He never hit us, and he didn't drink the housekeeping, and on Saturdays he'd walk with me on his shoulders up to a field with horses, and he'd show me how to feed them stale bread out of the flat of my hand, and then we'd drink Tizer, or dandelion-and-burdock out of the bottle, and he'd even let me burp the loudest, and he kept himself alive until I didn't really need him any more.

For a moment I thought I'd made a mistake. The man staggered towards me, his big red hands still clenched. He looked like a silver-back gorilla fronting up a leopard. But no gorilla gives off the stench of sweat and gut-rot whisky like this fellow. Out of the corner of my eye I thought I saw Spider smile. Show the cunt, he was thinking.

But then the man stood up tall, and straightened his tie, or rather put it crookedly on the other side of his collar.

'I only wanted a pint. Used to get a good pint of porter here. That's all I'm asking. A pint of porter.'

'A pint of porter is your only man,' I said.

He looked perplexed for a second, and then he roared with some kind of tune:

'A pint o' porter is your only man!'

'We've no porter, but I'll buy you a Guinness.' I opened the door for him, and we went into the Zip together. The forty or so people there were watching us in expectant silence. I steered my friend to the bar.

'Two pints of Guinness,' I said to Pelly.

'Coming up,' he said, not looking at me or my new friend.

'Used to get a good point of porter in here,' said the man again. 'Used to be a good pub back then. Not a patch on the Railway Arms, mind you. But a good pub. It's here that I met my Mary, God rest her soul. Met her and courted her. Good times we had of it.'

'She was your wife?'

'No; wife, no. She wouldn't have me, on account as I was just labouring, and not much chance of anything better. Why did you . . . I mean, what for did you not join in with the boys out there?'

'My name's Matthew Moriarty,' I said, and held out my hand.

'James Noolan,' he said. 'James, mind, not Jimmy.'

His hand felt like it was made of pork crackling.

'The thing is, James,' I said, when we'd settled ourselves, 'this isn't really what you'd call a pub any more. It's not the place for the craic. You're better off at the Black Lion, or the Red Bull up the road.'

'I'm barred.'

'What, from both?'

'Oh, aye.'

'What did you do?'

He smiled, mischievously. 'I lobbed the barman at the Lion through the window of the Bull.'

'That would do it. But you're not barred everywhere?'

'Well, no, I can still get a pint at the North Star, but that's a God-forsaken place for a man to have to drink.'

'Look around you here, James. You can see this isn't the pub you remember. It's gone. Look at the people. They're not your people any more.'

Noolan looked sadly around. His red eyes filled with tears.

'Mary herself wouldn't recognise it. She went to Wolverhampton. Where are your people from, boy?'

'Leeds.'

'No, not here. Where are they really from?'

'Donegal.'

'Donegal?' He sounded sorry. 'I never went there.'

He stood up, drinking back the Guinness as he rose. 'I'm away,' he said, for all the world as if the two of us had just slipped out for a quiet pint together.

At that moment Jonah came in. Errol and Spider stood behind him.

'Hello, James,' said Jonah.

'Jonah.' James nodded. I sensed he was suddenly on best behaviour. Dragging bouncers behind you like an ox pulling a plough was one thing, but showing a lack of the proper respect for Jonah Whale was quite another.

'They tell me there's been a spot of bother.'

'No bother at all,' I said. 'Mr Noolan and I were having a drink. He's on his way now. See you, James.'

Noolan waved over his shoulder, his gait a dignified shamble. Spider and Errol stood well back as he passed, although once he was through the door Spider did a quick Ali shuffle and a couple of sharp jabs.

'Serious piece of work, Jimmy Noolan, when he's had a drink,' said Jonah, smiling grimly.

'Pussycat,' I said.

5

Lamia

I suppose I was feeling pretty pleased with myself after the Noolan incident. I thought I'd done well, diffusing a tricky situation, giving a bit of dignity back to Noolan. And the truth is that there hadn't exactly been a surfeit of stuff in my life for me to feel good about, and I had to make the most of what came along. So I went shopping in the West End on Saturday morning and bought myself some new clothes: a sharp suit, a pair of black boots, a couple of shirts. I had lunch in a Vietnamese restaurant, and flirted with the waitress, who was charming and tiny and birdlike, and she brought many small dishes.

I thought about my life, and for the first time in a long time things seemed to be going the right way. I was back in academia, doing a job that I knew to be worthwhile. My students weren't spoilt brats looking for an easy couple of years before they went off to work in management consultancy; they were people desperately yearning for knowledge, prepared to make real sacrifices to achieve it. And now the bad side – the shitty pay – didn't matter because I could earn all I needed working at the Zip, and it turned out I was pretty good at that too.

At home that afternoon I even tried calling up some old friends and colleagues from my student and early teaching days up in Manchester, but the numbers had all changed, and all I got was recorded voices or a red hum.

Saturday night I was the Prince of Zip, doing exactly what Jonah had taken me on for. I circulated in the bar, I helped out on the door. I was in the mood to mollify Spider and Errol, so I said that I'd stand in whenever either of them needed a ten-minute break. It went down well. And working with just one of the guys at a time was easier. Without the group solidarity bullshit, Errol and Spider were both easier to talk to. Spider told army stories, stuff about serving in the Gulf and Northern Ireland. Errol spoke more about his DJing. These weren't exactly my kind of people, but they were OK, and it looked like we'd found a way of coexisting.

Nothing happened when I was standing in, but later a gaggle of eighteen-year-old lads tried to barge their way through the door, and I went to help. Just a bit of pushing, a couple of gestures. Spider wanted to go and properly sort them out, but I told him to leave it, said he'd made his point, flattered him about how coolly he'd handled it. Of course, it was Errol who'd done the real work, putting his arm around the gang leader and guiding him outside in a way that strongly suggested that resistance was futile, without making the kid totally lose face.

My woman, my Lamia, was there.

'She doesn't usually come in at the weekend,' said Pelly. 'She's here for you.' He pointed his finger, pistol fashion, at me.

'Hey, you're the one with the fan club,' I said, nodding to the two pretty girls sitting on stools at the bar. Pelly had been showing off his cocktail tricks, tossing the glasses, shaking his shaker, swizzling his swizzle stick.

The girls laughed, but didn't deny it. Mercedes wasn't on tonight. A mumsy woman called Helen was doing the tables. She was nice, in a grabbing-your-cheeks kind of way, but she wasn't Mercedes.

'Have you even spoken to her yet?' Pelly was still talking about my silent woman.

'She's not an easy lady to talk to. She told me to get her an ashtray last night, before James Noolan came in.'

'Hot stuff.'

'You want to go and take care of her, and I'll keep things cooking here?'

'Nah, I wouldn't trust you. You'd shake when you ought to stir.' He shot a white smile at the girls.

So I went to talk to the Lamia.

The Zip was full, and she was hemmed in with bodies around her. Somehow she still managed to convey the same serene isolation. No, 'serene' gets it wrong. It was a different kind of calmness. She was like an angel carved on a gravestone.

'Hi,' I said. She looked slowly at me, dragging her eyes from nothing. 'Everything OK?' I was already floundering.

'Fine,' she said, after what felt like minutes. And then she somehow concentrated her gaze, and for the first time ever I felt that she saw me. It was a difficult gaze to bear. 'You're new here.' As she spoke I could see the sharp white tips of her teeth.

'I've been here for a week. Feels like I'm a veteran. I've noticed that you come in most evenings.'

Stupid thing to say. How was she supposed to respond to that?

'What are you for?' Again, the tips of her teeth.

'For?'

'What do you do?'

'Here?'

'Here.'

'Well, I . . . it's a bit tricky.' Too many words, stuttering. 'They want to change the profile of the customers, make the place a bit classier, I suppose. More people like you.'

It was the clumsiest compliment I'd ever paid anyone. It wasn't even sixth-form. It was like something you'd say as a shy fourteen-year-old. I expected her to defocus again, to drift back into her private universe. Instead she smiled. It was a curious little smile, impish, young. Young, at least, if you concentrated only on her mouth. Its effect on the rest of her face was to throw her age into relief. The fine lines around her eyes deepened into wrinkles, the skin over her cheekbones became tissue thin and dry. And she knew it: perhaps she saw, or thought she saw, some reaction in my face, or perhaps she simply understood what smiling would do to her carefully composed beauty. Either way, the smile stopped. I went on, even more quickly, garbling my words.

'And so I'm here to help keep out the undesirables and to . . .'

But she wasn't looking at me any more. Nor, this time, had she simply slipped away. She was peering intently out of the wide window. Something about the way she looked made me spin around – I almost felt that someone was standing behind me with a hatchet. What I saw was a big black four-wheel-drive at the kerb. Not some cheap utilitarian box of a Toyota or Suzuki, not even a country-chic Land Rover, but one of the sleek and massive new Porsches, where even the pretence of off-roading has been abandoned, leaving just the simple, bruising statement of wealth and power. Two men in dark suits peeled out of the front seats.

Each took a rear door. On this side there stepped out the kind of thing you don't see much in my part of North London: she was wearing what looked like a real mink coat over the top of something short and diaphanous, like the shed skin of a mermaid; her long, rowan hair was touched with gold at the front; gold adorned also her fingers, her wrists, her neck. You see that kind of woman shopping for shoes in Knightsbridge or leaving a restaurant in Kensington or getting into a taxi on the King's Road. You don't see them in Kilburn. I guessed she was eighteen years old, and she still looked happy to be in the world. She slid out of the big Porsche like thick cream off a spoon.

Two men came round from the road side of the car. One was the man in black from the front. The other was a short, almost slight figure, with a deep tan and silver hair. He was wearing a grey suit with a faint metallic shimmer somewhere in the weave. He put an affectionate arm on the girl's shoulder. Affectionate or proprietorial. She was two or three inches taller than him, despite his Cuban heels.

'Oh God, no.'

My woman had spoken.

'What?'

'Don't let him in. Please, don't let him in.' She looked at me, her grey eyes full of terror.

'I don't understand. Why not?'

'You can't let him in. I'm begging you.' The emotion had animated her face, and again it had lost its sculpted purity.

I checked back. The group was walking towards the door. I could see Spider and Errol. They'd noticed them too, and were standing weirdly to attention, as if they were awaiting foreign dignitaries.

'OK,' I said.

And as I thought about it, there did seem something sinister in the party. The little man appeared harmless enough, with his thick head of carefully moussed hair: but then what sort of person goes about with two minders? But I'm guessing I would have let them in nonetheless, without the woman's obvious fear, without my desire to do something to please her.

I walked quickly, but trying not to show too much urgency. I got there just as Errol was standing back to let the silver man and the golden woman in. The two heavies, bland and featureless, were behind them.

'I'm sorry,' I said, standing in their way, 'not tonight.'

The man had been answering Errol's smile with a flash of his own chemically white teeth, vivid against his tan. The smile dipped and then returned.

'What was that, son?'

The accent was hard to place. There was something foreign in it, perhaps South African, but it was overlain by glottal-stopping Estuary.

'I said you can't come in.'

The smile was still there, just. The man was a head shorter than me, but up close I could see there was nothing frail about his thinness. I sensed the two men behind begin to edge forward, and I was glad to have Errol and Spider there. Except that Errol seemed to be trying to mouth something at me, and Spider was looking straight up into the ceiling.

'It's casual night. No suits.'

The man snorted.

'No suits?' He pronounced it 'suts'. 'I've never heard that one before. Come on, friend, we're just here for a quiet drink. I was told you'd just done the place up. I used to know it in the old days, and I'm telling you the rest of the world had to employ bouncers to keep the lunatics in, never mind out.' He smiled broadly again, showing all his teeth.

His tone was friendly, and I felt his charm, his strength. I wanted to smile back, to explain that I was only joking, that of course they could come in, have a good evening. The girl's face was beginning to set into a pout. I wanted very strongly to kiss her to see if she tasted as rich as she looked.

The man put his hand out in the same proprietorial way he had used with the girl, as if to gently move me out of his way. It was that which shunted me into psycho mode.

'Look, I've told you, you're not coming in. You and your boyfriends can piss off, and,' I said, pointing at his clearly much-pampered hair, 'take the chinchilla with you. Oh, but your granddaughter can stay.'

Nothing in the man's words or actions had justified any of that. I suppose that I could argue that what followed backed up my feelings about him; but then, if I'd known what was to follow, rather than insult him I'd have welcomed him in, taken his coat, polished his fucking shoes, if he'd let me. But my stupid words were out there.

'I'm not his granddaughter,' said the girl, stroppily. It was like when you guess a child's age, and they say, indignantly, 'I'm not five, I'm five and a half.'

The man looked at me now in a new way. I looked back. His eyes were pale and unblinking.

'Don't let him talk to me like that, Bernie,' the girl added, although I hadn't said a word to her.

Suddenly, faced with the man's pale eyes and quiet calm, I felt weak and exposed. Spider and Errol were in the way of the two bruisers, but nothing separated me from the silver man, and in that moment I began to realise my mistake.

Successful career criminals survive and prosper by being

the hardest fucking men on their patch. Ordinary citizens can never begin to imagine the levels of brutality they've had to pass through, the trials of strength and will. Any weakness gets discovered, and those who lack the qualities of physical courage, ruthlessness and technical skill drop away, find their niche lower down the food chain. If this man really was a top crook, then he'd barely need to tap his reserves of violence to crush me.

I felt a muscle in my eyelid begin to twitch, and I tried to blink it away. The man's thin mouth smiled again: no teeth this time, just a quick, wry flicker. Again I sensed the two minders move forward. Errol shifted his bulk to the middle of the doorway, blocking them. Spider stood to one side and a little behind.

The man's lips hardly moved as he said: 'No, Mandy. This gentleman's in charge here. He's only doing his job. Come on, we'll go up West. This place is still a shithole.' As he left he turned his head and said over his shoulder, 'See you now, boys,' his cheerfulness fully restored.

'Have you any idea who that was?' asked Spider when the Porsche had gone. Errol was looking at me like I was the Bearded Lady or the Calf with Two Heads.

'Dunno. Some estate agent? Owns a chain of flower shops?' They both laughed, nervous tension easing out of their shoulders. And out of mine. 'Look, I guess he was some kind of crook, probably still living off a bullion raid back in the eighties. Got his first break sucking Ronnie Kray's cock in nineteen sixty-three. But we handled him.'

'Nobody handles Bernie Mueller,' said Spider. 'He fucking handles you. And if you're not careful he'll handle your fucking head off. And I don't get it. I thought they wanted money in here. You probably just turned away five hundred quid in fucking champagne and caviar and fuck know's what.'

'Not that kind of money. That's exactly the kind of money they don't want.'

Errol said, 'Chinchilla,' and started to laugh. After a second, Spider joined in. There'd been some adrenalin pumping, and it's always a good feeling when it's still in the blood, and you haven't taken a clattering.

'So who is this Mueller, then, if he's not an estate agent?'

Errol answered: 'You're not that far out there, in a way. He owns most of the shit housing round here, streets of it, anyway. Me Auntie Eileen lives in one of his. He's OK as long as you pays your rent. If you don't, then there int no warning, you just wake up to find your head in a horse's bed, if you get what I'm saying.'

'But it's not just the houses, though,' said Spider. 'He's got a finger in every fucking pie going. All the decent slappers round here are his. And then there's all the fraud and that, the stuff they can't get you for, and if they try the fucking jury's got no idea what's fucking going on. That's the one to get into. Fancy some of that meself.'

I went back into the bar. I didn't return straight to the woman – that would have made me look too much like her poodle. But in five minutes I was there. She was fully herself again: untouchable and composed.

'They've gone,' I said, unnecessarily.

'I saw. Thank you.'

Silence.

'Who was he? I mean, I know his name, but what was he to you?'

She looked at me, waited again, weighing what she owed, what she was prepared to give.

'My husband.'

That was all I was getting. I don't know what I expected. She wasn't the bear-hug type.

The rest of the evening slipped by. People drifted away. Helen and Pelly were clearing up. Jonah hadn't come in. It was a pity: I'd wanted to tell him about my encounter with Bernie Mueller. I wanted to let him know how well I'd dealt with it, wanted to explain why he was the kind of person who'd put off the lawyers and media types they wanted in the bar. I suppose that my need for his approval said something about Jonah, and something about me.

Usually the Lamia would disappear before closing time without me seeing how – I'd see her in her place, then look away and back again and she wouldn't be there. Other people had noticed it too, and Mercedes said she was a witch. But tonight she was still there at ten to one.

'Late for you,' I said, trying to sound light.

'It's later than you think.'

'I see you do enigmatic to go with the mystcrious.'

That made her smile, but not much.

'Will you help me find a taxi?'

'Yes,' I said, after hesitating for a full three-tenths of a second. 'I'm finished here. More or less. Just let me have a word with . . .'

She stood up and handed me her coat: silk and cashmere, blood-warm and fluid in my hands. She shucked into it as I held it for her, and I felt the brush of her hip against my groin. Her perfume was dark and musky, and seemed to come from within her, reaching me from her pores, from the breathing of her skin.

I didn't look at Pelly and Helen, nodded briefly to Errol at the door – Spider, to my relief, wasn't there.

Outside the air was cold, and dry. I had only my suit, and I shivered. We were close, but not touching. I saw that she was tall: her eyes were an inch below mine.

'I know a good place for taxis along here,' I said, still keeping up the pretence that this was what we were about. 'Where are you headed?'

'There's somewhere here, just here,' she said in response.

We were on the Kilburn High Road. It was Saturday night after closing time. The streets were emptying, but there were still drifting groups of men, and other men lying across the pavements amid the fast-food cartons and rolling cans of Special Brew and Tennents Super. Cars and Transit vans still moved north and south, calmer now the grind of day was over. As well as the residential streets, the High Road is met by endless blind alleyways. Alleyways stocked with dustbins and blown trash and city filth, and Christ knew what else.

The woman was pulling my sleeve. 'Here,' she said. 'This is the place.'

She was moving into one of the stinking alleys. A dull blue light up high on a wall gave some illumination, but this was still a world of shadow and murk.

'No,' I said, 'not here.' But I was already getting hard. I knew what she wanted. I knew what she had always wanted. Or was it the other way? Had she always seen inside me with those unfocused eyes of hers, seen what was there, seen that it matched what she had, what she wanted?

So my Lamia led me into the alley, through the filth, our feet stumbling over the trash and the unlevel ground. The alley bent slightly, and soon the street was only a sliver of light, like a new moon in the desert. I put my hand under her coat, laid it softly on the curve of her back, swept it

62

down, along her thigh. I felt the buckle of a suspender. She gave a little gasp, and fell back against the wall, pulling me with her. I pressed my face to hers, and I could hear the hard urgency of her breath. She took my hand and put it to her breast. I felt her nipple with my thumb, and I pulled open her blouse and kissed the top of her breast, and then sank lower and took the nipple in my mouth. And now her hands were on my hips, and she pulled me to her, and her legs were around me. I put my hands on her buttocks, lifting her skirt. I slid my hands into her knickers, and clutched her to me, and she moved sinuously, and whispered, 'Fuck me' in my ear, and I laughed and said that that was exactly my intention.

And then, with a delicate little movement, she stepped out of her knickers. I undid my belt and she put her long-fingered hands on me, and then I was inside her, and I could feel her body from her neck to her ankles around me, and I tried to kiss her mouth, but she moved her head to my shoulder, and her lips to my ear, and I heard the strange sounds she made, like none I've ever heard from a woman. She didn't groan or pant or gasp, but she let out little sibilant hisses. Maybe she was just saying 'yesss, yessss', but it unnerved me. I tried to kiss her again, partly because to fuck without kissing is an offence against love, and partly to stop the noise, but still I could not find her mouth. And then her body began to beat and writhe to a new rhythm, and it was a rhythm beyond my skill to control, and I felt an inanimate thing, or like the victim of some rite.

And I opened my eyes and tried to look at her, but her body was too close to me, was part of me. And she was as light as the cigarette smoke I could smell mixed with the musk in her hair, and her lightness made her seem not human, but spectral. Except I could feel her bones, brittle and fragile. And I thought of the nest box of blue tits I found as a boy, deserted by the cat-stalked mother: eight tiny skeletons in a circle, their beaks pointing inward, something I'd have to face in my dreams for years afterwards, and which was back with me now. And my Lamia was dry bones, and her face a grinning skull, and her hisses were growing sharper, and her writhing uncontrollable, and I was choked by the dust and decay of her, and I thought again of the sepulchral angels, crumbling to white dust, and again of her skull, and the dust of her. And it was all mixed with the foul stink of the alley, and the rustling of vermin amid the garbage. And as what was left of my erection collapsed she came, or at least her hissing and writhing stopped, and she fell from me like a sloughed snake skin.

She was looking down. I put my fingers on her chin and tried to lift her face to me, but she shook me away.

'Could you get my knickers. They're over there,' she said, gesturing farther into the gloom.

'Sure,' I said, fastening my trousers. I didn't want to be in this alley for another second, didn't want to have whatever conversation I was supposed to have with her. But I would ask her name.

'Do you know where. . . . ?' I said, after a few moments of kicking about in the dark. And then I saw something white and gauzy, and picked it up, but when I turned around I was alone in the alley.

6

A Return

I felt pretty sordid as I picked my way out of that narrow, shit-smeared space. I hadn't done much of this sort of thing – the brutal, random, alleyway fuck. I still didn't know her name, didn't know anything about her, except that she was married to some kind of criminal called Bernie Mueller. Was married, or, I supposed, had been married. And that she was afraid of him, and didn't want to see him. Nor did it seem that she wanted to see much of me.

Still, I hadn't had much in the way of female company over the past six months. Since Sufi left I'd had a couple of dates, not including the defensive actions I'd fought against Dunyazad, but only one night of what could even remotely be described as sexual intimacy. That was with a girl of monumental proportions called Miriam, whom I'd met at a conference in Edinburgh. It was a broad-based humanities shindig, aimed mainly at youngish academics, with plenty of social interludes to help promote interdisciplinary harmony. Miriam approached me at a buffet, and asked me to hold her plate as she piled it high with sausage rolls and chicken drumsticks. Then she led me into a corner and sent me off to collect drinks for her while she talked about her struggles at Cambridge. At twelve o'clock she bundled me into bed and pretty well did what she wanted to me, which largely involved instructing me to do things to her that I didn't particularly want to do. She could be very persuasive. In the middle of the night she asked me whether I had any food. I didn't. We were staying in student accommodation and of course there was no room service so she told me to go and buy two pork pies from an all-night garage. It took me an hour to find one. When I returned she was snoring on her back. She woke up with a grunt and ate both the pork pies sitting naked on the side of the bed, her long red hair falling over, but in no way hiding, the largest breasts I'd ever seen on a live human being. After the pork pies she did what she wanted to me again, and then got in some more quality snoring.

She gave her paper the next day. It wasn't my field but I sat in. It was on Frankenstein. Mary Shelley gave her book the subtitle 'The New Prometheus', and Miriam's lecture was all about how Dr Frankenstein and Prometheus both brought gifts to mankind that could simultaneously help and harm – Prometheus his fire, and Frankenstein his new scientific discoveries.

In the Q&A at the end I pointed out (possibly too vigorously) that Shelley's subtitle was more likely to be alluding to the less well-known, but still far from obscure, myth in which Prometheus actually creates mankind, in the same way that Frankenstein creates his monster. Miriam didn't take kindly to my contribution, and that night there was no repetition of the pork pies or the doing what she wanted to me.

So that was pretty well it, sex-wise. That's why I couldn't help but feel some satisfaction, some taint of smugness, mixed in with the disgust and the mystery, as I left the stench of that narrow passage.

I couldn't sleep that night, thinking of the Lamia and Mueller, and also of Mercedes. It may not have been quite logical, but I knew that whatever it was that had happened in the alleyway had involved some element of betrayal. If I was going easy on myself, I might say that the betrayal was minor because, after all, nothing had happened between Mercedes and me; but a betrayal it remained, because I liked her, and I wanted there to be something between us. Mercedes was close to my physical ideal: dark haired, black eyed, olive skinned. And she was smart and she was funny and she had that thing of being maybe about eight per cent mad, which is just enough madness to make a girl inter-esting but not enough madness to make her strange and nowhere near enough madness to make her stab you in the night because the voices told her you'd been replaced by a double. I was worried that somehow word of what I'd done with the Lamia would get back to Mercedes, destroying whatever hopes I had. I was a fool.

But whenever I tried to concentrate on Mercedes, working on strategies, trying to come up with a way of asking her out, the Lamia kept coming back into my thoughts. I kept feeling her again against the dripping wall, kept sensing her becoming spectral to enter me, felt her bones crumble, felt her spores suffuse my nose and mouth and lungs.

I'd showered and brushed my teeth, but when I felt a tickle at the back of my throat I knew what it was. I coughed it free, and then worked at it with my tongue and then finally got it out with my fingers: a long, blonde hair, grey at the root, its lustre gone. *A circle of bright hair about the bone.*

The next day was Sunday. On Sundays I didn't do a damn thing, didn't drink, didn't smoke, went out only to get the papers. That evening one of my friends from univer-sity got back to me – somehow the message had reached

him. We had a good talk about college days, and he said
he'd come down to visit, and I said that would be good,
thinking I ought to get a sofa bed or futon or some such.
Talking to him made me want to get back properly into the
heart of things, back into research and full-time teaching.
I thought that maybe I should stop playing at being a
doorman, that maybe I should get on with what I was good
at. I resolved to talk to Jonah on Monday, to tell him I
thought it wasn't working out, that I'd stay until he found
someone else.

On Monday night I felt restless and decided to have a
quick drink before my shift – it was half-term, so there
wasn't a seminar. The first thing I saw as I pushed through
the doors of the Black Lion was Ju, natty in a kind of
Edwardian suit in blue velvet.

Somehow I wasn't surprised. I'd been thinking about Ju.
It was obvious that something hadn't been right with him,
and we went back a long away. That created obligations. I
kept meaning to call him. I didn't have his number but I
could have got hold of him through the label. But then I'd
never been good at making that kind of effort.

He was at the bar, engaged in an animated discussion
with a brutal-looking guy wearing Soviet-bloc denims. I
could see the veins standing out on the man's forehead, and
his blue jaw was set and rigid. Other eyes were on them,
not all friendly. I went over.

'United fucking Ireland,' Ju was saying, 'who the fuck
wants to be united with a bunch of fucking oligarchs?
Nationalism's just a trick to keep the working class pre-
occupied so the fucking landowners can carry on shitting
on them. You've got to try thinking with your brain and not
your spade.'

Maybe the fellow he was talking to would have enjoyed the chance of a nice open debate on the ironies of Irish nationalism, and maybe he was about to kneecap Ju. I wasn't taking the chance.

'Three pints of Guinness here,' I said to a bemused barman, as I put an arm round Ju. And then I turned to the man in the denims and said, 'Excuse my idiot brother here, he's just out of the nuthouse and his medication's not quite right and so he blathers and he doesn't know what he's saying and anyway his father played hurley for Wexford.'

The big fellow stared hard at me, but then he took his pint and went over to put money into a fruit machine, and the other faces about the place turned back to their business.

I looked at Ju expecting to see some pleasure there, but his expression was closer to shock. For the first time in our friendship it looked like I'd really surprised him, and I felt a gratifying little surge of satisfaction at having repaid him for his stunt in Power's Bar. His mouth was open and his eyes wide and manic. Then he wiped his hand across his face, and came out with a quick smile.

'Everything was cool,' he said, coolly, which didn't seem quite right.

'Hey, I knew you had it covered. But, you know, sometimes you have to think about what you say in a place like this. He a friend of yours?'

'Never met him before.' And he was normal again; normal for Ju, that was. 'But you, Matty. Good to see you again. Fucking good to see you.'

'What are you doing here?' I asked him. 'I know you claim to be a local, but I haven't seen you in here before.'

'I'm meeting a bloke,' he said. 'Just some geezer. But not for a little while yet. Let's have a sit.'

'Yeah, well, I'm only in for a quick one myself.'

We took our beers over to a table. The Black Lion was a great old Kilburn pub. The inside must once have been truly beautiful, with its gilded mouldings and curious reliefs showing nymphs and zephyrs and dryads engaged in various Dionysian pursuits. But it wasn't a museum and everything was scuffed and rucked or rubbed smooth by hips and arses in rough tweed.

Ju still seemed a touch nervous, and I tried to compensate by excessive heartiness.

'It's fantastic bumping into you like this,' I said. 'Ever since I saw you with those two guys in Power's, I wanted to . . . you know, get together, get pissed, sort out the world.'

'Fuck the world. Let's just get pissed. I'm early for my man, we've got an hour.'

'I can't get too drunk – like I said, I'm working tonight.'

'Working? Is this the security bullshit you talked about?'

'That about sums it up. I'm a hired heavy at the Zip.'

Ju spluttered beer foam in my face.

'Since when did you turn into a hard bastard? I thought you were Mr Ivory Tower. Something got fucked up along the way.'

'Ain't that the truth.'

'Tell me about it.'

So I did. It wasn't a happy story, but it had its blackly comic side, and Ju gave his own glancing commentary as we went, without getting in the way of the narrative. It was the first time I'd strung it together in a coherent way, and so for the first time I too was able make sense of it all. And as I told the story, which became the whole story of my life since I'd fallen out with Ju all those years ago, I felt the sinews and connective tissues of our old friendship begin to re-form, and our heads inclined together in laughter. Maybe I should have sensed that Ju's concentrated interest in what I was saying may at least partially have come from his desire to avoid talking about himself, to avoid hard questions.

And then Ju lifted back his cuff and showed his watch.

'Don't want you telling teacher it was me that made you late for school.'

'Shit, Ju,' I said. 'This has been all me. Let's meet up and you can pay me back for that hour of tedium.'

'It wasn't tedious for me,' he replied, seriously, and there was no taint of irony in his voice.

'Yeah, but still, I need to hear all about the new record, and all the rest of it.'

And Ju's eyes went out of focus for a second, and he said, 'Sure, you will, next time.'

And I stood up and we gave each other the kind of hug that men sometimes give each other, the kind that begins with jokey slaps, and then becomes serious for a moment, and then dissolves in embarrassment.

But before we separated, Ju said – whispered, really – 'It wasn't your fault.'

And then I dived off, leaving him to wait for his man.

At the time I thought his words referred to the stuff I'd just told him, about the way I'd loused up my life. But later, much later, I thought about it again, and I knew that he meant how our friendship had ended.

I was smiling when I reached the Zip, thinking that we'd made a real start, and that the next time I saw Ju the last of the awkwardness would have gone, and our friendship would be again as it once had been.

'What's so funny?' Spider was looking at me with his usual furtive blankness.

'Oh, nothing. How goes it here?'

'Quiet. Jonah's dropping round about ten.'

Errol loomed up behind him like a black iceberg.

'Evening, man.'

Mercedes was back. She was on a bar stool chatting with Pelly while she ate a plate of tapas.

'Looks good,' I said.

''S only *patatas bravas* and Spanish omelette. My mother could make it better asleep. You look happy for a change. But you should be sad.'

'Why?'

'You lady no in.'

'Hey, Mercedes, you know you're my lady.' I said it smilingly, but I let my eyes connect with hers. She was still for a moment before her face crinkled up.

'Steady, mate,' said Pelly, 'no-fraternisation policy in operation.'

For all my curiosity about her, I was relieved that my Lamia wasn't in. I'm guessing that she'd have said nothing about the encounter, but simply stared into her void as she always did. She wasn't going to be smiling the smile all of a sudden. And even my curiosity, wasn't that already partially sated? Hadn't I found out about her the things that all men want to discover: the smell of her, the taste of her, the feel of her, hot and wet? The world was full of other things to be curious about, and my Lamia's relationship with her husband, and the source of her melancholy and solitude, could wait their turn.

About half an hour into the night Errol came over and asked if I'd stand with Spider while he had a 'comfort break'.

Spider was half out in the street, looking up and down, nervous at being left on his own.

'It's Monday night, Spider. All the bad boys are home tonight watching *Emmerdale*.'

'Yeah,' he said, and let out a nervous whinny. 'Boring, innit? Could do with a bit of action just to keep me awake.'

'Sure, Spider. Well, don't tell the boss, but I like it quiet. I've got a joke. What do you call a fly with no wings?'

Spider looked puzzled. I think he may have thought that there was some link with his name. Finally he shook his head.

'A walk.'

'Funny,' he said, but he wasn't listening.

'It's the way I tell them.'

I was aware of a shadow over my shoulder, and I turned round. There was something familiar about the man in front of me. Navy blue suit, white shirt, neat hair, smell of after-shave. He looked like a rugby player. Bland, fleshy face. A broken nose, badly reset. He was wearing Ray-Ban aviator sunglasses, but that's not something you notice in London, even at night. What was strange was that he was just standing there, not trying to come in. Perhaps he was waiting for his girlfriend to catch up. Something like that.

'Help you?' I said.

He looked for his girlfriend each way up the street.

'I think maybe you can,' he said, his voice a little indistinct, maybe from the broken nose, as though he was making tiny *nngth* noises before each word. And then with a smooth movement he took something out of his pocket, and hit me across the side of the head with it. The pain didn't confine itself to my head, but filled my whole being, rampaging like a monster down my neck and into my guts. It hurt too much for me to cry out. The world greyed for a couple of seconds, and my knees buckled.

I tried to turn back into the lobby, looking for help from

Spider. Spider was on one knee, facing away, doing up a shoelace. 'Spi . . .' I said, my words sticking like paste in my mouth. 'Spi . . . hel . . .'

But then the guy with the cosh took hold of me. He dragged me out of the doorway, my legs still folding like broken sticks. I tried to struggle, but I was half gone from the blow, as weak as a stunned veal calf. His massive arm was a steel clamp around me. To any passer-by I suppose we'd have looked like two friends out for a night on the piss, one helping the other.

And then another shadow was at my side, and the two of them half dragged, half carried me. I knew where we were going. There was only one place that it could be, and I recognised the stench the second we entered the dog-leg alley.

The greyness was rolling back. But in its place the world was spinning. There was the sound of a man whistling. I couldn't get a fix on the tune, something simple, something old. I was on the filthy ground. I don't know whether they threw me, or just let me drop. Either way my face was in the fetid wet grit of the floor. And then my mouth filled with saliva, and before I could do anything about it my stomach spasmed and, in a dramatic spray, I vomited up the beer I'd drunk that evening. I thought my head was going to fall open, like a neatly spooned boiled egg.

'Fuckin' hell, Bernie,' a voice said, the thick *nngthing* voice of the man with the broken nose. 'He's puked on me Guccis. Dirty little cunt.'

'Don't you worry, Mr Liphook,' said another voice, the clipped South African cockney voice of Bernie Mueller, 'we'll get the boy here to clean it for you.'

I was on all fours. I looked up, trying to focus. In the blue light I could see the shapes of three men. I tried to speak, but before the words were out another spasm hit me and I retched again. And then one of the men kicked me in the stomach.

'Let's help get that up for you, son.' This was a third voice, as bland as a dentist's.

I rolled into a ball, partly as a reflex, partly to try to protect myself. I knew that I was about to take a bad beating, and I knew why. I'd taken plenty of stray punches in my time – mine was the kind of school where that was one thing you learned – but I'd never been beaten up by professionals. I knew it was going to be an ordeal, knew that it was the kind of experience that never leaves you, but I knew, or thought, that I was no coward, and that if I could cover my face and my guts I'd get through it.

And then they started to stamp on me. I think it was just the two heavies, but I wasn't looking. They stamped down through my feeble guard, stamped down into my guts, into my face. I managed to twist, putting my soft underside to the ground, and then they stamped down on my spine and kidneys, and on the back of my head. They grunted as they worked, each stamp rammed home with a guttural *ugh*. About then I started to cry, and tried to make it into some kind of noise that would reach the street.

Mueller said, 'Gag him, Mr Liss,' and one of the men forced my mouth open and tied a rag around my head.

'Hold him up,' said Mueller, and I prayed to Christ that it might be over. I knew that my face was a mess, and that the stamping had done something serious to my insides, but I thought if only it would stop here, then I wasn't going to die.

'Look at me,' he said.

I looked. Mueller's hair was as ridiculously bouffant as

the last time I'd seen him, but he was wearing a different face. His lips had pulled back from his teeth, and his nose was wrinkled in disgust. But even as I looked he was disappearing. I thought I was going blind, but then I realised that it was just that my swollen eyes were closing.

'You know what this is about, son, don't you?'

Because I'd embarrassed him in front of his girl? Because I'd fucked his wife? One, or both. I nodded.

'I don't like having to do this. But if word got around that I'd let some little poof like you keep me out of a place in which I had . . . an interest, then . . . well, I wouldn't be the man that I am.'

I tried to say that I was sorry through the gag. I don't know what it sounded like, but they seemed to understand it. Perhaps this was the stage at which people always said sorry. It made them laugh. It was the sort of congenial laugh you'd hear at a pub table with old friends sharing a joke over a pint.

'Bit late for "sorry", old son. It's retribution time.'

His hand made a little twitch, and I saw he was holding a knife. I began to tremble. I would have prayed but my mind was blank; I would have fought, but I had no strength.

'This'll help you to remember.'

Remember.

With a kind of exultant joy I realised that they weren't going to kill me, that I would live to tell the story.

Then Mueller reached forward. I didn't know what he was doing, until I felt the hot tearing agony of it, cutting through all the other pain in my body.

'There we go,' said Mueller, and held a piece of flesh in front of my face.

'Nice one, Bernie,' said a voice from behind. 'Very fucking *Reservoir Dogs*. Clean as a fucking whistle.'

'Thank you, Mr Liphook. What do you say, gentlemen – are we finished here? Or does our friend need a final reminder, like they say with the gas bill?'

'Another little reminder, I think, Bernie. The red one, if you get my meaning.'

'Yeah, you took a little something away, maybe you should put a little something back.'

'I think you might be right. Hold him steady, gentlemen.'

My hands were twisted behind my back, and now they pushed my head lower, bending me forward. Mueller moved behind me, and Liphook and Liss made room for him. Someone's hand grappled with my belt, and my trousers and underpants were pulled down. From somewhere I found the strength to struggle. I writhed and twisted, and tried to throw them off. Then one of them punched me twice in the back of the head, and I slumped again into semi-consciousness. I could still hear and feel the men, but I could no more have fought against them than flown out of the alleyway on angel wings.

'Hold him, boys. That's the way, nice and steady.'

'Go on, Bernie, you've got him. Fuckin' 'ave 'im.'

'Go on, boss, make him your bitch.'

'Why don't you pop round the front? Share and share.'

Someone pulled my gag off.

'There you go, suck this fat one.' It was Broken Nose, the one called Liphook.

I tried to move my face. A hand took hold of the hair at my nape and twisted.

'I said fucking suck it, or your other fucking ear's coming off. Suck it, you bitch, you poof, I said fucking suck.'

And he was slapping my face.

And then a voice came from somewhere.

'Enough.'

I knew the voice, but I couldn't find a place for it. And then I thought it was my dad come back to help me. But not my dad, because my dad was dead.

'What the fuck?'

I felt a shove, and I tripped sideways over my tangled pants, and I was lying crumpled against the alley wall, my bare haunches in the filth. I tried to see what was happening but my eyes were almost completely closed. I peered and saw the shape of a big man, saw the other three, one pulling up his trousers, one fastening his flies.

'I said *enough*. This stops now.'

It was a voice like the stone being rolled from the mouth of the tomb.

'This is no concern of yours, Whale. You know what this is about.'

'The boy's one of mine. That makes it my concern. If he made a mistake, he's paid.'

'Not enough. Whale, you know this boy can't leave this place. You know he can't leave.'

'The boy's solid. He'll not say anything. I'll vouch for him.'

'You don't know what you're saying, Whale. For the last time, I'm telling you to walk away.'

'Say the word, Bernie.'

'Mueller, you know I can cause some mayhem here, if I've a mind. So call off Cindi and Barbie here, and we can all go away happy.'

Then one of the men moved forward quickly. I don't know whether Mueller gave him a nod, or whether he was using his initiative. Either way it was a bad idea. Jonah reached into his inside jacket pocket and pulled out a hammer. He held the metal head in his hands, with the wooden handle hanging down. Then, with a swift straight jab, he rammed it into the man's forehead. He stopped dead. His back was to me, but I could imagine the look of surprise on his face. Then Jonah spun the hammer in the air, and caught it, this time by the handle. In one continuous movement, he stepped forward and swung the heavy hammer in an underarm arc and smacked it into the stunned man's groin. He went down, swallowing his agony.

'I said enough,' said Jonah. 'We've all had our fun, one of mine, one of yours. Away with you now, and leave me the boy. I tell you, he'll not speak. You have my word on that.'

'There was no need for you to get involved here, Whale.' Mueller's voice had lost its calm certainty. 'We've no quarrel, but you don't know what consequences might come out of this. You don't know what the payback might be.'

'There's been payback. You've cut the boy's ear. I don't know what else you did. You made your point. We can leave it at that.'

There was a pause. I heard the sounds of life out on the Kilburn High Road, the sighing of the traffic, someone's laughter, a distant siren.

'Have it your way, Whale. But is this worth it? What you've achieved, where you stand, for this sorry little shit? You should have heard him beg.'

'He's not a professional. It's my error that's led to this. Away now.'

Jonah stood back, and I saw the two men still standing walk past him.

'Get Liphook,' said Mueller. As their footsteps receded I heard Mueller whistle again his nursery-rhyme tune, insouciance recovered. And then, in a voice that echoed down the alley, he shouted, 'It's a life you owe me, Whale. A life.'

And then Jonah was bending over me.

'I'm sorry, Matthew, son,' he said. 'Jesus, the state of you.'

From there it becomes even more dreamlike, as I slip in and out of consciousness. He lifts me, and carries me towards the light. I'm aware of the road and the traffic. I think he stood in the middle of the road, until a taxi stopped. I remember nothing of the journey, but I remember arriving at the Royal Free, and a metal lift and then a bed. Jonah wasn't there any more, but there were doctors and nurses. They were talking to me, and asking my name, and I begged for something for the pain, but for a long time they couldn't give me anything, and then finally they did and I sank to the bottom of the ocean and lay in the silt with the bones of the dead.

PART TWO

Some Dull Opiate

7

The Dreamer Wakes

I was sitting on the bench. My hands were trembling, my guts twisted, my feet tapping and grinding at the dirt to some mad rhythm of their own, part bossa nova, part the junkie jive. My hands were filthy from the digging, the soil clogging my nails. My hair had grown long – covering the mark on me left by Bernie Mueller – and I'd grown a beard: a dirty yellow, smeared with brown. I didn't stink, but I wasn't clean. I was wearing a long overcoat, fuzzed and burred, the colour of a pariah dog. And beneath that my suit, the suit I'd bought six months before with the money from the job at the Zip Bar. But the suit was still stained with the filth of the alleyway, and with the sweat and grime of the months in between, and now it didn't look quite so sharp. And underneath the jacket I wore a grey shirt with a frayed collar, a relic of my old days of dull respectability in the Kilburn VAT office. Each layer was like a stratum of my own geological time, waiting to be uncovered and interpreted, telling the tale of my decline and fall.

And I knew that this was the lowest point, and in that fact lay both my despair and my salvation. Things weren't going to get any worse; things couldn't get any worse.

I'd first discovered the place by chance. I'd never much seen the point of Hampstead with its little streets, so inexplicably

pleased with themselves, and innumerable coffee shops, and
all the different places to buy scented soap, and the quaint
old houses that once might have held poets and composers
but now were home to Russian mafiosi and Lebanese
cosmetic surgeons. But the physiotherapist, a stout, badly
made-up South African, said that unless I took my shattered
knee for a walk it was likely to set solid and leave me not
just limping but crippled. She gave me a stick with a curved
handle at one end and a rubber plug at the other – the kind
of thing old men use to shake at noisy children – and she
told me that she'd beat me with it unless I put in some
miles. Somehow the message got through the heavy cloud
that fugged up my head.

Well, you can say a lot for Kilburn. If you want to buy
cheap batteries, guaranteed to sweat a blue-green ooze into
your radio, or you need to get your hands on a yard-length
of hairy brown cassava from a shouty man in a shop
smelling of fish shit and ox blood, or get yourself beaten
up in alleyways, then it comes out top in every poll. But
great walking country it isn't.

So, one morning, I started walking north-eastward,
through the dense noise of London towards the promise of
green beyond. I trudged blind to the external world, but
also a stranger to myself, thinking of nothing. Each day I'd
get a little farther, but there was no sense of triumph, or
even achievement. It was just the thing I did. After two
weeks of this I could manage to hobble for a couple of
hours, before I'd have to lie on a bench, or just slump to
the pavement to rest. Sometimes I'd trudge back again,
sometimes find a bus.

I never made it as far as the heath, which was always the
destination in the back of my mind. But one afternoon I

found the church and, more importantly, the churchyard of St James.

From the outside the church was severe and formal. Undistinguished eighteenth-century. Not hostile, but aloof. But the churchyard could not have been more different: half an acre of woodland, lost and dark and magical, overgrown, but not abandoned. Little paths wove through the trees and bushes, leading to half-hidden spaces that had slipped out of time. And that's where I found my place. The bench was set above and back from the main perimeter path. It was deep in the green shade, but looked out over the wall and across London. Wave upon wave of life flowed out there, murmuring and shushing. It was nice to know that it was there, and it was nice to know that it couldn't touch me.

I first came there on a hot August afternoon and the heat haze made it all seem dreamlike and unreal. Even the skyscrapers down in the City were like the ancient towers and pyramids of Babylon, of Egypt. The churchyard was alive with birds in subtle browns and olives, shimmering themselves invisible, only to appear again, branches away. Even the graves were kindly. They were too old to give any taint of mortality; too many years separated the grief of death from the smooth and mossy stones around me.

Yes, this was a wondrous place to sit, stoned out of your fucking skull on prescription painkillers.

The addiction had come on me subtly, although not without warning. The three days after Jonah got me to casualty remain only as fleeting images of white and gunmetal, shot through with pain like shrapnel. I was in intensive care. My spleen was ruptured, which, along with the internal haemorrhaging, was the main reason I was in there. Four of my ribs were broken, along with my nose and my right eye socket. My kneecap had been pulped, leaving bits of bone and cartilage floating around in the soup. Half my fucking ear had been cut off.

Three days were enough for them to know that I wasn't about to die, so they wheeled me to a normal ward. That was when they decided I was well enough to talk to the police. A man and a woman. He had pale eyelashes; she was small and Asian. I told them I'd been having a piss down the alley when I got jumped by two guys. Average height, average build, brown hair.

Why hadn't they taken my wallet?

Must have been scared off.

What, by the person who brought you in?

Sorry, I was out of it, didn't know who that was.

The police officers looked more annoyed than concerned for my well-being. Another unsolved crime to make the Kilburn station's figures look bad. They said someone would be in touch from victim support, but, mercifully, that never happened.

And then back to my slumping, half-sleeping world. The whole time I knew that I was floating just above a lake of fire. Only the opiates were keeping me clear of it. They'd hand me the two white pills on a plastic tray. After a couple of hours, I'd begin to feel uneasy as the effect wore off, and the fire would come closer, and I'd begin to search for the face of the man who came to help me, and when he came I loved him, and I loved the good drugs.

The day after the police, Jonah came. He looked uncomfortable.

'I told them I was mugged,' I said, to ease his mind. My

voice sounded woolly, as if my tongue had grown too big
for my mouth. I concentrated, working at articulation. 'I –
know – what – you – did – for – me. I – know – what – it
– might – have – cost – you.'

He looked down, and nodded.

'Ah, I haven't brought you flowers or grapes or any such
thing,' he said, gruffly. 'I thought this would be better, more
useful.'

He held out a brown envelope. It was as thick as a paperback book.

I tried to lift my arm, but I couldn't get it clear of the
covers. Even that movement was enough to dip me down
towards the fire, and my face showed the heat of it.

'I'm sorry, son. I'll keep it and give it to you when you're
out. It's . . . it's to help you by.'

He didn't stay much longer. I think he could sense the
effort it was costing me.

I didn't have to think for long about lying to the police.
Jonah had risked his life and livelihood for my sake. Without
him I'd have been killed. And not just killed. So I owed him.
The police probably could have nailed Bernie Mueller: I
knew his name, could identify him. There was a good chance
he'd go down for assault and battery. A couple of years,
with parole. Then, or before then, he'd have reached out.

But there was another reason I didn't want Mueller
arrested for beating me half to death and for the other things
he tried to do to me. I wanted him out of jail, because I
was going to kill him.

The next few days were the worst time. The memory of
what happened, my helplessness, the pain of it, the terror,
came back to grind and pound me. The mental horror was
always at its worst when the pethidine was wearing out, and

the physical pain melded with the mental, leaving me writhing and gnashing and, sometimes, screaming.

I would wake in the night, only the after-image of my nightmare still with me, but even that was enough to make me stuff the pillow into my mouth. There was an old guy on my right. I don't know what was wrong with him, but he was as thin and white and frail as old lace, and he'd always be awake, and he'd say, 'Easy, son, take it easy, they're coming now,' and I'd hear the clip of the nurse's heels.

And sometimes I thought about the Lamia, and desire would add its own taint to the mixture, and I'd be ashamed of the erection that pressed through the pain and fear.

But the drugs, the good drugs, would help.

And then, on, I think, the fifth day, I was moved again. This time a silent and melancholy black porter wheeled me to a different part of the hospital, and I found myself in a room so full of flowers it looked like one giant bouquet. Two nurses helped me slide from the trolley to the bed, and one, Malaysian or Indonesian, said, 'You got nice friends.'

There was a little parcel and a note.

Matty

Bumped into that big Scotch pal of yours – the one who looks like Boris Karloff. Told me you'd had a bit of bother. Came in last night, but you were sleeping. Didn't have the heart to wake you, but I did pull your bottom lip over your top one to make you look stupid. Seriously, I'm fucking gutted for you. Thought the least I could do was sort you out a decent room – don't worry about the cash, I'm expecting a bit of a windfall any day now. Gives me the added pleasure of knowing you'll be sweating about your socialist principles. Also left you a little something. In the box you'll find an MP3 player – don't get too excited, it's only a loan. Save you from going mental listening to hospital radio. It's easy to use, even for a Luddite like you. I've loaded up about 200 albums – a mix of stuff, some you'll like straight off, some you'll learn to like. Plenty of old mates in there. Plus some of the new stuff. Demos for my new masterpiece. Even some tracks I've more or less finished, bar the mixing.

Anyway, I'll try to drop by in a couple of days, check on how you are, take the piss, steal your grapes.

Ju

I was too doped to take it in. The nurse put the telly on.

The next day I played with the music player. It was a cool toy, white and shining chrome. The nurses and doctors all stopped to admire it, in between telling me how lucky I was not to be dead or brain damaged. And it wasn't that hard to get to grips with the menus and options.

As Ju promised, there were plenty of old favourites, tracks we'd danced to as kids, or argued over, endlessly debating lyrics and guitar lines. There was also a fair amount of deeply weird stuff that Ju must have known would annoy the hell out of me. Dutchmen clanging hammers against dustbins; wailing Icelandic folk songs; Hong Kong pop, including a Cantonese cover of George Michael's 'Careless Whisper', which made me laugh out loud.

And then Ju's new material. I only knew it was him because the player told me in a line of scrolling text. 'Ju Flaherty's Magnum Opus', it said, in black on pale grey, in the space for 'Album title'.

It was all a bit rough, with plenty of offstage laughter and fluffed intros, but the sound was clean. The influences came from everywhere, and the tracks jumped around: some perfect pop pastiche, some grungy guitar, some sleek dance tracks, with Ju's tell-tale sinewy bass lines, some stuff you couldn't categorise. Ju wasn't a great singer, but he could carry a tune, and his voice worked well enough amid the layers of guitars and keyboards. Masterpiece? No. But it was OK.

There was one track which lingered. It came in with a raging torrent of discordant clanging and clunking, a guitar nagging and whining like a dentist's drill, a bass that made my screwed spleen ache. Beneath it a tune, or the ghost of a tune, carried by a thin, childish voice which stayed just on the edge of consciousness, swamped by the sheer noise around it. And then, one by one, the instruments on the backing track fell away, until all that was left was the sweet voice, full of innocence, but with the shadow of something dreadful still hovering, and you realised that all along the voice was singing:

> I had a little nut tree, nothing would it bear,
> but a silver nutmeg, and a golden pear.
> The King of Spain's daughter, came to visit me,
> all for the sake of my little nut tree.

I didn't know why it moved me so, but I found tears welling in my eyes whenever I played the track, until finally I couldn't play it any more.

Ju never came to reclaim his iPod. I was looking forward to seeing him, and I used to hope he'd show at the right time, after the first stupefaction had passed, but before I started to get edgy. I thought of some things to say about his music, and I spent long hours composing critiques of the other stuff on the machine. And, whatever the mess it made of my principles, it was good having my own TV, my own room, where I could lie amid the dying flowers, dreaming of biblical vengeance.

After three weeks I was out. It would have been sooner, but when I told them I was on my own they held me back. A young doctor said that in the old days they used to keep cases like me in hospital for months, but they'd found that people healed much more quickly at home. It took me an hour to put my clothes on. My leg was in plaster, and I'd been hobbling up and down the ward on crutches for a few days, but the walk to the taxi was the farthest I'd been, and it hurt. I took two pills in the cab, even though I was supposed to wait until bedtime.

For the next week I tried hard to keep to the programme. Two in the morning, two with lunch, two at night. But all the extra moving around I was doing, even just the getting out of bed to make tea, was shaking me up. I'd reached the point where it took a direct knock or jolt to my knee to make me weep with the pain, but there was enough background discomfort to mean that there was never a moment when I didn't want the relief of my peth. And it was still a magical thing: I hurt, I took some pills, I didn't hurt any more. Who wouldn't say yes to that?

The day after I was back Jonah came round. It took me six minutes to get out of bed and to the door.

'Good to have you, ah, *home*, Matthew,' he said. He wasn't a man who readily gave away his feelings, but I sensed him recoil from the stuffy sickroom air, perhaps even from my face, weirdly hued and swollen as it was. When he'd come to see me I was still bandaged up; now my face looked like some new type of exotic fruit, purple and pulpy.

'Can I get you some tea, or anything?' I asked. It seemed only polite.

'Ah, no, no. I came because, well, here you are.'

He held out the brown envelope. I took it.

'Is this my redundancy? No, hang on,' I said, touching the scar tissue at the bottom of my right ear, 'it's a *severance* payment.'

Jonah looked blank – I mean blanker – for a moment, and then smiled, shaking his head.

'I see. Severance. For your ear. I'll say this for you, laddie, you've a spot of something about you. Maybe we should say you were covered by our medical plan. But I wouldn't have thought you'd be wanting to come back.'

'I think we can learn to get along without each other, me and the Zip Bar.'

Jonah stayed for twenty minutes. He made the tea. It was awkward for both of us. There were clearly things that he wanted to say, but even at the best of times he had no natural fluency. It was as if each word had to be carved anew.

'Matthew,' he finally managed after a couple of false starts, 'where you've *been*, what's been done to you, it can go one of two ways. I mean how it, ah, *affects* you. Either it can destroy you, and you'll never know yourself again, and you'll be lost to yourself. I've seen it happen. You know, the truth is, boy, that sometimes I've made it happen, and that's my work, and that's what I chose, and I'm not proud, though I'll say that I never did harm to a good man, or to a man whose only vice was an empty head. But it can go another way, the things done to you. It can mean that you carry with you the knowledge that you've survived the worst thing that can happen, you've taken it, and you're still here, still acting, still an *agent*. So you fear nothing. And the thing is, son, and this may seem a harsh judgement upon poor suffering humanity, the thing is that you have the *choice*. You can choose courage, or you can choose cowardice, the way of losing yourself – don't pretend you haven't got a choice. There's always a choice. Necessity is for rocks and brute beasts. Read Sartre, read Camus, it's all there in black and white.'

In other circumstances it would have made me smile – a man who carried a hammer in his pocket talking Camus and Sartre like an earnest sixth-former. But I wasn't smiling much at that time.

And then there was something I wanted to tell *him*. Because, you see, I knew it wasn't the worst they could do to me. They could do it again.

After he left, the first thing I did was to find my pills. The second was to open the envelope. The third was to count the money. There was two thousand four hundred and fifty-five pounds in crumpled notes. I almost checked the bottom of the envelope in case I'd missed any loose change. I guessed it was some emergency stash of Jonah's.

I couldn't decide whether it was generous or niggardly. Generous, I supposed, if it was Jonah's own money. Niggardly if it was the company. After all, I'd been doing my job when it happened. But then the peth began to kick in, and I stopped caring about it.

Later that afternoon I called the college and explained the situation to the personnel woman. She told me I should be eligible for sick pay, but she didn't sound particularly pleased about it.

So that was it. I had nothing else to do but lie around stinking up my flat, using the peth to dull the pain and to blur the memories. There was nothing much to eat in the flat, but then I didn't have much of an appetite. I found a packet of dried stuffing that had been in the cupboard when I moved into the place. That kept me going for a couple of days. And then Jonah came round with a box of groceries. He opened the windows. When he'd gone I spent ten minutes trying to close the sashes again, but I didn't have the strength.

The following morning there was another knock at the door. I thought it was Jonah again, and I was beginning to find his visit annoying. But when I finally made it to the door I found Dunyazad there.

'That big man let me in,' she said, pushing past me. 'What a bad mess.'

I didn't know whether she meant me or the flat, so I just said, 'Yeah, sorry.'

And before I knew what was going on, Dunyazad had begun to clean up. It took her a couple of hours, for most of which I begged her weakly to stop. Then she made me some kind of a stew, and then she left, saying she'd come again in a few days.

And that set the pattern for the first month of my recovery. Between them Jonah and Dunyazad kept me alive, not that it earned them much in the way of thanks.

The pethidine tightened its hold on me. After that first month there was no real pain to speak of, just a gammy leg. But there were still the mental horrors, and more significant even than those, the pethidine had acquired its own logic, its own necessity. And boy, is it a shit drug to get hooked on. No real high, at least not after a few weeks, just a release from the onset of withdrawal, plus the gauze it throws over the thoughts you don't want to have.

The GP got wise after a month, and no amount of begging could get him to give me anything stronger than Nurofen. And so I found a man who could help me out. Kilburn is good for that sort of thing. He asked whether there was anything else I needed. He said there were better things than peth. He offered me free samples. Brown and white. But I was faithful to my friend. And it helped that it was cheap. For ten pounds a day I had what I needed. Jonah's envelope hardly seemed to notice it. The man was kind and considerate and solicitous, and he had a big strawberry birthmark on his face, so I pitied him, and was happy to give him my money.

And of course my other needs diminished as the peth took over my life. Food came once a day out of a can. Sometimes I'd eat peaches; sometimes it would be soup. I would spend most of the day watching TV. At times the figures that moved on the screen fascinated me, and I would be concerned for the welfare of the characters. There was a schoolgirl who was plain but clever. She liked a boy who was handsome. Her friends helped her to look nicer, changing her hair and throwing away her glasses. His eyes were opened and he saw her truly for the first time. But she decided that if he only liked her now that she was pretty, he must be shallow, so she rejected him. And now he was desolate, and his friends convinced him that he must read books to impress her. It was very sad. But mostly I watched without seeing, and the light from the set was just a pattern, as abstract as a kaleidoscope.

Dunyazad continued to come round once or twice a week to clean for me. I could sense her concern growing, but my main wish was that she'd leave me alone. Her presence came to seem selfish. She'd make me move so that she could plump the cushions on the sofa. She told me they'd got someone in to cover my classes, but she said that he had no panache, and so she had stopped going. I'd try to clean myself up on the days she came, to stop her nagging me. But I was beginning to look a mess.

'You should shave your face,' she said, one afternoon. 'Get a man to cut your hair. Or I could do it for you.'

'Look at this,' I replied, drawing the hair back from the side of my face. 'Look at it. I said look at it.' I think I was shouting.

'OK, Matthew. I'm sorry,' she said.

I felt bad after that, and I didn't begin to feel good again until she'd gone, and I took my pills.

If Dunyazad was an inconvenience and a bore, Jonah was a trial. Luckily his visits diminished, once he saw that I could get around, but he'd still appear once a fortnight or so, bringing books, wanting to talk. He read, I'm sure just so that he could talk to me about it, the *History of the Peloponnesian War*. He wanted to know if the Athenians were supposed to approve of the account by Thucydides of the ultimatum given to the Miletans: we are stronger than you; unless you submit, we will kill or enslave you all. Was Thucydides attacking this attitude? Or was he holding it up as the only way to fight a war? Wasn't Athens supposed to stand for freedom, and Sparta for slavery and brute force?

Right then I truly couldn't have given a fuck, but I murmured something about Thucydides making up the speeches, putting clear arguments into the mouths of his characters, when who knew what the truth was. And then

I suggested he do some more reading on the subject before he bothered me with it again. He went away, his big shoulders slumped. But before he left he turned and said: 'I've been reading some books about mathematics, you know, to fill in some of the gaps. A man that knows only philosophy and trouble, he doesn't really know much. There was one fellow, his name I can't remember, he said that sometimes when you're trying to find the solution to a problem that seems insoluble – in mathematics, you mind? – you should raise your eyes to the next level up, try to go for an even greater problem – if you understand me. A greater problem of which the lesser forms a part. And on the way to tackling the bigger problem, whether or not you beat it, you might find that you've solved the lesser. Am I clear?'

'Sure, Jonah. Clear as you like. Clear as anything.' I hadn't taken any of it in.

One time he did come with something interesting: a replacement for the hospital-issue stick he'd seen me hobble about on. It was a dark-wood cane, with a handle cast in some dull metal. Although the design on the handle was worn almost smooth, I could just make out the sockets and hard jaw of a skull. But it was the weight of the thing, not the camp theatricality of the skull, which astonished me.

'What's it made of?' I asked, turning it round in my hands, enjoying the dense mass of the stick.

'Blackthorn. But the core's hollowed out, and filled with lead.'

'What's it for?'

'You need to ask? For hitting people.'

'Oh.'

'Son, maybe you still feel shamed about what happened. But let me tell you, other things being equal, two men are always going to beat one man. There's no shame in that.'

'I know, I know . . .'

'But listen, son: a man with a stick is a different proposition altogether. A man with a stick, a stick like that, mind, is not something to be taken lightly. A blow from that, given right, will put a man down, and there's an end of it.'

'Like the knuckle-duster. I still have that, you know.'

'Yes, but with the stick there's no need to get close to a man.'

'I'm not looking to get in trouble, Jonah.'

'I'm not saying you are. But it can help to make you feel safe. It's for your soul.'

And it did. Make me feel safer, I mean. But not as much as the peth.

I only ever went out for my walks, which I'd combine with a trip to my dealer. And I'd take my stuff up to the churchyard and ease myself out of the world, watching the hours pass, so silent and still the squirrels would run over my legs, and birds perch on the arms of the bench, and sometimes I'd feel, when it was time to leave, that my feet had grown roots, and I'd have to wrench them from the soil.

I'd come to love my pethidine. It was a true and loyal friend, it helped me to cope, it never betrayed me or let me down or failed to deliver on a promise. We could have stayed together for ever, one of those quaint old couples you see still doing the shopping, or sitting in the park feeding the pigeons.

But if my pills were reliable, the man who sold them to me was not. One evening he wasn't there. I looked for him, relaxed to begin with, but soon the tension and the fear grew until I was running from pub to pub, cold and sweating, and not even a four-pack of Tennents Psycho gulped in the park could calm me. Finally I found someone who could help me. Unlike my guy with the birthmark and soft, nervous hands, this man was big and intimidating.

'Don't want that peth shit,' he said. 'Never even heard of that shit. You take this. Now, you come back when you want more. Come back to *me*, you hear. I'll see you right.'

He pressed something into my hand. I looked down, dumbly. It was a twist of cellophane with brown resiny grains inside. I walked away, meaning to throw the twist into a dustbin when I was out of sight. But I couldn't find one, and so I went home. I sat in the kitchen and looked at the heroin. It fascinated me. It looked innocent, like brown sugar, or like the incense we used to burn in Mass at Easter. It was the job that all the altar boys coveted: walking behind the priest, swinging the smoking brass burner – what did we call it? *Censer.* I was nearly always given the job, because I was the most devout of the boys, and my hair was then still pale blond, and everyone said I looked like an angel.

It was two in the morning. I was beginning to get stomach cramps. I went to bed. I twitched and jerked and thought of the boot stamping down on my face, thought about the man – which was it, Liphook or Liss? – who tried to put his cock in my mouth. I managed to get to the basin before I vomited some thin black bile. I went back to the kitchen. My arms and legs ached, and my head was pulsing. I was thirsty, but the water had a foul taste, like the brine from an old tin of tuna. Tea was better. I made tea. I smoked all the cigarettes I had left, seven of them, and then I went back to the stubs and smoked them again, down to the filter.

I opened the twist. I touched it. It was soft and crumbly. I sniffed at it. I couldn't smell anything, but I put my nose too close, and touched it with the tip, and then I recoiled, and brushed at my nose. The pethidine was just a purified form of this stuff. If that was true, then could there be any real difference between my pills and this? It could keep me going until the morning, when I'd find my man. Then tomorrow I could start getting clean.

But how could I take it? I had nothing to inject it with, and even if I did, I wouldn't have known how to use the gear. I knew there was some performance with a spoon before you injected. You mixed it with something. A memory said ascorbic acid. Vitamin C. Could that be true? And then some liquid to dissolve it. Water? Couldn't just be water, could it?

But there were other ways. I found some tinfoil, which must have lain dormant under the sink for a good two years. You put the heroin on top, and heated the foil from below, and then inhaled. No injections, no blood, just the end of my pain and sickness.

My hand shook as I held the cheap disposable lighter. I crunched away at the flint. Nothing. I fiddled with the little lever that changed the height of the flame. Nothing. I found some matches by the side of the cooker. Would a match burn long enough to make it work, to melt the heroin, to set free the truth it held? I struck and the match broke. Fumbling, I dropped the box and the matches scattered across the dirty vinyl flooring, skittering and bouncing like children released from school.

In a rage I scrunched up the foil and the brown dragon with it, and hurled it towards the bulging black bin-liner in the corner. It bounced off the wall and rolled slowly back to me. It was as if the stuff wanted me to have one more try, to show a little gumption, to stop being such a yellow fuck and just get the job done.

I wish I could say that there was some kind of revelation, a flash of light, maybe a ghostly visit from Dad, or even a real one from Jonah, some actual event that made me change. But it wasn't like that. In a dramatically undramatic way, I felt the evil energy go out of me, and I knew that I couldn't do this, and that I had finished with the drugs, any of them, all of them.

Without looking at it, I picked up the ball of foil and put it in my pocket. I left the flat and started walking. It was light, but the roads were empty. It was a Sunday, I realised. I didn't need to decide consciously where I was going: my feet knew. I was still limping, but I had my stick, and it took me an hour and forty-five minutes to reach the churchyard. I walked through the trees, lush now in damp late summer, and found my bench. I dug with my stick and then with my hands in the leaf mould and loose soil behind the bench, until I had a hole as deep as my arm. Then I put the heroin into the hole and refilled it, stamping down the earth, and covering the scar with leaves.

So that's how I came to be here in the churchyard of St James, sweating blood like Christ in Gethsemane, except the sins I was suffering for were all my own.

I breathed deeply and tried to let the beauty of the place ease away the pain coursing and churning inside me, tried to use its peace to silence the voices that screamed and jabbered in my head. But, despite the beauty and the peace, the pain remained, and the chemical anguish remained. Ride it out, just ride it out, I told myself; this is no worse than a bad dose of the flu.

The trouble was that it was a bad dose of the flu that I could cure as simply as clicking my fingers. But I wasn't going to do that. I was staying clean.

I felt a kind of elation, and I may have jabbered a bit. And then the bells began to ring.

8

The King of Spain's Daughter

The bells startled me. But that wasn't surprising: every nerve was already screaming and jittering, emerging back into life after the imposed dormancy of my pethidine months. I stood up, and birds exploded from the bushes around me, pigeons clapping heavily as they ascended, blackbirds screeching their alarm. I was shivering, despite the warm sunshine that filtered through the leaves, and I could feel that my hair was dank with sweat. My scalp itched. The fuzzy wool of the coat would have been intolerable on my neck if I hadn't been so cold. And then the bells surged again, and caught me again, the peels gushing in and around me like water, or like flowing gold, and I was like Danae, ravished by golden light.

I was walking towards the sound. Suddenly I saw that there were people, and I came out from the spell of the music, but only partially, and these people also seemed to be flowing with the bells and the golden light.

But they didn't flow near me. I re-entered myself, and saw that the good folk of Hampstead changed course when they saw me, swerving to avoid any contact. I looked down at myself, and I understood why. I backed away towards the wall of the church, sorry to have embarrassed the worshippers. I was fidgety, and keeping still was difficult, and I moved from foot to foot, and shuffled, and my hands were clasping and unclasping. I didn't immediately walk away because there was something fascinating in the mundanity of the people. On the whole they weren't smartly dressed: most of the men were in friendly sweaters and unassuming slacks, the kind of clothes that aspire to inoffensiveness and comfort. Only one or two of the elderly men wore suits. The women were old and eccentric or young and mumsy – there were a surprising number of kids among them, and I guessed that this must be one of the churches with a school connection. In London competition to get into the decent church schools is pretty hot and the churches are ruthless in exploiting this to up their congregations.

But cynicism didn't predominate in my thoughts as I skulked in the shadows. My main thought was that this was a beautiful scene, ordinary people coming together to celebrate something beyond themselves. I wanted to walk among them, sharing their common purpose and love.

And I looked down to see a small child, perhaps six years old, standing before me. She was wearing a pretty summer dress, and she had a little white plastic handbag over her arm.

'Are you Jesus?' she asked me, in a matter-of-fact way.

'Oh, I'm so sorry.' A small, smiling blonde woman, plump as a cushion, nodded and bobbed behind the girl and pulled her away.

I felt the beard on my face, and the hair hanging down to my shoulders. Jesus. Yes, I supposed I must look a bit like a child's idea of Jesus. If I drew back my old coat, could I point to the glowing red Sacred Heart? I would have found it funny if I'd been less raddled.

But then the Sacred Heart of Jesus and the girl left my thoughts. Two women were approaching the church. One was young, early twenties, I guessed. Tall, but a little hunched, as if ashamed of her height. She wore plodding brown shoes and a thick skirt and a knitted top, as flattering as old carpet. Her eyes were cast down, and it was difficult to work out whether her face was attractive. Her nose was thin and fine, but her jaw was heavy. And her hair was a long, lank, tangled greasy mess, as if a mermaid had surfaced through an oil slick.

It wasn't the big, greasy-haired girl who caught my attention, however. The other woman walked a step in front of her, and you knew that the girl belonged to her. The woman was all elegance, from the little black hat with the ghost of a veil, down through the cream of her blouse and the narrow pale blue of her skirt, right to the stilettos that clicked like jazz percussion on the paving.

If she saw me, she did not recognise me, or did not acknowledge that she recognised me. Others among the congregation greeted her, but they received nothing but brief nods, and then the pair were through the big doors of the church, and my Lamia had gone to pray.

I was alone out there. I squatted down on my hunkers, possessed by another bout of shivering, and then my stomach went into cramps, and I staggered from the church and into the quiet of the trees and pushed my way though the bushes, brambles scratching at my face, nettles ecstatic at my wrists, until I found what I was looking for – a space entirely enclosed – and then I vomited, and then I slumped, and shook, and wept – not tears of the soul, but tears of the body, the kind wrenched from us by disease.

When my eyes had cleared I looked down. I was lying on a flat gravestone, sunk some inches below the level of the grass surrounding it. The names carved into the stone were weathered almost completely away, but I could see that a family was buried here. I could just make out one name, not the latest but one preserved by chance in the middle of the list. Louisa Jane Drummond b. 1791 d. 1802. Beloved daughter, beloved sister. I couldn't leave my filth over the grave of Louisa Jane Drummond. I remembered that there was a standpipe in the churchyard, and an old bucket by it. I went and filled the bucket with the icy water and I washed the grave as best I could, and then I went back to the pipe and filled the bucket again, and washed myself, and then drank like a spent camel.

I felt calmer after that. Still shaky, but purged. I knew that I ought to go home, to shut myself in my room with my stash of cans and sit the week out. But I couldn't do that just yet. I went back to the church. I half expected to find a clerical bouncer at the door, there to keep people like me out. And then I was in the wide high space of the church. Other than the great cathedrals, the places you visit on school trips, I'd never set foot in an Anglican church before. It wasn't the same as the church I'd served Mass in every Sunday from the age of seven to sixteen. There weren't any statues. There weren't the stations of the cross. The altar was different. And the stage was crammed with players, endless priests and sub-priests (or whatever they were called) in vestments up there, with a choir as well, singing as I entered. This church was older, and more beautiful, and less gaudy, but it lacked the feeling of desperate piety that inner-city Catholic churches have, the feeling in the air that *this* is the *only* solace, the last hope that the people have. Back in the Church of the Body of Christ in Leeds, the aisles were full of the scrubbed poor, meek and afraid. It wasn't about joy, it wasn't about celebration: it was about clinging to something entirely necessary; necessary, but slipping away.

This church gleamed with satisfaction and contentment. The middle classes were here to socialise, and God was the best kind of host, attentive but invisible.

A woman in a black cassock came towards me, smiling: this was a church full of smiles. She gave me a hymn book and a missal, and made a broad gesture, as if to say that all God's children were welcome here, yes, even you. I looked around, blinking. There was a pew at the back dotted with other figures as out of place here as I was. Men with white tufted hair and grimy jackets, the tramps and quasi-tramps of the parish. Yes, that was where I belonged. I stood at the end of the pew. Two faces turned to me, blankly. One man had a pair of spectacles melded together from two separate pairs. His jaw moved in circles as though he were chewing. The other had bare feet with sandals, and his toenails curved down like talons. I could smell the men, faintly pissy. It could have been worse. Perhaps they found my stench more repellent. It was all grimly, horrifically satisfying, and I sensed the rightness of being here, among the bums.

And three rows in front of me, I saw the woman, and the girl I took to be her daughter. Their heads were together, as they shared the hymn book. It was a hymn I didn't know, and I couldn't find a tune in it, but the sound was comforting, like the breathing of a benign giant. The girl's greasy hair kept falling over the page, and the Lamia brushed it away impatiently. I could hear their voices, not strong, but high and pure.

Although the spirit of the church was more social than sacred, there was something movingly spiritual about the two women. Perhaps it was just that they possessed, embodied, that feeling of religious hunger that I recognised from home. They were calling on God to help them, and it wasn't just a hand with the mortgage, or an intervention with the school governors, but salvation that they needed.

The singing stopped, and one of the priests began to speak, and then we sat for the readings. I could not take my eyes from the two in front of me. I thought about the alleyway, thought about what we had done. For the first time the memory brought with it no surge of desire; nor any disgust. It was too long ago, and that was a different Matthew Moriarty.

And as I sat there thinking, something strange began to happen. The young girl's hair began to change. It was too slow and gradual for me to observe the process, but, moment by moment, the hair was losing its dull dark colour, and changing also its shape and texture. The lankness rose from it, like mist from a meadow, and with tiny steps the hair became silken, and the colour changed to deep red-gold. And as the hair transformed itself, the girl stood taller, uncurling like a clenched hand unfurling into the light.

The hair had not been greasy, but wet. She must have washed it that morning, but left it too late, and when her mother hurried her from the house it had not dried, and perhaps it was the embarrassment of the wet hair which had forced her into that bent-over posture.

But sitting behind the two women, observing the transubstantiation, I could only think of its magic. People rose around me, and for a second I thought it was in collective awe at the beauty of the girl's hair, and I stood with them. But it was only for the Gospel. And slowly the Gospel story penetrated me: it was the story of the woman taken in adultery, and Christ is asked by the Pharisees what should be done, and as they speak he writes with his finger in the dust. What does he write? It doesn't tell us. It is such a human moment. He must be thinking, trying to devise a way of saving the woman without countermanding scripture, and finally he says that he who is without sin should cast the first stone.

It's a lovely story, the one story in the Bible that has always moved me, the one story that makes me think that there is some truth, beyond mere consolation, in the Christian myth. But now, bathing in the golden light from the girl's hair, it was too much for me. I stretched out my arm, reaching over the backs of the pews towards the girl, yearning to feel the soft gold silk in my fingers, desperate to work my fingers through the hair until I reached her face, and then I would gently turn her face to me.

'Steady, son.'

A hand was on my arm. I turned and looked into the face of the man next to me, the one with the sandals and the talons.

'You'll not get your biscuit, or your tea.' His voice was cracked and hoarse.

'What?'

'Afterwards. They give you tea and biscuits, if you're good.'

The man smiled at me. His face sagged inward, as though there were no hard bones, just the soft flesh of him, the white skin, the grey gums, hanging off a gelatinous frame.

And I peeled away from him, a hysterical laugh rising in me like a geyser, and the heads that turned towards my raucous, clanging laughter would have seen only the long lank back of my head, and the coat flowing behind me.

9

Getting Clean

The week that followed was a tough one. I was lethargic, yet agitated; hungry, but without appetite. The muscle pain wasn't so bad, after the first two days. More in the way of an ache. One new development was boredom. I hadn't been this bored since I was a child. As an adult there are always things to be done, and when all the things you have to do are done, then there are lots of things you want to do. People write books I want to read more quickly than I can read them, so how can I be bored? But when you're kicking opiates, even low-grade stuff like pethidine, nothing interests you, and you have no concentration, so time crawls by, and it's as if you're seven again, and locked inside on a wet Sunday, with nothing to do but watch the rain run down the windows, and you think the day will never end, or the year, and that you'll never be old enough to buy what you want, or do what you want.

A tough week, but only a week. It made me wonder about addiction, and the people who become addicts. True, pethidine's a shit drug, and you don't get much of a high out of it. I've spoken to heroin users, and when they're relaxed and think you're into them, they'll tell you how great it is, how *simply fucking fantastic* it feels. Compared to that, the peth can't offer much, but still, it is, you know, OK. So, with heroin, you have the pull of the high as well as the push of the raw addiction.

But for all that, withdrawal's pretty much the same, whatever you're on. And, like I said, it's a week. So why don't more people do it? The answer must be that it's because they like it, because the world you live in when you're a junkie is just that little bit better than the world you live in when you're clean. It's full of problems, but all the problems are soluble. You might need to steal, or lie to solve them, but that's beside the point. The problems of real life, the life the rest of us lead, are infinitely more complex. You can't solve the problem of who to love and how to live by shoplifting from Safeway. You can't make sure you're on the right career path by stealing your mother's purse, or lying about what happened to the housekeeping.

One thing that helped, or at least distracted me, was the recollection of the girl. Over and over again I saw her hair become lustrous, watched her body straighten and grow before me like a flower opening to the sun, and somehow she became a symbol for me of the way things ought to be, of a kind of goodness.

I'm not saying it was the world's healthiest obsession, but it was better than dreaming of pethidine. Anyway, in a week I was clean. Or clean enough. There are still times when I think about the warm ease of it, about the peace you can find, about the way problems dissolve, and you and the drug are alone and happy in your universe.

I was lucky in that neither Jonah nor Dunyazad showed that week. I didn't want anyone to see me in that state, didn't want anyone to know what I'd become. On top of that I suffered a shuddering, racking remorse at my appalling treatment of Dunyazad, and if I'd been presented with her in the flesh God only knows what kind of tearful scene might have followed.

And then something happened that I really wasn't expecting: the telephone rang. It had been so long since I'd used it I'd forgotten I had the damn thing. If the line rental payments weren't on direct debit I'd have let myself be cut off. As it was, it took me eleven rings to find the phone. It was under a jumper by the side of the couch.

I very nearly said: 'Kilburn VAT office, how can I help you?', which was my call sign back in the bad old days. I stopped myself, but then didn't know what to say. I settled on a wary 'Hello?'

'Is that Matthew Moriarty?' American accent. I knew the voice, but reached for the face, the name.

'Yeah, that's me.'

'Oh, hi, Mr, er . . . can I call you Matthew?'

'Sure.'

'Great, Matthew. My name's Coen. We met, you remember? In that bar, the Power or something? I . . . we were with Ju Flaherty?'

'I remember. Hello. Yeah. What can I do for you?'

'Well, the truth is, Mr . . . er, Matthew, there's a situation that's come up, over . . . concerning Ju, yeah.'

'A situation? What do you mean?'

'Hey, it's cool. So far, we think. It's that Ju has sort of disappeared. Not, I mean, in a sinister way, you know? Just that we can't get a-hold, and we need to.'

'Well, I'm sorry about that, Mr Coen.'

'Hey, it's Jack, you know, it's Jack.'

'Jack. I'm sorry, like I say, but what's that to do with me? I haven't got him, if that's what you mean.'

'Got him? No, I see, you're kidding, ha ha.'

'Or seen him. It's been months since I last saw him. We went for a quick drink. He was meeting someone.'

'Oh, I see. And you haven't spoken to him since?'

'No. He left some flowers, and paid for a private room when I was in hospital . . .'

'Hey, I'm sorry to hear that. When were you sick?'

'It was about six months ago. I wasn't sick. I had the shit kicked out of me.'

'That's really bad. And Ju, er, helped you out with the room?'

'Yeah. I didn't see him – I was out cold when he visited – but he sorted out the room for me. I haven't even had the chance to thank him. I meant to. I was going to get hold of him through you lot at the label, but then, well, stuff came up.'

'Hey, Matthew, don't worry, I know how it is. Look, there are, er, things about this we really need to talk with you about, you know, over. We'd really like to meet about this. Do you think there's any way you could come in?'

'What, you mean to the studio?'

'Hell, yes, the offices here in Holland Park. Just dive in a taxi, get a receipt, we'll take care of all that.'

'But I don't know how I can help you. I told you that . . .'

'Look, Matthew, the truth is we're pretty desperate, and we're kind of depending on you to try here. You know Ju was fond of you, and you two go back a long way, and I just kind of think, if you came in, then there's something in this for everyone. Am I making myself clear?'

'Was. You said was.'

'What?'

'You said that Ju *was* fond of me.'

'Just an expression. Look, can you come here?'

'When?'

'What about today, this afternoon. If you've nothing on.'

'I've nothing much on.'

'OK, then?'

'OK. Where exactly are you?'

It was eleven o'clock; we arranged to meet at three.

Why had I said that I would see them? I didn't have the faintest clue where Ju might be, or how I'd go about finding him. And why should they think that I would?

So I didn't think that I could be any practical help, but that didn't mean that I wasn't interested in Ju, and where he might be. The people at the label were obviously worried, and that bothered me. And perhaps more than any of these things, I was lying when I told Coen that I didn't have *much* on: I was as naked as the day I was born. Time lay heavily on me, and at least the trip down to Holland Park would eat some of it up.

I looked at myself in the bathroom mirror. I'd got up that morning and pulled on the same clothes I'd worn the day before: my old jeans and a green jumper with three big moth holes on one of the arms. It had been a present from my mum when I was in my first year at university. I'd only ever worn it when I went home. Now it had become a regular, the cheap wool worn as soft as vicuña. My hair was clean, but hadn't been cut. The beard was still there. It looked blonder than the hair on my head. I looked more closely, and it seemed that the paler strands had some white in them. I ran a bath. A haircut could wait, but that beard had to go.

I soaked until the water went tepid, and then I soaked some more. Getting rid of the beard saw off three of my old and rusty disposable razors. I hardly recognised the nicked and blotchy face that finally stared back at me. It would be a lie if I said that I wasn't pleased. I'd shaved away a decade.

I rummaged about, trying to find some clothes that didn't look like they'd been discarded by a finicky tramp. A pale jacket from a suit (trousers long gone) made from some kind of man-made fibre: rayon, perhaps, or polyester, or spent nuclear fuel rods. A white shirt, crumpled, but clean. A pair of chinos, hanging loose on my now scrawny hips. I had to bore a new hole in my belt to keep them up. I finished it off with an orange tie, made from some other industrial fabric. It set up a disquieting static hum whenever it brushed against the jacket.

I lunched on dry pitta bread and tinned peaches. Before I left the flat I had a brainwave. I still had an old file of receipts and other miscellaneous rubbish on top of my bookcase. I pulled it down, and found what I was looking for. Ask a London cabbie for a receipt, and nine times out of ten he'll just tear you out a blank one. At least, if you tip him he will.

How much would the cab fare to Holland Park be? About fifteen quid? I wrote it out for seventeen fifty, and signed with a cryptic flourish. And then I walked down to Quex Road and waited for the bus.

Holland Park is the kind of London I should hate. The money is old, the buildings grand, the vistas wide. Nobody like me lives there. No blacks, no dogs, no Irish; except for the dogs, which you get your Croatian nanny to walk while the baby sleeps.

Should hate, but can't hate. Perhaps it's because the big red-brick houses were built by and for artists, and something of that relaxed and confident bohemianism still inhabits the air; or maybe it's just that the sun's always shone whenever I've been there. And OK, so that was only twice, once to visit an exhibition at the dying Commonwealth Institute, and once to sit on a bench in the park, while a pretty girl called Lucinda told me that she didn't want to see me again, but she still wanted to be my friend, and I didn't mind at all, despite my counterfeit distress, because back then I assumed another Lucinda would be along soon, although if I'd had a little more under-standing I'd have seen that it was exactly that attitude which had put Lucinda off, and that in fact the supply of Lucindas was very soon about to dry up.

10

Music Business

I'd always enjoyed public transport. You give yourself up into its hands, and for the time you are there, you are free, without responsibilities or commitments. It's a time to read, or think, or slip into neutral, without the nagging feeling that you should be doing something else: fixing the dripping tap, hammering out another work file, saying the right thing to the woman you're supposed to love. And, if you want, you can watch the other people: the big black woman squeezing angrily down the aisle, looking to see who she can crush against a window; or the old man, just out for the ride, happy to be there; or the mother, folding a pushchair with one hand, a flopping baby in the other; or the madman, eyeing up victims; or the secretary putting on flawless make-up despite the bumping ride; or the solitary schoolchild, not in with the gang, trying not to show his desolation.

I jumped out on Kensington High Street, and walked up through the park. There were still a few late lunchers: shop-girls with salads, twenty-year-old men with sparse facial hair leaning into sandwiches, as if into a strong wind. I walked past the bench where Lucinda had dumped me, and smiled at the ghosts there.

I'd scribbled down the address on the back of an old electricity bill. It took me twenty minutes of strolling to find the street. The building itself was set back from the road, with a car park taking the place of the pleasant gardens of the houses on either side. If it wasn't the wackiest building in Holland Park, it was giving it a shot. There were four floors of red brick, with a cupola, and a crenellated tower, and high chimney stacks. It reminded me of another Gothic house I'd stayed in once, lost in a fold of Cornwall.

The outside was still nineteenth-century (with a nod to the fourteenth), but the inside, going by the lobby at least, was pure twenty-first. The floor was polished black granite, like a frozen oil spill, and the walls seemed to be made of stainless steel.

A woman smiled at me from behind a beech-wood desk shaped like a tear.

'Can I help you?' She wasn't the kind of rigidly glammed-up receptionist you usually find in big corporations. She was little, and cute, and wore her black hair in two high ponytails. Her fingernails were painted black, but you got the feeling it was an ironic nod to the Gothic surroundings rather than a sign of musical allegiance.

'I'm here to see . . .' I'd gone blank. 'Fuck!'

The girl put her head on one side.

'I'm afraid Mr Fuck isn't in today.'

I blushed. 'Sorry. I mean I forgot his name. It's here somewhere.' I found my scrap of paper. 'Jack Coen.'

'Jack? Oh, you were right first time. Take a seat. Someone'll be right down.'

So, they took a relaxed view of things at Hellbent Records.

I sat on what looked like a low leather bed. My knees came up to my ears. I didn't know whether I should be sitting, or whether I ought to lie on my side, like a Roman at a feast. I stood up again, and thumbed through the music magazines on the coffee table.

Two minutes later a tall skinny youth in jeans, trainers and a T-shirt telling the world to *go fcuk* came and mumbled something about following him. He wasn't a shaking hands kind of guy. We got as far as a glass wall; the youth put his index finger on a black oval set into the wall above a keypad. Nothing happened. He wiped his finger on his jeans and tried again. Still nothing happened.

'Never fucking . . . they think technology is . . . you know, but I think it's . . . mmmm, er, not a slave, but our sort of like master. You with me? This thing ever work for you, Sukes?' he called over his shoulder.

'Try washing your hands next time. It can't see through spunk.'

'Yeah, funny, shows what you know, you, er, dyke, you never even get it on your hands.'

He punched in a code to the keypad, and the glass door obediently swung open. He didn't bother hiding what he tapped in: 666, the number of the beast.

'Lift or stairs?'

'How high are we going?'

'It's only the third floor, but the lift is well cool.'

'So you people still say cool?'

'Ah, it went out about ninety-eight, but it's having a mini-revival, you know, in the, er, right environment, you know, *climate*. But if you ask me,' he said, visibly warming to his subject, 'it's acquired genuine classic status, at least since the great renaissance of the early nineties, so it'll never be completely in or out again, and that means you won't ever sound uncool for saying cool, if you get what I'm saying, the way you would have sounded uncool for saying cool in, say, nineteen eighty-four.'

'You've given it some thought.'

'Yeah, well, it's my thing.'

The lift *was* way cool. A glass tube on the outside of the building. It had been rigged to make a *Star Trek* thrumming noise as it moved.

'Cool.'

'Cool.'

It took four seconds.

It opened out into a hallway. There was another security door, and another failed performance with the finger.

'Fucking useless technology, man.'

'Yeah, I get it. Master not slave.'

The security number was the same.

We were in an open-plan space, with perhaps twenty ovoid desks, arranged in some kind of pattern (prime numbers? Fibonacci sequence? Chinese zodiac?), half of them loaded. Faces turned. One or two swivelled their Eames office chairs (what are they? – a thousand pounds each?) completely round to get a better look. It seemed there wasn't a lot else happening at Hellbent Records today.

The average age looked to be about twenty-five. The girls were all pretty, and dressed like students given the run of Daddy's credit card. The boys seemed to come in two flavours: haplessly casual, like my guide (whatever his name was – I'd come to think of him as Spunk Finger), or designer smart, you know the sort, perfect short hair, black sweater, heavy black lozenge-shaped glasses, weird shoes. For some reason the sloppy ones were all strangely elongated, as though they were some kind of gas, seeping from cracks in the floor, and the designery ones were all short and squat, as if they themselves were the product of a bigger designer sitting somewhere else, churning out copies of himself. I guess their mothers loved them.

Music was playing. Nothing I recognised. Trippy, with a woman breathing over a theremin. Several of the men, unhappy with the choice, were indulging their own tastes through earphones plugged into their computers.

Most of the faces had become the backs of heads, but one or two lingered, perhaps trying to work out whether my long hair and random clothing were something new, the kind of thing they'd kick themselves for not being in on. I felt the top of my head in case the static from the tie-and-jacket combo was making my hair stand on end. I seemed to be OK.

'Just, er, follow me, and I'll, you know.'

I followed Spunk Finger through the room. At the end was a square glass box, the insides of which were obscured by thin Venetian blinds. The name plate on the door read *Billy Adams*.

'He said just to go straight in,' said Spunk Finger, and so I did.

Adams had his hands behind his head and his feet on the desk. He looked momentarily startled, and began to take his feet down, but then stopped and put them back again.

'Heard of knocking?' he said, but didn't put much into it.

I thought about blaming Spunk Finger, but just said: 'I got the impression this was a laid-back, my door's always open kind of place. I can go out and try again, if you like.'

Adams paused, weighing me up, and then smiled. 'No need to act the stroppy cunt. Sit down. I'll get Jack in. This, by the way, is my man Thurber. He's in charge of . . . well, shall we call it security, eh, Thurber?'

'Whatever you like, Billy.'

I hadn't seen the faintly menacing figure standing behind Adams. He'd been looking out over the office through a gap in the blinds. He must have seen me walk through the room. He was wearing a dark suit, but tried to compensate with a Loony Tunes tie. I didn't know whether it was his desperate attempt to fit in with the laid-back music business, or simply some idiosyncratic lapse in taste; or, for that matter, the gift of a child, which rendered it Pierre Cardin in his eyes. He had the worst acne scars I'd ever seen: his face looked like it had been gouged and scooped and slashed by gardening tools. He walked forward and put out his hand.

'Good to meet you, Mr Moriarty.'

His voice was English, but slightly accented. For a second I thought of Mueller, but Thurber's variation seemed more a layer above his English rather than below.

Adams made a loud klaxon noise.

'First blooper, Thurbs. Moriarty here's a scholar: you've got to doctor him.'

'Apologies, *Dr* Moriarty.'

'Matthew's fine. It's not like I'm a doctor of anything useful.'

'Thurber here's not just a pretty face either, you know; he's got a Harvard business degree, or so he tells me.'

I made an effort not to wince. But that at least explained the accent. There was a quick knock, and Coen came in, breathless.

'Sorry if we dragged you off the shitter, Jack, but as you can see, our . . . *dick*'s here.'

'Ha ha, that's right. Hi, everyone.' He did a sort of nervous wave at Thurber, and shook my hand, saying,

'Really great to see you again, Matthew, really great.'

Coen and I sat in front of the desk, with Adams behind it. Thurber remained standing, looming at Adams's side.

For some reason I thought it was important that I say something: there wasn't much for me to say, but I didn't want to appear to be too passive.

'This is slightly weirding me out,' I began, which was true enough. 'So what if Ju's slipped away for a while? I just don't get what it's to do with me. I mean, I've told you I don't know where he is . . .'

'Matthew, Matthew,' said Coen, leaning towards me until our shoulders touched, 'no one's weirding you out, as you put it. Let me tell you first why this is an issue for us. That's if I may, Billy?'

'Go ahead; wouldn't want to stop you when you're in the zone.'

'Thanks. The thing is, we've put a lot of money into Ju's new project. We call it the Nut Tree album, but that's, you know, just our working title, on account of one of the songs that Ju and Billy liked. And it's looking good, you know, sounding good, and we're all very confident about it. Just need a couple more weeks in the studio . . .'

Adams took over, forgetting about Coen's zone.

'Some of the vocals are shit, need redoing. The whole lot wants mixing, bit more texture here and there. Sort that and we've got your modern classic. As it is, it's just *noise*, as my dear old dad would say.'

I don't know why, but I didn't mention at that point that I'd already heard the work-in-progress on Ju's iPod.

'OK, so you need to find him. So what?'

Thurber stepped up and leant heavily on the desk.

'The reason you're here is because you're a friend of Ju's,

and if what I understand is right, he hasn't got many of those, and because, so I hear, you've got some experience in the security field.'

'Security field?' What the hell was he talking about? Unless . . .

'Don't be modest now, Matty,' said Coen. 'Ju told us about your undercover work for the government. And when we met you that night in the . . . what was it called?'

'Power's Bar.'

'Sure, Power's Bar . . . you said you had a new job in the security sector.'

'I was just . . .' What exactly the fuck was I doing at the Zip? . . . 'just advising them about some trouble they were having.'

'Yeah, sure,' said Adams. 'You were passing on your expertise. Well, that's all we want.'

By now my mind was hitting overdrive, working out the angles. I had old and strong ties to Ju, and if I could help him then I would, but there was also a chance here to help myself.

'So you want me to find him for you?' I sounded as non-committal as I could.

'Look,' said Coen, 'we don't know if something bad's happened to Ju, or if he's just feeling burnt out and needed a break. There's nothing heavy here, we can't make Ju work, even if you find him, unless he wants to, of course. But we want to know what's happening. There's a lot of money at stake, leaving aside art for a moment.'

'And don't worry,' said Adams, 'we're not asking this as a favour. We'll pay you. Whatever your daily rate is, plus expenses. We can think again in a couple of weeks, if nothing turns up.'

My daily rate. What the fuck was my daily rate? A hundred pounds? Two hundred?

'I charge two hundred and fifty pounds a day. Plus expenses.' Screw the lamb; gimme that sheep.

Coen and Billy Adams exchanged glances. I thought I saw a hint of a smile, and kicked myself for undercharging them. But this was all a mad fucking business. I didn't know anything about finding people. It was a joke to say I'd worked in security, a joke to say I'd worked undercover for the government. I'd spent a miserable year as an intelligence officer at Customs and Excise. When I'd been transferred to field work, I'd been involved in precisely one surveillance operation, when I reported a colleague for his lazy racism, and found myself shunted to the wasteland of Kilburn VAT office. I wasn't James Bond, I was VAT man, the clipboard crusader.

But that two hundred and fifty pounds a day sounded good to me. Even so, I didn't want to con anyone.

'You understand, don't you,' I said, playing it straight, 'that I'm not a professional? You'd be better off finding someone who did this sort of thing for a living. I haven't even got a fucking raincoat.'

Thurber, who had been leaning forward, listening intently to everything that had been said, stood up straight, making a growling sound in his throat as he did so. Then he walked away from the desk, and opened a gap in the blinds again to look out.

'We've thought it all through,' said Coen. 'We think that a friend has the best chance of finding him. Jeez, you even live in the same part of town. But that's not the main thing. We think there's a chance he may have gone back up to Manchester . . .'

'Leeds.'

'Sure, Leeds, and you guys hung out up there together. The stories he told about it . . . the stories.' He shook his head, smiling at memories he didn't have.

'Plus,' said Adams impatiently, 'we don't want the press to get hold of the story about Ju disappearing. That's why we haven't gone to the police, and we certainly don't want any shit about private detectives being hired. But you, you're just looking for your mate. Probably owes you money, eh?'

'About fifty-five pence, as I remember.'

Adams looked at me blankly.

'Bag of chips, can of Vimto. Nineteen eighty-two.'

'Yeah, whatever. So, you in?'

'Expenses, that's travel, food, everything?'

Thurber grunted again from his place at the blind. It wasn't the kind of thing you'd ask if you knew what the fuck you were doing.

'All the usual crap. Deal?' Adams thrust out his hand. It seemed rude not to take it.

'I'll need some names. Friends, anyone he was working with on the album. Have you got a studio here?'

'Nah,' said Adams. 'We usually use Abbey Road, you know, for the fucking history. Nothing like having all those ghosts around to help you out.'

'Is that where Ju was recording?'

'Ju? Ah, well, we did a bit at Abbey Road, but then, well, it wasn't working out so great there, so we thought we'd go for a different feel.'

'So where'd he go?'

'Red Shift.'

'Never heard of it.'

'Oh, it's up and coming. Nice little operation. Just an

engineer, and the engineer's assistant. Nothing too, you know, overpowering. Thought it might free Ju up a bit, take the pressure off.'

'And it's cheaper.'

'That wasn't the main issue. Jack, can you sort Matty here out with a list of all Ju's contacts?'

'Can do, but, you know, Matthew, we've already spoken to these guys. They don't know . . .'

'Jack shit,' cut in Adams.

Coen forced out a laugh. 'No, sure, they didn't know Jack shit.'

'Still, I should have a chat. You never know.'

'You never know,' said Coen, smiling hopefully.

'And I'll, er, I'll need something in advance. Say a thousand.'

'Can we do that out of petty cash, Jack?' said Adams.

'I guess we can rustle it up.'

At that point Thurber made his moan, and stumped out of the room, saying something about coffee. Adams and Coen each sighed with relief.

'Thank Christ that miserable fucker's out of here,' Adams said. 'Trouble is, he's been dumped on us by Matsushika.'

'How come?'

I didn't really care about the internal relations at Hellbent, but Adams seemed to want to talk about it.

'Well, we had our bit of trouble, meaning America didn't have no fucking musical taste, so all the money we put into launching our bands there was so much bog roll. Matsushika stepped in, because, you know, even your archetypal faceless bureaucrats know that a bit of cred can't do any harm. And for a long time I seriously think they forgot they owned a hunk of us. They had enough problems of their own with the Yen turning to shit and God knows what other slanty-eyed bollocks going on. But then, and it had to happen, one of their accountants found us at the back of the filing cabinet, and had a good sniff. And, yeah, so we weren't exactly what you'd call a tight ship. Stuff goes missing from record companies, that's all part of it. So they sent dear old Jackie boy here to lend a hand. That right, Jack?'

'Well, Billy, that's not quite how I, er . . . well, you know I live for the music.'

''Course you do, mate. And that's the problem. You see, Matty, after a while they began to think that Jack the lad had gone native, so they sent a minder to mind the minder.'

'Mr Thurber?'

'Oh yes indeedy.'

'He didn't seem too impressed with the idea of hiring me.'

'Not his fucking call. And, now he's gone, there's something else. He's a bit of a stickler, good old Thurbs. Likes things done properly, likes the paperwork, likes to know that every fucking "i" has its dot and every "t" a cross, and so sometimes he crosses his "i"s and dots his "t"s.'

Coen laughed.

'So what?' I said, not knowing where we were headed with this.

'So,' and this was Coen taking up the argument, in his usual smiling, nodding way, 'the thing is that if you find anything, and I'm confident you will, completely confident, then I, we, want you to come to us before you go to anyone else.'

'Sure, I get it. I work for you.'

But Coen wasn't finished.

'And that includes, should you find anything, anything at all, going to the police. Am I, I mean are we, clear?'

'I don't know what's made you think I was thick; of course you're clear.'

'Oh no, we don't think you're thick. No, you're a smart guy. It's just that we need to know what's happening, so that we can manage whatever comes up from a . . . from a PR perspective. So we need a heads-up, a time to get things straight. We're not asking you to compromise anything. You just tell us, and the moral responsibility is ours, OK?'

I was getting bored.

'I think I OKed all this ten minutes ago.'

And the two of them looked satisfied, and I signed some papers without reading them, and soon I was walking out of the office with Ju's London address, feeling happy about the way life can open up for you.

At the lift I heard a gruff voice.

'Moriarty.'

'What can I do for you, Mr Thurber?'

'I just want you to know that I think this is a waste of time. We should get the police involved, never mind the publicity. The least we should do is to get in a – to use your word – professional.'

'All very interesting. And all your problem.'

'Just keep me informed, OK?'

'Er, no.'

'What?'

'I'll report back to Adams. He can tell you what he wants.'

'Look, I don't know just what kind of stupid bastard you are, but any cretin could see there's something wrong with this whole arrangement. You're getting mixed up in things you don't understand.'

'The world's a complicated place, Mr Thurber. There's plenty I don't understand. But don't call me a bastard again. Got that?'

He stared hard at me, and then walked away without another word. He didn't seem very frightened by my threat.

I walked out into bright sunshine. I went and found a bench under the trees in the park and sat down to have a proper think. Just what had I taken on here? Finding a friend. Was that all? I didn't need Thurber to tell me that there was more to this, but exactly what was beyond me. And the last time I'd taken on a new job, a job offered out of the blue, like this one, well, the outcome hadn't been all that I could have wished. I smoked a cigarette, and let the problem wash over me. And then I lit another cigarette, and looked at my hand. For the first time since I'd swallowed the cold turkey, my hand hadn't shaken when I held the match. That was something. Hell, no, that was a big thing, a thing worth clinging to. If this job helped me over the next few weeks, gave me something to fill the space, then it had to be worthwhile.

And could I really find Ju Flaherty, my mercurial old friend? No, I thought I probably couldn't, but there was always the chance that I might, and an even greater chance that I might find something else valuable along the way.

And two hundred and fifty pounds a day.

Plus expenses.

I ground out the butt on the grass and jumped at a tut loud as a pistol shot. A middle-aged woman with big hair and a look of mild sexual affront on her face was sitting next to me – I'd been so lost in thought that I hadn't noticed her. She was looking at my foot. I felt myself blushing.

'Sorry,' I said, and flicked the butt into a Royal Borough of Kensington and Chelsea rubbish bin. I was smiling as I walked away. Yes, I really was re-entering the world – the world of other people, of social embarrassment, of hope.

11

Los Caprichos

I knew it was futile, but when I got home I tried calling the number Coen had given me for Ju. I let the phone ring on in my ear, expecting either nothing or, at best, the click of the answering-machine tape. Fifteen rings I counted, and then twenty, enjoying the pleasure of doing something and nothing. I was thinking about a girl I used to know called Louise and the cool green Gola trainers she used to wear, and the white socks pulled up to her knees.

Then someone picked up the phone.

'Hello,' I said, 'hello, Ju?'

Breathing, breathing. I thought it was the breath of a girl, some woman at Ju's address. Could the mystery have been solved already? Had Ju nipped over with a girl for a fortnight to Amsterdam, getting whacked on Scooby snacks? Or it was a wrong number.

'Hello, please, I'm trying to get hold of Ju . . . Ju Flaherty. Is he . . .'

Click.

Fuck it.

What to do? It was getting late. I had Ju's address, but I'd have to go and buy an *A–Z* to track it down. And I wanted to check out Ju on the Net, find out exactly what I was dealing with. And then I had a stack of chores. When you're a junkie you let things slide, but now I had milk to buy and eggs and shampoo and some stuff to clean the grill. I grabbed my jacket and went out into the gloom, still unsure what I was going to do next.

My first stop was an Internet café. I got dozens of hits for Ju Flaherty. He was on the official Hellbent Records site. A moody picture and a discography. And then there were fan sites. None devoted just to Ju, but there were mentions in relation to the old Manchester scene, and some fun pics of Ju posing around with the Happy Mondays and the Stone Roses, the images smeary with the smell of ganja and the acrid taste of speed. And then there was a more recent picture, a paparazzi snap of Ju and some good-looking guy. Ju had his hand up to ward off the flash, but the other figure was staring straight at the camera, with a look somehow both indifferent and engrossing. There was a caption: *Christian Holbach and musician Ju Flaherty attend the opening of the new Saatchi gallery.*

The impression I got from the Net was of Ju's declining status over the last decade, with a sudden brief media flores-cence in recent months, although that didn't seem to have much to do with music. There were no reviews of gigs, no excited buzz about the new record.

I left the café and bought an *A–Z* at the newsagent's and some household stuff at one of the cheap shops on the High Road. I was still wearing the stupid clothes I'd put on for the interview with Hellbent and now I had two big bags emblazoned with the legend that you could have 'Everything For One Pound!'. I meant to get home, dump the stuff, change into something less ugly, then find out about the voice on the phone.

And then I saw her. I hadn't seen Mercedes since before my beating. I had no way of knowing whether she'd tried to get in touch with me while I was convalescing. Perhaps she had given it no thought at all. Now she was striding towards me, her hair black and shining under the street lights, her step high and quick. Men stopped and turned as she passed them, and even the cars slowed to get an eyeful. I looked at the tacky bags and my idiot clothes. My mouth was dry and the noise of the world faded. I wanted so to talk to her, to joke and laugh and ask her whether she was doing anything at the weekend, and hell, why didn't we go for a pizza. But I couldn't face her now, couldn't watch as her eyes took in what I was wearing and carrying, the gaunt, poor look of me. I was outside the Colin Campbell, a nothing pub for old men. I turned away from Mercedes and entered its gloom.

The next morning I soaked the worst of the hangover away in the bath, and by ten I was ready to go. I tried phoning Ju's number again, but it seemed the girl had learnt her lesson, and no one picked up. I was already half out of the flat when, on impulse, I went back to the kitchen, opened the cutlery drawer, and grabbed the knuckle-duster.

Twenty minutes later I was getting out of a taxi at Egremont Street. The houses were white stuccoed Georgian, a mix of semis, with longer lengths of terracing. It was the kind of street that had gone to pot in the fifties and sixties, the grand houses divided into smaller and smaller flats, each five years seeing the place slide down another notch. But that had all changed. Now a house here would go for millions. The cars in the street were a mix: a couple of MPVs, a tidy old Merc convertible, a Mazda toy racer, plus a twenty-five-year-old Ford Escort, and a battered purple car without a badge, which might have been a Simca or a Yugo. So, I guessed, there were a couple at least of the flats still occupied by tenants who could remember when the place was a dump.

I found number 14B. Steps led down to a basement flat, which was 14C; 14B was the ground and first floor, 14A the rest of the house. I rang the bell. It was the continuous-buzzer kind, and I kept my finger on the button. After a couple of minutes I switched to a random pattern, which I thought might be especially irritating. Still nothing. I looked through the letter box, but that only showed me the communal hall, and a big pile of unopened mail, kicked to one side. I went down to the basement flat and rang the bell there. A couple more ding-dongs and the door opened on a chain. I could see an old lady through the gap. She was wearing a dressing gown, and there were bandages round her ankles.

'Hello, I'm sorry to bother you, but I'm trying to get hold of the guy in Flat B, Ju Flaherty. He's a friend of mine.'

'Who?'

'Ju Flaherty,' I shouted, 'he lives in Flat B. Do you know where he is?'

'What?'

'Never mind. Sorry to bother . . .'

'I don't want any.'

There was no reply at 14A. The house was a semi. I walked along until I found a gap, blocked by a wooden fence with a locked gate. There was a brick wall on one side, and I used that to help me crawl up and over the fence. My stick had become as natural a part of my wardrobe as my shoes, but that didn't mean it helped me when it came to getting over fences. My knee didn't enjoy the climb, or the six feet I had to drop down from the top of the fence, and I had to rest for a few seconds on the far side, crouching and panting like a scared cat.

I was next door to Ju, and had to scoot across the garden and scramble over another low fence, courtesy of a sagging compost heap. I wasn't especially worried about the police. If someone called them, sure it would be embarrassing, but I could explain what I was doing, and send them off to Hellbent to check, if they didn't believe me.

So now I was in Ju's back garden. It was neatly kept, with a mowed lawn and lavender bushes at the edge, and a patch of mature trees at the bottom. Not very rock and roll, but then I supposed as the garden was shared it might be one of the other residents who did the gardening.

It took me a couple of seconds to figure the layout. What was a basement flat at the front was at ground level at the back. French windows opened on to a concrete patio. I thought I saw the old woman move around through the windows, shuffling through the gloom within, but it might have been my imagination. There was a wrought-iron staircase spiralling up to the next flat – Ju's, I hoped. I walked up the stairs to a window and a door. The window looked into the kitchen. I could see that it was the kind of kitchen designed to be as sleek and aseptic as an operating theatre, but things had gone wrong. Dirty plates and cutlery were lying piled on every surface. Drawers were open, rubbish spilled on the floor from untied bags, and the windows themselves were dirty, and two bluebottles buzzed at the panes, and the husks of more were on the sill.

I remembered that one of the things about Ju was his almost neurotic tidiness. He used to share a bedroom with his terrifying thug of a brother, and their room looked like it needed some serious therapy: one side was soiled underwear and crumpled tissues, and the other was books and records in military order, and T-shirts ironed and folded. The brother, Jed, would mess up Ju's half whenever he could be bothered, in the same way he'd thump or kick Ju whenever he thought about it. Ju hated his brother, but also idolised him. I met Jed only once at the house. One Saturday morning Ju and I were sitting on his floor, playing singles on Ju's Dansett record player. Jed, who must have been fifteen or sixteen then, was supposed to be working down at the meat market, hefting pig carcasses and haunches of beef. He burst into the room.

'What are you two poofs doing?'

'Nothing'

'Well, fuck off and do it somewhere else.'

Then he came over and stamped on the record player, breaking the arm, and, more importantly, carving a trench in the vinyl. And the record? The *Spinal Scratch* EP by the Buzzcocks, the third punk record ever released, and one of the greatest. It's got Howard Devoto singing like a fucking demented android, his words too quick and clever to register, and Pete Shelley's guitar sawing away in a frenzy, and some drummer whose name I forget drumming up a storm back somewhere in the mix. If it had been the first 1976 pressing, then the destruction would have been an act of unforgivable cultural vandalism; it was the re-release from 1979, however, so it was just straightforward sadism. Jed knew exactly what he'd done, and waited for the response. Ju sprang up and rushed Jed, and Jed slapped him so hard that he lifted Ju up off his feet, as if he'd blasted him with a shotgun.

I could see into the room beyond through an open door, but there was no movement. I knocked on the outside door, and then slapped at the window. Still nothing. I was about to go when, on impulse, I tried the door handle. The door opened. It struck me as odd, but not that odd. Even in London people sometimes forget to lock the back door.

I wondered whether I should shout out, but decided against it. I was excited, a little afraid, and I had to dry my sweating palms on my thighs. I remembered enough about the law from my old days in Customs to know that if you walk into an unlocked house they can't get you for breaking and entering, but I suspected there were other offences. I had a nagging feeling that trespass had been made a criminal as well as a civil offence. The police would understand me trying round the back of the flat to check on my old friend, but going in, creeping about, that might appear to them to be something sinister. I gripped my stick more firmly.

I walked into the next room, a wide open living space, with white leather sofas, and Barcelona chairs, and a plasma TV hung on the wall. There was nothing idiosyncratic or individual here, nothing to mark Ju's history or his passage through life: it was the kind of decor you'd see in any style magazine, requiring only enough money to make it happen.

Of course, the magazine would have tidied away the crap. Two pizza boxes, lolling open to show the nibbled crusts; sweet wrappers; Coke cans – the sort of stuff you'd see in a household of lazy students. There was an ashtray full of Rizla butts. I had a sniff and got a noseful of marijuana ash. But the room didn't smell of it, beyond the general mustiness, which meant it must have been a while since the joints had been smoked.

I moved on through the flat, annoyed by the flies, still nervous that the police were about to kick down the front door and catch me doing whatever it was I was supposed to be doing. The living room led into the hall and adjacent staircase. I walked quietly up the stairs, although I hardly expected to catch anyone up there. The wall by the stairs was lined with a series of Goya etchings. I looked at each one as I ascended. A colossal satyr squatting on the world, holding a grinning man by the ankles; a woman alone in a cell, enveloped by the darkness; plucked chickens with the heads of men cowering under the blows of two sturdy women; men carrying donkeys on their backs; a heretic sitting before the Inquisition, a dunce's cap on his head; witches performing barbarous acts on children. I remembered that the teenage art student Ju had spoken about Goya, utterly perplexing, not to say boring, the rest of us. So perhaps here at least was something of his, although these were hardly comforting images.

I looked in the bathroom at the top of the stairs. The lavatory was full of paper, the cabinet full of make-up. I didn't think it was Ju's, but then you never knew with him. There were two more rooms. The first held a single bed. It was the only tidy room in the flat. I opened the wardrobe. It was laden with clothes all still in their dry-cleaner wrappings. On a shelf at the bottom were nine pairs of men's shoes, size eight.

I'd begun to have a bad feeling about the last room before I opened the door. I'm not saying that I knew what I was going to find there, but there was something about my creeping progress through the flat which made it inevitable that a grim discovery would lie in wait for me.

She was sitting back against the wall at the foot of the bed, her legs wide apart, her head slumped forward on her chest. A mass of curly brown hair fell over her face. She was wearing a long skirt and a tight-cropped T-shirt, showing her bare midriff. The needle was still hanging from her left arm, like an arrow in St Sebastian.

I felt under the mad profusion of curls and touched her cheek. It was cold. I wanted to see her face, but I was worried that the body would move, that I would leave some trace of myself.

This wasn't my first dead body, but it was my first dead woman. It shouldn't matter, but it did.

She'd been alive this time yesterday, and now she was dead. Had my phone call had anything to do with it? Perhaps I'd panicked her, driven her to get a fix. I couldn't see any track marks on the arm with the needle. Had she been a smoker or snorter, who'd just moved up to play with the big boys and girls?

I sat on the bed and tried to get my head straight. I knew that I should call the police right away. But I'd told Adams and Coen that I wouldn't do that, that I'd tell them, and leave it all in their hands. The issues, moral, practical, buzzed in my head. Maybe I still wasn't thinking clearly after my months of doped apathy. If I waited for them here it would cost me a lot of time, a lot of explaining. I'd automatically become a suspect, which would in turn be a waste of police time. And what good could I do? All I knew was that she was alive yesterday and dead today. That this was where Ju Flaherty lived, but that he'd disappeared some time before. All that they would find out anyway. And I had that nagging, Kafka feeling that if I stayed, if the police came here and linked me to the girl, then the wheels would turn inexorably, and justice would crush me. My heart was racing, my skin cold and clammy. I needed to get out into the air.

I ran down the stairs, past the Goya prints. Then I came back up again and wiped the door handle to the wardrobe in the spare room with my shirt-tail. As I went back down

I noticed one of the etchings for the first time – I don't know how I'd managed to miss it before. It showed an armless man impaled upon the sharp branch of a tree. His wild face looked back over his shoulder, staring at the artist, at the viewer, with glassy eyes. I was out of there ten seconds later. Despite my knee, I ran down the street like a shoplifter, and didn't stop till I reached a payphone on the Edgware Road, near Little Venice.

I dialled 999, but as soon as the operator came on I slammed the phone down and I was away, running again, with my limping, shambling gait, about as conspicuous as a man can get in London. But there was a banshee at my back, and I fled to escape her howling.

12

Brainstorming

I suppose that criminals must get used to the feeling of being outside the law, the edgy, churning feeling in your guts, the terror that you'll be discovered, exposed, punished. It's a childish feeling, a relic of the days when your parents were the law, and they held absolute power and knowledge, and they would always find out what you'd done.

If you leave aside my father's occasional drunken brawls, my parents never broke a law in their lives. Once, in a sweet shop after Mass on a Sunday morning, I tried to conceal one bar of chocolate under another as I held them out to the shopkeeper. My dad saw what I'd done, and exposed me in the shop, and then calmly took me home and hit me on the bare arse with his belt five times. It was the only time he ever hit me, bar the odd playful cuff, or the way he used to flay the skin off my cheeks by rubbing his bristly jowl against me.

So, stepping outside the law was hard for me, and the night after I found the body of the girl was a long one. As soon as I'd got home I'd called Hellbent, but neither Billy Adams nor Jack Coen was there. Before I knew what was happening I found myself put through to Thurber.

'Look, Moriarty, this is . . .' is as far as he got.

I wish I could say I was more concerned with the girl than with my own fate, but it was a damn close-run thing. I kept wondering about what her face looked like. And her posture: it was a strange way to sit to shoot up, her legs splayed like that. Had she perhaps been a gymnast, or a yoga freak?

Later I dreamt of the impaled man. I went into the world of the etching, and tried to lift him free of the branch. It entered at his arse, and the point of it came out at the back of his neck, and he was begging me to help him, but he was slick with blood and sweat, and I would half lift him from the cruel branch, but then he would slip from my arms with a groan. And then he closed his white eyes and opened them again, and when they were open the man was no longer the shaggy-haired desperado in the Goya print, but Ju Flaherty, and with that image in my head I woke up.

It was half past five, but I knew I wouldn't be doing any more sleeping, so I got up and made myself coffee, and sat at the cheap trestle table I used as a desk. I wrote down everything I knew about Ju, everything that Adams and Coen had told me, everything from the Internet, everything I knew of him from my time as his friend. I did mind-mapping diagrams, and flow charts, and drew boxes with arrows, and worked out a timeline, and then tried brainstorming myself, hurling concepts around, writing down every madcap idea. After an hour I had twenty pages of useless crap, but at least I wasn't looking at Ju impaled on a branch.

What I knew was simple. Ju had been working on an album. It was a big one for him, a big one for Hellbent Records. They had invested a lot in him, and this was his chance to move from respected musician – a musician's musician, to use the old cliché – to big star. And then two weeks ago he'd disappeared. And then a girl had died in his flat.

I didn't think Ju had anything to do with the girl's death. Unless he had transformed into someone who wasn't Ju at all, he hadn't been near that flat since he'd vanished – he just couldn't live in that kind of squalor. So who was she? I gave her a story. She was Ju's girl, someone he picked up for sex, but she hung on in there, well past her sell-by date. And he'd disappeared without a word, and she'd waited like Tennyson's Mariana while the moss grew on the flower pots, and he cometh the fuck not. She'd despaired and killed herself, or done the usual chick stunt of the half-hearted suicide attempt, a grubby little attention grab. But then I stopped myself. It wasn't fair. I was blaming the victim, and it came out of my guilt.

I refocused on the paper before me. I'd written THURBER, and underlined it twice. Thurber wasn't happy about having me work on the case. Could it be that he had something to hide? But then I was thrown back on the question of why Coen and Adams wanted me to help them find Ju. Could they really believe that I had a better chance than a professional investigator – even if I accepted their claim that they didn't want the publicity they'd get from bringing in the police?

Thurber was right when he said that something about this didn't smell right. At nine I called Hellbent. Adams wasn't in yet, but Coen was.

'Hi, Matthew, great to . . .'

'I went to Ju's flat. I found a girl there.'

'Did she . . .'

'She was dead.'

Silence.

'I said she was dead. D-E-A- . . .'

'I heard you, I heard you. Who was she?'

'How the hell should I know? Did Ju have a girlfriend?'

'It's the music business, Ju had lots of girlfriends. How did she . . . I mean, was she . . .'

'I think it was an overdose. There was a needle. She looked . . . I don't know, fuck, peaceful.'

'Did you call the police?'

'No. But I wish to fuck I had.'

'No, that was cool, that was, er, wise. Yes, that was the right thing to do. We'll handle that, we'll take care of it, don't you worry, no, siree. And so there's no way the police can link this back to here, to Hellbent?'

'Not through me. But they'll know it's Ju's flat, and they'll know he's one of yours.'

'Sure, sure. But Ju wasn't there?'

'Of course he wasn't there.'

'And you haven't got any leads yet about where Ju is?'

'No.'

'What will you do next?'

'I'll call the names on the list you gave me.'

'I told you, we've already done that.'

'You might have missed something.'

'I guess we might.'

'Then, if nothing comes out of that, I'll try Leeds. His family there.'

'How will you find them?'

'It's a small city.'

'OK, then.'

'OK. And you'll pass all this on to Billy?'

'Sure.'

'And Thurber?'

'That's for Billy. But I can't think why we wouldn't want him to know this.'

I read through the list Coen had given me. One name leapt out at me: Christian Holbach. I called the number, and an electronic voice told me to leave a message. Reading on, I recognised a couple of the other names, but these were mostly second-division musicians, the crowd that Ju had risen out of. I picked one at random, a session drummer called Drew Mortlake. He'd been in a band called Sturm in the early nineties, a British take on the Pixies. No one liked them, the critics because they were Pixies lite, the public because they sounded terrible. But he was a good drummer, and Ju didn't play the drums, so he'd done the job on Ju's album.

The call began with a mumble.

'Hello, is that Drew?'

Another mumble. He might have said 'Yeah'. Might have said 'fuck off'.

'I'm a friend of Ju Flaherty. I'm trying to find him.'

There was a choking fit at the other end, followed by the sound of someone coughing up a bucket full of phlegm.

'Sorry, mate, that's better.' The voice was clear now, educated, upper middle class, slumming it. 'Caught some kind of chest infection off my little boy. You're looking for Ju? Aren't we all. Elusive little cunt. I'm supposed to redo the drum track on "This Is Worse," but I'm booked to start work on Cliff's Christmas single next week.'

'I know you've already spoken to people at Hellbent, but I'm asking you to think carefully if Ju said anything at all about going anywhere.'

'Not a word. We packed up a couple of Fridays ago, and he was just your same old Ju, and I think I even asked him what he was up to at the weekend, you know, the way you do, and whatever he said it didn't stick in my head, but it certainly wasn't, you know, "Well, I'll be disappearing for God knows how long" or anything like that.'

'Did you know Ju's girlfriend?'

'Girlfriend? Well, if he had one he didn't talk about her. He was always pretty focused on the work.'

'OK, Drew, I appreciate you talking to me. If you think of anything at all can you please call me on . . .' and I gave him my home number.

'What's your mobile?'

'Mobile? Ah, it's . . . I haven't got it here. Can never remember the fucking number. I'll get back to you with it.'

I put sorting out a mobile at the top of my to-do list.

I had similar responses from the other people I managed to get through to. I didn't get the feeling that any of them knew Ju that well. None of them knew about a girlfriend. When I tried the Red Shift studio I just got a message. I thought it might be worth a trip down there to talk to the engineer and the rest of the crew.

Red Shift was in glamorous Hackney. That meant a walk up to West Hampstead and a trip round on the North London line. On the way to the station I stopped at a phone shop on the High Road. The eighteen-year-old assistant wanted to sell me a two-hundred-pound Nokia with a built-in organiser, camera and nose hair trimmer, along with a contract that would keep me happy as long as I spent more than three hours a day on the line chatting and texting and didn't mind the direct debit for £49.99 leaving my account every month. I did mind, and I settled for a no-name refurbished brick and a stack of pay-as-you-go vouchers. The sales guy looked like I'd sexually assaulted his mother.

13

Red Shift

I didn't know Hackney well, and didn't particularly want to rectify that. The locals may think differently, but to me it was just derelict buildings and empty faces and people who'd prefer it if you were dead, although they personally couldn't be bothered the fuck to make it happen.

It took me a good hour to find the studio, which was in a basement at the end of a row of crummy houses, near a sweatshop. I knew it was a sweatshop because just as I got there three police cars and two more unmarked vehicles came screeching up. Uniformed officers and guys in suits got out and jogged into the building. Two of them tried to climb a wall they'd have been better suited, anatomically, to walk through. Thirty seconds later the place exploded into life, with bodies, mostly female, mostly Asian, leaping out of windows and flying through the side doors. The police grabbed some, others ran hurtling down the street, saris a-flutter. A fat Asian man, still with a tape measure round his neck, was led away.

It was all quite a spectacle, humorous but for the thought of the misery of the workers.

I hammered on the door to Red Shift Studios. The bell was hanging by a wire, and didn't look like it was going to do me much good. I tried shouting through the letter box, and then I hammered some more. When I opened the letter box to have a second go at the shouting, I caught a glimpse of denimed groin, and then the door opened, leaving me looking pretty stupid, still bent double.

'If you think blowing me's gonna get you a cheap studio rate you're chasing the wrong fucking monkey up the wrong fucking tree,' said one of the weirdest voices I'd ever heard. It was a cracked wheezing drawl, like Mick Jagger gargling turpentine. It was followed by a honking, snorting, gasping peel of laughter.

I stood up, trying to look dignified. The man standing there could have opened the door in 1972 and not appeared out of place; or at least not looked any more out of place. His hair was straw coloured and dangled down over his shoulders. He was wearing a loose shirt covered in what might, some years ago, have been flowers, but which had now faded to abstraction. His trousers were stripy and tight and stopped at his calves. He was carrying a joint, as fat and long as a good cigar.

'I've come to see Charlie Mercer.'

'So now you've seen him, and what do you reckon?' he said, and did a funny little jig on the spot.

'I think he looks like a dickhead. Can I come in?'

Charlie Mercer let out another of his baroque laughs and stood back. And then, as I was about to walk past him, he stepped back in front of me. His jaw projected belligerently.

'Nah, man, I mean, what do you want? Can't just let any dude in off the street. I've got, like, literally five hundred million quid's worth of gear in there, and I can't just let any fucker in to walk off with the shit. Do you hear what I'm saying?'

I've always had the kind of personality that sets itself up in contrast to whoever I'm talking to. The stiffer my company, the looser I get. Among fools, I become wise. Confronted with this insane old hippy, I felt like a bank manager.

'Mr Mercer, I'm not here to steal your gear. I'm a friend of Ju Flaherty. He's gone missing and I'm trying to find him. From what I can establish, you were one of the last people to see him. Can we talk about this inside?'

Charlie Mercer took a toke on his carrot, and shook his head.

'Oh, yeah, Ju. I love that little dude. Come in, man. But I've just gotta finish up something with Janine, if you're with me.'

I followed him in, and found myself in some kind of storeroom. Bits of drum kit, old keyboards and other musical detritus were piled up in no sort of order. There were boxes and boxes of cabling, and big speakers with gaping holes where woofers had once sat.

'This way, man. Sorry about the lack of, what do you call it, discipline. You know they wrote a book about chaos theory? Could have found out all they wanted to about it here. Took Janine on so she could help me sort this lot, but she can't tidy for shit. Rolls a mean spliff, though.'

He held out his arm behind him, and I took the joint, without thinking. Once it was in my hand I thought I might as well use it. But then I saw that the end was damp and brown, and I handed it back. We came to another door. It had a little window. Charlie knocked on it, and waved.

'This is me second line of defence,' he said. 'This door could withstand a chemical, nuclear or biological attack. I got it from a catalogue, one of them for the survivalist nutters. There's some freaks out there, I'm telling you. You know,' he said, looking deadly serious, 'you can buy anthrax mail order? And I'm not talking about the band, 'cause I wouldn't wipe my arse on them, and I've been to Glastonbury every year since 1977, so there's not much I haven't wiped my arse on.' More wild laughter. I'm beginning to warm to Charlie Mercer.

The door opened. A black woman, somewhere in her mid-twenties, stood there. She was tall and thin and stroppy looking, and had the greatest Afro I'd ever seen. She looked groovier than Sly and the Family Stone put together.

'Take the fucking key next time.'

'Yeah, sorry, Janine, babe. Come in, man. Don't mind Janine. Her bite's worse than her . . . you know.'

We were now in a small waiting room, with battered comfy chairs and a long low sofa pocked with cigarette burns and disquieting ochre stains. There was a big window which looked on to the studio mixing desk. Beyond the mixing desk was a space with a couple of electric guitars and a massive bank of keyboards. To the right of the desk there was a glass wall, through which I could see two more rooms: a big one with a drum kit and grand piano and a couple of acoustic guitars, and a smaller one set up with microphones and a music stand. There was a gormless-looking fat boy sitting at the piano.

'Sit down, man, can you?' said Charlie. 'We're just wrapping up in here.'

'How long will you be?'

'Aw . . . ten minutes tops. Just some kid getting a demo together to send in to *Pop Idol*, or one of them. He's putting in a bit of piano to give it some class. Trouble is, you know, there's a bit of the old all-the-right-notes-but-not-necessarily-in-the-right-order shit going on.' Charlie followed that with another mad guffaw, dropping his joint in a small avalanche of ash and sparks down his shirt front.

Half an hour later I was still listening to the fat boy's plinks and plonks, and Charlie's increasingly exasperated 'Yeah, great, Cuthbert, but let's try it one more time. And this time, Cuthbert, get it right, yeah?'.

Ten minutes later he came back into the waiting room.

'I'll let Janine tidy it up in there. She's better at the computer bamboozledry anyway. You know, I'm still happier with the old wax cylinders.' Laughter again, and by now, despite the wait, I was joining in. Perhaps the heavy dope fug had got to me. Anyway, when Charlie spliffed up again, I actually did join him, figuring that it might make things flow a little more between us.

'So, you're looking for Ju?'

'He's an old friend of mine. And the label are worried.'

'Not surprised.'

'And he didn't say anything to you about going anywhere, about needing a break?'

'Hey, we all need a break. Gets intense, you know. Yeah, that's the word, intense.' He nodded sagely. 'Intense.'

'But he didn't say anything . . . specific.'

'About fucking off? Nah.'

'Did he have a girlfriend?'

'I thought you were his mate?'

'We were at school together.'

Charlie leaned forward to take the joint from my fingers, but stayed close to my face. His breath was like an old building.

'You know, I did love that little dude. He had something. I mainly get has-beens or never-will-bes here. I'm not stupid, I know that. When I started out I thought . . . thought that this was the beginning, that . . . doesn't matter. But Ju was different. He played beautiful bass, but it was more than that. He could see the stuff, you know, see the music in his head, like the whole architecture of it.'

Charlie lost himself for a few moments, wandering perhaps in the broad aisles and high domes of Ju's architecture.

'How were things with the label?'

'Hellbent? Bunch of royal twats, if you hear me. Ju shouldn't have been here. He should have been at Abbey Road. And it was mad, I mean *mad*, economics.'

'What do you mean?'

'Well, they signed him up for serious money. Then to stint on the recording . . . makes no sense. Like buying gold Rizlas and filling them full of rabbit shit. But I still say we were getting somewhere, me and the little dude. We had a simpatico thing going, me and him. And the studio didn't even want to pay for this place. Drip, drip, drip. Hard to get a rhythm going when it's drip, drip, drip. Ju ended up paying out of his own pocket, just to get more time. And who does that? And I'm cheap, but I'm not that cheap.

'Look, man, you're gonna say this is crazy talk, but I've got this theory, right? I never even really spelled it out to Ju, because, well, I didn't have it straight then, and anyway, it would have napalmed his creativity, if you hear me. I think . . . I mean I don't think that the fucking label, Hellbent, even wanted him to make this record.'

'What? Why not? All the money they'd splashed out, it'd all be wasted.' Charlie was right about me thinking it was crazy talk.

'You're not doing the economics. Now, you and me, we have faith in the Ju dude. No one needs to tell me he's a genius. And seven years ago, or whatever, you know, the world agreed, or that bit of the world that matters. But things have moved on. Economics, we're talking here. The money they paid out, that's all been written off. That's old money. You can't spend old money. It's like Confederate dollars: counts for sweet Gene Vincent. But new money is new money. Releasing Ju's record, marketing, distribution, you're talking fucking stacks of it, man. And Ju had all this tight in his contract. They had to do right by him, give him the push, the full fucking treatment. Millions. New money.'

I was losing patience. It was only a matter of time before Charlie linked it all to the Roswell incident and crop circles.

'So this shit really does make you paranoid,' I said, holding up the remains of the joint.

Charlie was suddenly all offended dignity.

'Hey, I'm just flying a fucking kite.'

'OK, Charlie,' I said, soothingly – I didn't want him to clam up, just to cut out the bullshit. 'What did Ju think of it all? He'd know if he was being strung along, wouldn't he?'

'I told you, he didn't think it, I thought it. You know his big pal at the label, Billy Adams? He gave Ju the works about cash flow and what have you. Ju's a clever little fucker, but he isn't clued up when it comes to deviousness. You know, they say it's old hippies like me that don't get the modern world. Well, Ju was like something from the time of lords and ladies, man, he was . . . what's it . . . chivalrous. Yeah.'

Charlie lay back in his chair, lost now in hopeless melancholy. But then he shot forward again, laughter shaking his skinny frame.

'We had one big night after a session here. Just the two of us. He knew some weird places to get wrecked. And it was taxis all the way, none of your fucking night buses for Ju. I thought I'd seen it all, but he opened my eyes that night. Some of his mates, though. . . . There was one geezer, Christian . . . something.'

'Holbach?'

'Yeah, that's it. I remember his name, 'cause it was funny, you know, Christian and Ju. But I didn't take to him much. Thought he was your authentic bad influence.'

'Did Ju ever talk about Leeds; about maybe going back up there?'

'Yeah, he was from up there, wasn't he? But you didn't get much of that roots shit from Ju. He wasn't tied like that at all. He was a free spirit, man, I'm telling you. You think he might be back there?'

'It's an idea.'

'Oh.' Charlie was looking serious again.

'What is it? Have you thought of something?'

'Nah, it's nothing. But, you know, he had to get the cash from somewhere. He might have done a couple of deals. I don't know if he had a man up there. I'm not saying he did.'

'I don't get you, Charlie. What kind of deals?'

'I'm not saying he was doing deals. He might have done a couple of deals, but I'm not saying he did. Not the kind of thing I'm into. I like my weed, and anyone who's against it just hasn't looked at the . . . the *science*, you know, for – what is it? – multiple sclerosis and what have you. And no one ever got stoned and went out and kicked someone's shit in, but do they go on about lager? And the old Bolivian marching powder, well, you can play on it, that's the truth, and you can play well on it, but you can't play well for long.'

'Hang on, Charlie, are you telling me that . . .'

'I'm shtum,' he said. 'Zipped. Oh Christ, Janine's giving me the eye. You don't want that. Get on the wrong side of Janine and that's it, you know, she just hits the delete key.'

'Please, Charlie, believe me, I'm his friend. I want to find him. I don't want trouble for him.'

'I've said it all, man. What's your name?'

'Moriarty.'

'Cool name. I've said it all, Moriarty, man. Shtum. Zipped.' He glanced nervously up at the window. 'Coming, Janine,' he said, although I couldn't see her there. 'Jesus, she's made, what's it, Billy Bunter cry. If he wets my keys I'm gonna fucking eat him.'

Charlie stood up. I'd had my time.

'Thanks for your help,' I said.

'No problemo, Moriarty, man. And when you find the little fucker give him a bollocking from me. Tell him to get his skinny little bum down here. We've got work to do. Come along yourself and we'll all get shitfaced together.'

He came with me to the door. When I was halfway up the steps to street level, he shouted out, 'Oi, I nearly forgot to tell you something.'

I turned back, hopefully.

'What do you call an . . . no, that's not it . . . yeah, how do you titillate an ocelot?'

'I don't know, Charlie,' I said.

'You oscillate its tit a lot.'

His wild laughter followed me down the street, and I grinned, despite my disappointment.

14

A Down Payment

I took the train back to West Hampstead, and sat at a
table outside a café. The sun was warm, and the street
was full of pretty girls. I smoked a cigarette to help me
to focus. I had something to add to my twenty pages of
useless notes.

I couldn't swallow Charlie's wild claim that the label
was deliberately sabotaging his project. It was a classic
dope-head delusion. Blame the big bad guys for messing
up your life.

That left Charlie's other theory. Piecing together the
scraps he had given me, it seemed possible, maybe even
likely, that Ju had got himself mixed up in a drug deal.
The studio had starved him of cash, and he'd had to find
the money himself. It wasn't a pleasant thought. Perhaps,
as an old friend, I should have tried harder to give the
evidence some other interpretation, but the truth was that
there was nothing in Ju's character that made me think
that he'd allow the law to get in the way of his ambition.

It wasn't much of a revelation to find out that Ju was
into coke. He was in the music business, wasn't he? I
remembered the night we'd met in Power's Bar, the way
he'd leapt on me. It was like the old Ju, but more so: he'd
been intensified, and that was the coke working.

I didn't have any issues with Ju taking drugs. And coke

was probably less destructive to the core of personality than pethidine. But, as I knew, buying drugs means giving money to bad people. And selling drugs means that, even if you somehow manage not to become a bad person yourself, well, then you're in bed with them, and when you get into bed with bad people you end up fucked. For the first time my curiosity, at most my mild concern for Ju, had turned into fear.

I kept thinking of Leeds. London is a big place, a good place to get lost, but Ju wasn't a Londoner, whatever he might like the world to think. He was as much a provincial as me. If things turned desperate, then I thought he might run back home, even if he despised that home, hated and resented it. And I didn't know what else to do. I couldn't just wander the streets of London hoping I'd bump into him.

The dead girl, the Mariana. She was the central, shocking fact in all this, but my mind kept rolling away from her. Was it that I didn't want to believe that Ju was responsible for her? Selling a bit of coke was one thing, but supplying his girlfriend with heroin? The theory I wanted to believe was that Ju had nothing to do with the girl's death. He'd already vanished. She was one of the hopeless, a groupie, and he'd slept with her, perhaps let her stay. He couldn't have known she was a junkie. No one knowingly gets involved with an addict, no matter how beautiful they are. Maybe he found out about her, and that's why he left. Maybe he left and that's why she got fixed up with the junk. I was sure that Ju hadn't given her the stuff, and hadn't been there when she died. Ju was selfish and blinkered and driven, but he wasn't an evil man; I knew he wasn't an evil man.

I walked back home and called Hellbent. At long last I got hold of Billy Adams. He immediately sounded cagey.

'Hey, Mr Moriarty,' he said quickly, before I had the chance to speak. 'Mr Coen has appraised me of the, ah, circumstances. We're glad you're keeping things confidential. That's how we'd like them kept, from now on.'

'OK, sure. I wanted to let you know how I'm getting on. I've got one or two ideas . . .'

'Look, Mr Moriarty, I've got every confidence in you, every confidence. I trust your judgement. Part of leading is knowing when to delegate, and this one's down to you. Just get back to me when there's a result. I don't need to know the, ah, minutiae of it. Are we understanding each other here?'

'That suits me. But you said to keep you . . .'

'And you have, you have. Let's get some completion here, then we can . . . then we'll all be happy. OK, then, goodbye.'

It was hardly recognisable as the same person. I guessed that Thurber was at his shoulder. That, or Adams thought his calls were being tapped. Or Hellbent could be one of those organisations where all calls are recorded, and he didn't want anything . . . incriminating, on the record.

Whatever it was, it looked like I was off the leash. It was late afternoon. There was nothing much more I could do that day. Nothing much more that I could do to find Ju, that is. I did have one other job, but that had to wait until later in the evening.

I left the flat at 10.30. It was a Tuesday, and Kilburn was quiet. The air was still holding on to the warmth of the day. I'd thought carefully about what I was going to do, although it didn't really need much planning. This wasn't one of those operations requiring split-second timing, or the elaborate manipulation of diverse elements. The main task was to dip into the well of my hatred, drawing out just enough of the hot, burning liquid to help me get through it, without taking so much that I lost my clarity.

I hadn't been back to the Zip since the incident. The only person connected with the place I'd spoken to was Jonah. Seeing Mercedes in the street had pulled the place back into my consciousness, and I'd spent that night in the Colin Campbell thinking about her, about the feel of her sliding past me with a tray of food, thought about the curve of brown skin above the cup of her bra. But those images kept losing out to the others: the sole of a boot in my face, the man trying to shove his cock in my mouth. And another image: the image of a man bending to tie his shoelace, feigning deafness, his traitorous back turned.

What I was planning needed only a few seconds, and hesitation was the only possible danger. The violence that doormen deal with escalates, sometimes steadily, sometimes suddenly. But it never, or seldom, comes out of the blue.

I walked quickly past the bar on the other side of the road. They were both there. Spider, as I'd hoped, was leaning on the door frame, looking bored. The massive dark shape of Errol was visible inside.

Errol was the unpredictable element here. I still didn't think that he was in on it, but that didn't mean that he cared much about me, or that he'd stand by while I did what I had to do to Spider. But even if he chose to help his colleague, I could do most of what I planned before he had the chance to intervene.

I crossed over. Spider was leaning with his back on the

right-hand door post. I walked slowly, leaning on my stick, my collar up, my head down. If he turned, he might be mildly curious, but he wouldn't be alarmed. He didn't turn. I heard him say something to the invisible Errol. Errol laughed, but as often with him it sounded as though he were trying to be convivial, rather than genuinely amused.

I was two feet away. I lowered my grip on the stick to free the heavy nub of it for a swing. But my hands were wet with sweat, and my fingers felt thick and stupid. I dropped the stick with a ringing clatter on the pavement. Spider sprung round, as I bent to pick it up.

'Give you a hand there, mate,' he said, and I felt him bend towards me to get the stick. He reached it first and raised his eyes to me, holding the stick out. There was a second of puzzlement, another moment of recognition. I put my hand in my pocket, and it slipped into the knuckle-duster as though it was always meant to be. As we both began to rise I drew back my hand and hit him with all my strength, a huge, heaving blow, aimed at the point of his chin. My aim was out by a fraction and the heavy brass connected with the jaw to the left of the chin. His own momentum, along with the force of the punch, threw Spider upward and backward, and I fell back in the same way, so we must have looked like a couple of circus acrobats. I felt the blow along my arm and into my spine, and it was a good and satisfying feeling. I picked myself up, and stood over Spider. His eyes were wide open, and he was conscious, but he couldn't move or talk. There was something changed about his face. The left-hand side was melting. I realised that I had smashed his jaw, probably broken some teeth. He wouldn't be getting up for a little while.

Then something hit me from the side. Errol grabbed

my jacket and threw me against the wall. He took hold of my hair, and pulled back his fist. I'd always known that this might happen, and it was a price I could pay. Then Errol looked into my face. There was the same movement from puzzlement to recognition. And then he straightened up, and nodded at me.

'What did you hit him with?'

I held up my fist, still encased in the knuckle-duster.

'I'm not letting you hit him again.'

'I know.'

'You'd better go now.'

I nodded, and walked away.

'Hey,' Errol called out. I turned, and he threw my stick to me. I caught it, and again nodded my thanks.

PART THREE

Ilium on the Aire

15

An Elegiac Couplet

As ever I tried not to get too depressed by the rent boys and spent whores of King's Cross. I found a seat on the train without too much bother: mid-week, middle of the day. When we got going I went to the buffet and grabbed a couple of beers. I'd brought some books with me but I found it hard to settle. If I was ever going to get back into teaching I had to keep my hand in. So I read the Loeb edition of the collection of epigrams known as the *Greek Anthology*, trying not to tut over the slackness of the translations. But presently I tired of the work, and put on Ju's iPod, and sat back to watch the green world pass by.

Scarecrows. I began to notice scarecrows. I'd thought that farming had moved on from the raggedy man in the field, but here they were. I counted them as I listened to Ju's music. Some were full-blown Worzel Gummidges, in old hats and coats. Other were reduced to abstraction, triangles on metal rods. Twelve by Peterborough. I stopped counting at Doncaster with my score at twenty-seven.

After my two cans of beer, I went and bought another couple. More passengers joined the carriage. An Asian family, passing out the samosas. A loud businessman shouting into his mobile, compensating with obnoxiousness for not making it into first class. A little girl in the seat in front played peek-a-boo with me, until her mother made her face ahead. For the rest of the journey the girl would steal glances, smiling at her own boldness.

And then we pulled into Leeds station, and a painted wooden eighteenth-century gentleman said: *Joshua Tetley welcomes you to Leeds,* and I did feel welcomed.

I hadn't been back for ten years. My father died when I was nineteen; my mother eight years later. At the end she went to live with my Aunt Maggie in Selby. I visited her there when I could, counterfeiting a good life for myself to help ease her days. She was sorry that my teaching career didn't work out, but she was pleased that I had a good steady job in the Civil Service. She'd ask me about girl-friends, and I'd always laugh, and tell her not to hassle me, and I'd say that there were so many pretty girls, and that I'd settle down soon.

In the station I thought of the odd nights I'd spent there, too drunk to go home, afraid to face my parents. There was a heated waiting room back then, with benches you could sleep on, as long as you had the money for a ticket. I looked for the room, but it had gone, replaced by a line of vending machines.

It was only when I was out on the street that I realised I didn't know what the hell I was supposed to do next. I'd understood that I wasn't going to find Ju by wandering around London, so why did I think I was going to find him by wandering around Leeds?

I paused in the middle of the pavement, completely at a loss, unsure even which way I should walk. Where would he be, if he had come back to Leeds? Where else, but home. I had no idea whether Ju's mother still lived in their old house, but I could at least start there.

Maureen Flaherty had been a big, blousy woman,

attractive, I think, but not popular on the estate, at least not popular with the other women. And thinking back, perhaps she was more than just attractive. To me as a fifteen-year-old she seemed impossibly old – she was perhaps in her late thirties then – and so I could not see her beauty. She dyed her hair, sometimes blonde, sometimes red, and her roots were usually showing. She wore short skirts and high heels and smelled, as my mother never smelled, of some sweet cheap scent.

Ju's dad wasn't around. Ju never spoke about him, and I didn't ask. I didn't even know whether he was dead, or had run off, or whether Ju knew who he was. Back then illegitimacy was still a stigma, and most of the families on our estate, however dysfunctional, had two parents. If no one ever called Ju a bastard, it was because of his brother. If you called Ju a bastard it meant you were calling Jed a bastard, and if you called Jed a bastard, then he kicked your fucking head in. Ju and Jed were so different it was always possible that they had different fathers. Ju was small and fine featured and quick; his brother huge and slow, with red hands made to hold a cleaver.

If Ju's dad wasn't around, then nor, for a lot of the time, was Maureen. She worked random hours in a bingo hall, and Ju and his brother had to fend for themselves. After we became friends I spent a lot of time at Ju's house, hanging about, watching the telly, listening to records. It was more fun there than in my house, with Mum nagging about homework. Once we went into Maureen's bedroom and looked in the drawers. We found her underwear. Stockings, suspender belt, nothing like my mum's big knickers and thick tights. I remember the excitement of it. Ju was also excited, but his fascination was more, I think, for the objects themselves, rather than for any erotic association.

Sometimes we'd go to his house and Maureen would be there. She'd kiss Ju on the lips, and talk to me in a way I didn't quite understand. She'd say, 'Ah, that's not little Matty Moriarty, is it? You are growing up, aren't you? You'll soon be a man, like your dad. Are you looking forward to being a man?' And I would mumble and blush, and Ju would be as embarrassed as I, and we'd disappear upstairs or go out and roam the streets and low fields by the beck.

Ju didn't come to my house very often. My mother thought he was a bad influence, and in some ways she was right, and in others plain wrong. If Ju taught me how to shoplift and spit, and showed me the gap under the fence where you could get down to the railway lines, then he was also the only friend of mine who had an interest in books and culture. He woke me from the dream of the ordinary, and made me lift my eyes to the wider horizon, and not just to check for police cars.

As I was already in town, I thought I might as well look around, see how the place was getting on. If Maureen Flaherty still lived at 52 Elton Street, then she wouldn't be going anywhere in the next couple of hours.

I could see straight away that Leeds had grown richer. Of course, it had been happening steadily since the late eighties, but I hadn't been away for such a long gap before, and the change was shocking. There were new shops and trendy bars wherever I looked. The old Victorian arcades, long the glory of Leeds but for most of my time a sad and fallen glory, were born again, glittering and filled with gaudy men and women. The shops were the same shops as in London, which seemed a pity, but better that than the gaps and shells like rotten teeth that I remembered from my youth.

I strolled down by the Aire, through the old docklands. It had been a complete no-go area when I was a kid, a wasteland of empty warehouses, with the river stinking and polluted at its heart. Now it was all smart restaurants and expensive apartments, and handsome gays holding hands, and even fishermen, with rods stretching out over the scumless water. I remembered my dad taking me out to some slow, brown river in the countryside and trying to teach me how to cast, and how the fisherboys on the banks kept the maggots in their mouths, partly through bravado, but also to keep them warm and active to tempt the roach and tench. We had jam sandwiches, and my dad took one and chewed it, and then spat the mess on to his hand and squeezed it and then pressed the paste to the hook, saying it was the best bait for carp. But he never caught anything that day.

I came back to the town centre, and as I wandered through the streets and arcades, the ghosts began to return. I could see myself and the other kids in purple blazers: it was a saint's day, and we'd been set free early on the town. I could see them all, Pete and Benny, Phil, John and Johnny, Chris: quick of foot or ponderous, light fingered or honest. I was there too, my pockets stuffed with stolen pens. But they could not see me, and their faces shone with joy and streetgladness.

I thought that I must meet one of them again, somewhere in these Leeds streets. It was still a small town, and surely one of my old friends must be here today, wandering like me, haunted by the ghosts. But then I realised that I was looking for bigger versions of the ghost children, and that I'd have no idea who they were if I did see one of them, grown now. My eyes began to fill with tears. I was near a pub called Whitelocks, hidden away down an alley off Briggate, one of the main streets. My feet carried me in, with little help from my consciousness.

Although I'd come here in search of Ju, we'd stopped being friends by the time I became interested in pubs. The ghosts in Whitelocks were the friends from my sixth-form college, and our jokes were different jokes, and I loved the ghosts less, although I still loved them. I supposed I must have looked pretty strange to the other punters: a long-haired man with a stick and red-rimmed eyes, staring into the shadows as if the shadows were alive. I can't even swear that my lips weren't moving, and it wasn't that I was talking to the ghosts – I was remembering conversations and impassioned debates and mad cadenzas on the passing obsessions of eighteen-year-old boys.

I had four good friends then. Lorenzo was a small, delicate-featured boy whose dad managed a pizzeria. Sixth-form college had saved him from a school almost as brutal as mine, but he had been given a far worse time than I had, because of his name. James Brougham had every imaginable speech impediment, and when he finally managed to get something out it was usually pretty offensive, and I never worked out whether it was because of his frustration at his impediments, or whether that was simply how he was. Nick Buckingham was reasonably cool, but didn't like me. He thought I was a fraud, that I only talked about the Greeks and Hannibal because I thought it made me sound clever. But he admired how I used to dance to the Smiths, a swaying stumble he dubbed the Dying Buffalo. My best friend in the group – hell, he was everyone's best friend in the group – was Paul Manston, and when my thoughts finally came round to him I had to turn away again, because of the way I let him down years later, and I couldn't spare the psychic energy to go after him now.

Instead I went farther back, and I remembered my first drink: a warm can of Colt 45 beer (I haven't seen that for a long time. Do they still make it? Is it available in some out-of-the-way corner off-licence in a village in Wales? I'd go for the chance to taste it again. Yes, even to Wales). It was at Ian McGill's party, ruined for me by the knowledge that Jane Ray was being groped by a Neanderthal called Miller behind a bedroom door. And I remembered my first proper pint down the road in the Marquis of Granby, how I hated it, apart from the foam, and for years afterwards I drank cider, until my taste buds had matured enough to enjoy the bitterness of the hops and the sweetness of the malt and the creaminess of the head and the glorious knowledge that it was all those good things and one more besides, because the thing was that if you drank enough of it it would make you drunk.

I checked the clock on the wall behind the bar. It was five o'clock. Two hours had slipped by. This was no good.

I walked down to the bus station. It had changed, and there were new electronic boards telling you when and where the buses went. The numbers were all different, and the buses now came in every colour but red, but I stopped myself from lamenting it for fear of turning into a miserable old cunt. I found a bus that went down the Selby Road. It trundled out of town, past the big new Department of Health building the locals called the Kremlin. Fifteen minutes later I was getting out at the bus stop before the climb up the hill to Halton. I crossed the busy road, and followed the footpath over the beck – the viscous brown stream that ran through the estate and on into the tussocky fields until it lost itself in quagmires.

I stopped at the little bridge and had a look down at the stream. If the Aire had been sanitised, the Wybeck was still studded with pushchairs and shopping trolleys, and even the old brown scum survived. I spat down into the water and watched the white dissolve into the brown.

So many of my childhood memories followed the sinuous brown line of the beck. The stream was as dense with meaning, with stories, as the Scamander or the Styx or the Lethe, but unlike the Lethe, this was the river of remembrance, not forgetfulness. Battles fought, games played, baubles found and friends lost. And Ju was in those stories, a presence as light and fleet footed as Hermes, the gods' messenger, trickster, joker.

It was time to think about him, and to remember, not just the friendship, but the end of the friendship.

That was the thing I'd been avoiding. Ever since we'd re-established a link, I'd shied away from thinking about why the link had been broken in the first place. It wasn't even that our friendship had run its course. We became friends when we were fourteen. It was all over before we were sixteen. Less than two years.

It happened like this.

There was one good thing about Jed, and one good thing only: he had a crossbow. Ju said that Jed sometimes let him look at it, but he warned him that if he ever touched it then he'd be dead, and when Jed made that kind of threat you listened. The crossbow became an obsession of Ju's, and so it also became one of mine. It was lethal and it was unobtainable, and so what could have more glamour, more allure?

And then Jed got sent to reform school, and Ju came to our back door.

'I've got it,' he said, and I knew what he meant. The crossbow wasn't unattainable any more. The crossbow was attained.

For months we'd talked of hunting the rats that teemed in the beck. We'd decided that the best place was a dumped fridge, like a half-sunk aircraft carrier, its deck a perch for the rats to groom and fuss on. The rats stood out clearly against the white, an easy shot. Ju had been saving up for an air rifle, stealing pens and watches to sell at school. But the crossbow was better than a fucking pellet gun, oh yes.

'Got to be early, five at the bridge,' he said. This bridge. There was none of his usual volubility. This was serious.

I slipped out of the house and into the morning, before the milk, before the dawn. The air was dense with cold. He was waiting for me.

'Is that it?' I said, stupidly, pointing.

'No, it's a bird, give her a shag.' Again, unlike Ju. That kind of crudity was Jed speaking.

But there it was, at last, the fabled crossbow. Wood, worn smooth; steel, bright and springy; wire taut as a harp string. My God, but it was beautiful.

'You do this,' he said, pulling hard at the bowstring. A click. And then he fixed a bolt in the groove. 'Cost two quid each, don't lose 'em or he'll kill us when he's out.'

So down we went, following the mud path that wound with the stream below the bank. The walk was half a mile and we two hunters did not speak. The thrill of death was on us: we were tense and reverent, our heads bowed in the pre-dawn. It felt like some ancient rite.

The dog threatened to ruin things. It kept snuffling and whining round us. Just some hollow mongrel, the colour of sick. The gypsies had left it behind when they'd gone. The field by the beck was one of their stopping places. They came like unease, without reason, without harbingers, to this field. One morning you'd wake up to the caravans and junk. A forlorn horse in tattered flares. A pram. A deckchair. Buckets. Loose stuff, the things you'd get by shaking Leeds and seeing what fell out. And always the death of fire, not fire itself; the burnt-out end of everything.

There might have been a season to their wandering, some calendar or number key. Did shamans read the bones or find a pattern in the fire, and give the secret sign to trace ancestral pathways? Or just the fairs in Hunslet, Armely, Stanks? The gypsy kids would line up, outside the honeycomb school fence, staring at us, watching intently, without curiosity; fingers, like the hooked and scaly feet of birds, poking through the wire.

We didn't like it. The hard kids who should have met their gaze, whose role this must have been, were scared, although no threats were made, beyond the mute challenge of their presence. These thin faces, skull-shaved, smoke-tanged, were too strange. What age were they? Ancient. Seven, nine, twelve, fifteen. A tiny one, old as Osiris, born three years ago. One holds a tab, one holds a stick, one pisses in the beck, but they are here to stare, to watch us at our play. And I remember someone saying, 'They call us *meat*.' And we scattered.

But the gypsies would go as mysteriously as they came, and this time they'd left this lame yellow dog. There was something wrong with its back leg. It was only being friendly, but we didn't want it with us. I threw half a brick and it ran off, stumbling and shambling, looking back anxiously over its shoulder.

I can hear the sounds still as we picked our way along the bank: the flapping of our flares, the Nylon scratch of parka on parka, the sucking of the mud, the first car horns from the Selby Road, sounding like distant cattle.

Ju's hand comes up. The place. The whiteness of the sunken fridge, just visible in the gloom. He turns and signals 'down', his finger pointing to the earth. We squat, toads on the bank.

And there we waited for the rats to come. I had some chocolate, and Ju some cigs. He passed me one, lit from a nicked Zippo. I prayed I wouldn't choke and swallowed deep into my guts. It was Ju who taught me to smoke.

Anyway, I don't know whether it was the flame, the smoke, the rustle of the paper, or just our breathing, but no rats came.

Ju held the crossbow all the time, his thumb rubbing against the grain of the wood. I'd never seen him like this before. To me it was nothing more than a fucking well cool weapon, an opportunity for adventure, but for him it symbolised *something*. His freedom from Jed? The power he'd always craved?

I was desperate for a go, but I knew that I was lucky, in a way, just to be there, and I didn't want to push it. Finally, when it was nearly time to go back home to get ready for school, Ju gave me the crossbow. Then I thought it was a sacrifice beyond compare, but now it seems the acceptance of defeat.

I nestled its gunlike weight, its intricate mass, its coils and cogs. I'd never felt anything this perfect before. I knew it would be mine only for a few minutes, but that made it all the more precious. I could feel the power of the thing, thrumming in my hands. Light came but still no sun; no rats.

'I need a piss,' said Ju. He stood up and sent his stream in a high arc across the beck. Just then the sun rose slyly from the earth. Its light caught Ju and blackened him, but then something magical happened. Through the arc of yellow piss, by some prismatic twist, a rainbow appeared, shimmering in the air like a kingfisher.

'Look, look,' said Ju, his voice crackling with the joy of it.

I thought then that his exultation was rainbow-bent, bliss at the thing he had made. But mulling over it now, on the footbridge over the same beck, it occurred to me that he could not have seen the rainbow too – surely the prism had to be between the viewer and the sun to work? So now I thought his joy was at the feat of pissing all the way from shore to shore. Either way it was a good moment, although it could not make up for the rat famine.

Then, as he put himself away, Ju's face changed.

'Watch it,' he said, sharply.

I was pointing the crossbow right at him.

'Sorry.'

I felt embarrassed, a fool. I heard a wheezing, snuffling noise and padding feet, and when I looked I saw the mongrel dog, tracking over the field towards us, eager again for companionship.

'Watch this,' I said to Ju. I meant to fire the bolt way in front of the wretch, just to scare it off. But I hit it in the neck. The dog managed the first quarter-second of a yelp, before the bolt spun it back into the long grass.

I found that I was laughing, a nervous, high-pitched laugh. Ju snatched the spent crossbow from my hands, and we both ran over to the dog. The bolt had gone through its windpipe. It was moving its legs. Brown eyes looked up at us, trying to understand what had happened.

'You'll have to kill him now,' said Ju.

It was about then that I started to cry.

'How? With that?' I pointed at the crossbow.

'No. I'm off home,' he said, and turned his back on me.

I think he was annoyed that I was crying. I was fifteen and I was crying. And he hated that I'd killed the dog, which was doing us no harm. I'd put a stink on the crossbow, ruined it for him.

And now I was alone with the dog. I bent down and stroked its nose. It tried to lick my hand. Blood oozed around the bolt. I thought it would gush if I pulled it out. I didn't know what to do. I walked away and then came back again. I saw a white plastic bag caught in the grass. I covered the dog's face with it, and stepped down hard on its thin skull, sobbing and crying all the time. Without looking at what I'd done, I ran home.

And that was the end of the friendship between me and Ju Flaherty. We never really shared a gang of mates, so there wasn't much awkwardness. We just stopped hanging out together. I felt desperate about it for a couple of months, but I didn't know how to approach him to make things OK again. If he'd given me a sign, anything, if he'd even fought me, I would have thrown myself into his arms. But there was nothing, not even hostility. He had his own tough friends, and I had my nerdy ones. We never discussed the crossbow or the dog or the prism his piss had made.

'All right, love?'

I'd been standing on the bridge with my eyes closed. I opened them. A woman with a pushchair, her baby asleep with the dummy falling out of its mouth. The woman was all angles – chin, cheeks, elbows. Perhaps she had made herself thin because she was otherwise plain, or perhaps that's just the way she was.

'Sorry, yes, fine. I used to live here.'

The woman smiled quickly and moved on, duty or curiosity satisfied.

I waited until she dwindled and then followed her up into the estate, with the school looming to my right. It appeared the same as ever: the four storeys of the main block, with the high water tower and the low wide mass of the gym. All that glass and concrete must have looked like hope, like the future, when it was built in the sixties. And the old social club was still there. It was built at the same time as the school and in the same brutalist style. That was where Chris Sumner had painted his famous Renaissance knob, thus rewriting the rule book for obscene graffiti for a whole generation.

I turned away, and followed the road as it bent away from the Body of Christ. I was now in the heart of the estate. Here things had changed as well. Most of the council houses had obviously been bought by the tenants, and a riotous profusion of decorative styles had taken over from the old red-brick uniformity. There were porches with Ionic columns; trellis-work; stone cladding; gnome-encrusted garden ponds. I knew that there were still rough estates in Leeds, the places where the underclass festered in hopeless apathy, but that didn't fit Wybeck. True, every now and then there'd be a blot, a house with boarded windows and junk in the garden, but overall the Wybeck estate had prospered. When I was growing up there was still genuine poverty here, with children malnourished, and houses furnished with packing crates. I once went into a house and when I looked down to see what I was standing on I found not carpet or lino, or even floorboards but raw earth. It was a family living literally in the dirt. Now most houses had satellite dishes.

But it was still different from the centre of Leeds, never mind London. Men in shiny shell suits and moustaches looked at me with blank inquisitiveness, sometimes with unconcealed hostility. Young boys, naked from the waist up, ran out shouting, and stopped silently to stare. Women looked out of their windows, not bothering to conceal themselves behind the curtains. And then I noticed that a little tribe of children had begun to follow me. This was still the kind of place where a man with long hair and a stick counted as entertainment. Whenever I looked round they'd stop, and perhaps this game of Grandmother's Footsteps was the point of the thing. Would I have done the same thirty years ago? Impossible to say: no one unusual ever showed up in my day. We had a mad lady who pushed an empty pram around, and the children would sometimes throw stones at her, and she'd shake her fist and tell us not to wake her babies.

I lost my way a couple of times and had to backtrack, and I tried to ask the kids whether they knew the way, but they scattered before me, disappearing into gardens and alleys. And so it took me twenty minutes to reach Ju's old house. It was a semi and, strangely echoing the old division between Ju and Jed's bedroom, it contrasted sharply with the house it joined. That was one of the smart ones: its brickwork newly repointed, rose bushes in the garden, the white plastic of its window frames gleaming in the last of the afternoon sunshine.

Ju's house, I mean the house where Ju had lived, where I prayed that Maureen Flaherty still lived, was a mess. There were net curtains in the window, but they'd half fallen. The patch of garden was nothing but nettles and weeds, and whatever paint was left on the woodwork was rapidly peeling and flaking away. There was no sign of life on the inside, but I knocked anyway. The door opened almost straight away, and I was startled into taking a step back.

My first thought was that Maureen hadn't done too badly: she was still recognisably the same handsome woman. She was probably sixty. Not much more. She still dyed her hair, but, of course, the roots were grey now and not rowan. And she still smelt of cheap perfume, although now the Tramp or Charlie or whatever it was she got from the market was mixed with other odours. She was wearing a pair of purple slacks and a jumper with a design of beads on the front. Her feet were bare and dirty. She looked vacantly at me, swaying a little.

'Mrs Flaherty?'

'What do you want?'

'I'm looking for Ju.'

'He isn't here,' she said, holding her head up high. 'You've already been told.'

There was still something grand, magnificent almost, in Maureen Flaherty, still something in her of the young woman who, at eighteen, must have dazzled. If you are middle class, then beauty can do good things for you. It will give you confidence, and you'll be happier; you'll have more choice in who you sleep with, in who you marry. But these things are gilt on an already comfortable life. If you are poor, then beauty can entirely transform your life, give you the things that otherwise would be beyond your reach, beyond even your hopes. But if it doesn't transform you, if you make the wrong choices with your beauty, and all it leads you to is a child when you are still a child, or to other things yet worse, then beauty is a curse to you, and the ache of its loss can never be assuaged. But for all that, the memory of the power you once had will still be there.

'You already . . . I haven't spoken to you before. I mean, not since . . .'

'You or one of you.'

'Mrs Flaherty, I'm a friend of Ju's . . .'

'That's what they said.'

'I knew him from here, from school. I knew you. I'm Matthew Moriarty.'

She concentrated on my face. Her lips moved before she spoke.

'Is that Magda Moriarty's boy? The Pole?'

'Yes.'

'I'm sorry she died. I heard she died. Will you come in?'

The inside of the house smelt faintly, but only faintly, of urine. When I used to come here with Ju the place was quite smart, full of flimsy new furniture bought from catalogues at £4.67 a week over thirty-six months. Now in the living room there was a sagging old chair, a wooden stool, a TV, a three-bar electric fire. That was it. There had once been a case full of Reader's Digest condensed books and a nearly complete run of a children's encyclopaedia. There used to be prints of swans and horses on the wall.

'Will you have a cup of tea?'

I could glimpse some of the squalor in the kitchen, but to turn down a cup of tea would insult the woman beyond endurance.

'I'd love a cup of tea; a cup of tea would be grand.'

She went and put the kettle on. I remembered lying on the carpet with Ju, watching *Tiswas* on Saturday mornings.

Maureen would bring us tea and toast, and she'd be in her dressing gown, and sometimes it would fall open a little to show a glimpse of a big breast. Once I came round too early, and I saw a man coming out of the door, and Maureen called him back, and she kissed him passionately on the lips, and he smiled at me when he passed me, cowering behind the wall.

'Milk and sugar?' she asked from the door.

'Just milk. Please.'

She came back.

'Sit down.' She gestured towards the chair, but I sat on the stool. I sipped the tea. She hadn't let the kettle boil, and the liquid was tepid, and hadn't taken up the taste of the leaves. But the cup was china and clean, and I guessed that it was something she had kept in case she should ever receive a visitor, and she did not want to be shamed by an old cracked mug.

'Matthew Moriarty.' She smiled as she uttered my name, and she lost some years, but at the same time I picked up the smell of gin on her breath. There wasn't much Irish left in Maureen Flaherty's accent. It used to dip and soar, but now it was plain flat Leeds. 'I remember you and Ju together. The tricks you got up to. But I thought you were good for my boy. I didn't want him to follow Jed. I never could do anything with Jed, but he only ever had bad friends. Ju was lucky to have you as a friend.'

'I was lucky to have him. He didn't need me; he was always going places. But, you know, Mrs Flaherty . . .'

'Oh, Jesus, it's Maureen. You're not a boy now.'

'Maureen, he's in the middle of something important in London, a new record. And he's taken himself off somewhere, and I've got to find him.'

Her eyes hardened. 'So you're not looking for him for yourself?'

'I am looking for myself, but also for the record company. You said that someone else had been looking for him – what happened?'

'I wasn't in. They bothered the Paisleys next door. They were asking where I was, where Ju was. The Paisleys didn't tell them anything. Nice smart man, Noreen said, posh.'

'But Ju *was* here?'

'I never said that.'

'I know he came to Leeds. Would he come to Leeds and not visit you?'

Maureen Flaherty's eyes filled with tears. She got up and left the room, and came back with a toilet roll.

'Ju's a good boy. He sent me money, you know? Every month. But I had a problem with the drink. I never told him about anything. He didn't come for a long time. I went down once to London, and Jesus but a good time we had of it. He took me to *The Phantom of the Opera*. Have you seen that show? Ah, it's a great show, but the man . . . the man wasn't in it. You know the one I mean.' She wiped her eyes and blew her nose on the toilet paper. Bits of the tissue stuck loosely under her nose. 'Would you like a drop of something stronger?' she said suddenly, perhaps noticing that I wasn't drinking the tea, perhaps just too much in need of it herself to fight the desire.

'I'll have a drop, yes, if you'll keep me company.'

And then she went to the kitchen again, and came back with two glasses half filled with gin, and this time my glass was not clean. Her hand shook as she passed me the drink.

'But he came here, two weeks ago?'

'Yes, he came here,' she said, and gulped. 'And he saw

the state of the place, saw what had happened.'

I imagined the scene. It was depressing enough even for me, and she wasn't my mother.

'What about Jed? Couldn't he help with . . . couldn't he help you?'

'Ah, Jed's not so bad either. But you know, there were things that he saw when he was a baby, things a baby shouldn't see. I was more wild then. So Jed . . . ah, Jesus.' She was crying again, heavy gin tears. 'And you know, he was away for a lot of the time. You know, away in the jail. But he gave me money too, when he had it.'

'So Ju stayed with you here?'

'He stayed here for the night. He said that if things went the way he wanted them to go, then he'd buy me a new house in the country, back home in Ireland if I wanted, and I could have a new start. He said I was only a young woman, or that I was only middle aged, and that in London things are different. But he wasn't even really here to see me. He was really here to see Jed.'

'Jed? But why Jed? Was it to, I don't know, get to know him, or something, to . . .'

'Ju knew Jed well enough. He wanted something from him. I don't know what. I don't want to talk about it any more. Tell me, Matthew Moriarty, what do you do in the wide world now?'

And she was flirtatious again, leaning unsteadily forward in her chair, as if her breasts could still captivate and her unblinking availability still arouse.

'I just do odd jobs, Mrs Flaherty.'

'Odd jobs? And you were meant for all kinds of great things. Call me Maureen, I've asked you to call me Maureen.'

'Where's Ju now, Maureen?'

'He went away again. I don't know where he is.'

'Did he say how long he planned to stay in Leeds?'

'Is it only questions you know? Would you like me to refill that?'

I passed the glass to her, the smudge from my lips added to the film of other smudges there. When she settled I asked her again whether she knew where he was.

'He was here one night. The next day he went to see Jed. That's all I know. He said he'd make things better for me, said he'd take care of me. And he said he could help Jed too.'

'Does Jed still work in the meat market?'

Maureen Flaherty laughed, and then lost herself in helpless coughing.

'Jed doesn't do that sort of work. Not on animals, anyway.'

Again the laughter, more savage now; again the choking.

'Where can I find him?'

'Hell.'

'Maureen, I'm trying to help Ju. I love Ju. I think he's in trouble, and to help him I first need to find him.'

As I knew it would, the use of the word 'love' sobered Mrs Flaherty.

'Unless you're a mother you don't know the meaning of love. I worked eighteen hours a day for those boys. I didn't begrudge it. I don't begrudge it.'

'Please, Maureen, please, where can I find Jed?'

'He'll be in a pub. You could try . . . what's it called? . . . the Rat, in Chapeltown. That's the one.'

'The Rat?'

'Rat and Parrot. It's where he . . . it's where his friends are.' She spoke with bitterness, and something like fear.

'Maureen, one last thing.' I was thinking about the girl

in Ju's flat, her lovely hair falling forward, her legs splayed, the needle. 'Does Ju have a girlfriend?'

'Matthew, are you teasing me?'

'No . . . I . . . Did he never mention a girl at all, when he was last here . . . a girl staying at his flat in London?'

Mrs Flaherty looked almost happy for a moment.

'Did you know of some girl?'

'I think there might have been a girl.'

And then the smile faded from Maureen's face.

'You didn't know Ju that well, did you, Matthew? Or you didn't know people at all. I'm very tired all of a sudden.'

'I'm sorry, I'm very sorry. Maureen, before I go, there's something . . . something for me, not really about finding Ju. Could I see his bedroom again? We spent a lot of time there as kids and I . . . I'd just like to see it.'

Maureen looked half puzzled, half amused.

'Go ahead. You remember how to find it.'

I left the sitting room and went up the narrow stairs. The carpet was loose and worn and treacherous. I remembered the pattern from twenty years ago. There were only three rooms upstairs: the door to Maureen's room was open. The bed was unmade, the sheets stained. An ashtray was upturned on the floor, raised up by the pile of ash and stubs it had once contained. There was a portable TV on the floor in the corner. Unlike everything else in the house it was new and expensive. I guessed it was a gift from Ju, perhaps brought with him two weeks ago.

I went into Ju's room. It was exactly as if I had popped out to use the toilet twenty years ago, and just come back in. At least Ju's half of the room was the same – Jed's was a blank space. Ju's model aeroplanes still hung from the ceiling by threads; his pile of Marvel and DC comics was still under the window. Of course, his records had moved with him, so that was one gap, but there was the home-made bookshelf – bricks and planks of wood – with *A Clockwork Orange*, and *The Catcher in the Rye*, and his *Portable Henry Miller*, the books we were talking about before things fell apart.

'He's OK, isn't he?'

I hadn't heard or felt Maureen O'Flaherty come up behind me, and I was startled.

'Yes, he's OK,' I said, with what confidence I could muster. 'I'm sure he's OK. Ju's always OK.'

After I left Maureen Flaherty's house I walked down to the Wybeck Arms, and asked the barman whether he had a number for a minicab. I got my new mobile phone out and after some random button-pressing found out how to make a call. I had a quiet pint while I waited. I'd been drinking all day, but I'd been taking it steady, and I didn't feel too bad.

I'd had some good times in the Wybeck. It's where we'd meet up before school discos. It hadn't changed much. Perhaps there was more colour now. I remembered mainly brown.

'Matthew Moriarty.'

I'd been vaguely aware of the small guy two tables away, taking furtive glances. It was early and there was only a scattering of punters, who were all male, and I wondered whether perhaps the Wybeck had metamorphosed into a gay pub behind my back (a London friend had told me that Leeds, taking its cue from Manchester, had become a much gayer place than heretofore).

I turned and looked at the speaker. There was something

mole-like about him, with his short black hair, and his weak eyes peering through thick spectacles. He was hunched over the table, his strong, stubby arms encircling an iceless glass of whisky. He was smiling and nodding to himself.

'Do I know you?'

'Pillock!' He chuckled.

'What?' I put an edge of hardness in my voice.

'Pillock.'

He was grinning widely now, and his eyes had completely disappeared. I shifted my guess from gay to nutter. But the nutter seemed to know me.

'One jay.'

Code for something? Should I reply with two magpies?

When I still didn't react, the smile began to die on the mad mole's face.

'Simon Pollock. I sat next to you in IJ. Only for maths. Everyone called me . . .'

'Pillock. Or Pilchard. Yes, of course I remember you. It's been a while.'

I remembered him, but only just. Apart from the pillock/pilchard thing, there was nothing else there, nothing at all.

'Do you remember, in maths we had to sit according to the alphabet? There was no one in between Moriarty and Pollock. Then you got moved up. And that was it.'

I got up and went to sit at his table. It seemed the least I could do to compensate for the absence of memory.

'What are you doing now, Simon?'

'Work in the kitchens at St James's.'

'Jimmy's? That's, er, nice.'

'Dump, really. Still training, you know, *retraining*, as a chef, but all they let me do is peel the spuds.'

'Well, it's . . . something.'

I didn't know what else to say. For some reason – a mix-up, or because of my address, or because I'd done something wrong – I started out in the bottom class at the Body of Christ. After a term I was up, leaving the others behind. Some of my first friends there took it as a betrayal, a desertion, and it's true that I was a lot happier out of the reach of some of the monsters and mutants down there in the primordial ooze.

'Did you ever reach a million?'

'A million what?'

'Have you forgotten that an' all? You said you were going to count up to a million. You kept score every day. Told us about it. You got up to thousands before you moved up. I always hoped you'd reach a million. I sometimes used to count a bit for you as well, just to sort of add them on.'

Was that me? Did I really tell people that I was counting up to a million? If I did, was it some nasty, superior little joke of mine? Did I invent a plausible total each day to impress the kids with? Or was I really doing it, really going to sleep each night counting sheep, really walking to school each day, counting my steps, tallying it all up, striving to make the magical seven figures? It felt familiar, like a smell you know but can't place.

'Jesus, Pillock, maybe I did.'

He looked happy that I'd slipped into using his nickname.

'I heard you're in London. What are you doing back?'

'I'm looking for someone. Fuck, what do I mean someone? I'm looking for Ju Flaherty. You remember Ju? Little kid, punk, spiky hair.'

Pollock was smiling again.

'He was here. He was here two weeks ago. I didn't know

you and him was mates. I saw him here, but I didn't talk to him. I didn't know him, but I recognised him. I never sat next to him, like I sat next to you.'

'Was he with anyone? How did he seem?'

'Just on his own. Didn't look too chuffed. Sort of sad, if that's it. Otherwise maybe I would have said hello.'

He'd been here, right here. 'It's a shame you didn't talk to him, found out what he was up to.'

'Yeah, well, I . . . I didn't know him.' He took his glasses off and wiped them on his jumper.

'Do you see anyone else from the old days, Pillock?'

'Oh, aye! There's still a few come in here. Jonno, and Bilco, them lot. Fat Gaz! He's here most nights. None o' the lassies, though. They've all moved on. Or don't come out down here.'

'And you, Pillock, did you ever get . . .'

'Married? Nah. Still playing the field. You know, ducking and diving an' that. Listen, can I get you a drink? What you having?'

'Another time, Pillock. I've got to try to find Ju.'

He was instantly resigned to another disappointment.

'Sure, yeah. Where're you going to look?'

'I'm meeting Jed – remember Jed, his brother?'

'Phew, yeah. Psycho.'

'I'm meeting him in the Rat in Chapeltown.'

'Taking your life in your hands a bit there.'

'A man's gotta do.'

And then the taxi driver called out from the door.

'That's my taxi.'

'OK, yeah, next time.'

I thought about asking him along, down for a drink in Chapeltown. But there was a chance things might get difficult. I didn't want to have to worry about anyone else. In truth I didn't even want to think about him. There was enough quiet tragedy around me as it was; I didn't need another layer.

'But give us your number,' I said, feeling embarrassed at so obvious a gesture of compassion, 'and I'll call you next time I'm here. We'll have a couple of pints together.'

'Oh, great, yeah.'

I gave him my pen and a scrap of paper, and he wrote his number down, and we shook hands and I left the pub, expecting never to see him again.

16

Dissecting the Rat

The taxi dropped me outside the Rat. It was only seven. Early, I guessed, to hope to meet Jed, so I thought I'd have a stroll around. I'd heard something about Chapeltown being regenerated. Maybe that was true, but it still looked like a shithole to me. Perhaps that's just because Chapeltown isn't my Leeds. For my generation, Chapeltown meant the race riots of 1981. If you didn't live there, there was no reason to visit, unless it was for drugs or poxed whores.

I'd only ever set foot there twice. When I was a young boy, nine or ten, I went with my dad, who was going to see the Jewish tailor who made him a new suit once every five years. There weren't many black or Asian faces on my estate, but here the streets were full of them. I felt frightened, and stuck close to my father's side, and the tailor, who was at least six hundred years old, gave me a boiled sweet that had gone soft in the bag. The second time I went to a party, with Ju. It wasn't long after the riots, and there were still tarry stains on the streets from the burnt-out cars. We were both gaudy punks then, and the Rastas and tough Asian kids jeered at us, and I was glad when we made it safely inside the house.

Leeds has always liked to shoehorn its immigrants into Chapeltown, keeping them safely away from the affluent areas, Roundhay, Headingley, Alwoodley. The Irish came in the 1840s and 1850s, driven by the famine. The Jews came from the 1880s, fleeing pogroms and poverty. West Indians arrived in the 1950s and 1960s, when Leeds had its post-war boom, and there were jobs for all. A little later Bangladeshis and Pakistanis arrived. When there was work, things were good in Chapeltown. Unlike the kind of vast new estate where I'd been brought up, it had real shops and businesses – like my dad's tailor. But under the Thatcher blitzkrieg that all changed.

Every wall I looked at now was daubed with ugly, witless graffiti. For the most part it was nothing but names: no flourish, no artistry, just 'Baz' or 'Spag' or 'Ham'. The once ubiquitous 'Leeds United' had vanished, as if even that vestige of community spirit was no more. Nothing left, just Baz and Spag and Ham. In ten minutes I saw two police cars slowly cruising, looking for trouble. One stopped by a group of black kids, hanging out by a bus stop. They seemed to be chatting in a friendly way, and then one of the boys bolted and the car doors flew open and the police were after him, while the other boys stood watching.

And yet this was clearly a more tolerant community than my own had been. No one stared at me, after the first glance to see whether they knew me, or whether I represented a threat. Chapeltown's always had its share of students and a smattering of resident bohemians, taking their chance, drawn by the spirit of the place and cheap rents. All it really needed was a slice of the financial action that the centre of Leeds was getting, a bit of trickle-down, and the entre-preneurial spirit among the people would do the rest. Perhaps it would happen.

I found myself in front of a house bearing a round blue plaque, the sort used in London to mark the houses of the great and good. It read: 'Frank Kidson MA, 1855–1926,

Musical antiquarian and folk-song collector lived here 1904–1924', and suddenly I was back in a different Chapeltown, one full of auto-didact scholars and earnest working-class intellectuals. But by now it was getting darker and I thought that I should return to the Rat.

The Rat and Parrot looked like a lot of money had been spent on it ten years ago, and then nothing since. The fittings were grimy and tarnished, the legs of the tables looked like they'd been chewed by dogs, and every flat surface was pockmarked with cigarette burns, as though the punters were too pissed or careless to hit the ashtrays. There was a pool table with gashed baize and broken cues, and a dart board with half the numbers missing.

I went to the bar and got a beer. The barman was of the big, shuffling, uncommunicative sort with a sweat-stained polo shirt stretched tight over his belly. The selection of drinks was worrying: mainly lager, ranging from cooking to head-fuck strength, and a couple of fizzy bitters. Thugs don't sit around discussing the finer points of real ale.

I sat at the last free table. It wobbled when I put my glass down, and my beer spilled, puddling like blood on the table. There were no beer mats. Sooner or later the beer was going to work its way over to me and dribble on my trousers. I went back to the bar and asked for something to wipe the spill up with. The barman stared silently at me for at least seven seconds and then stumped off like an ogre towards the Gents. I didn't quite know what to do with myself, and so went back to the table. I was about to wipe it with my hand when the barman came back and dropped a scrunched mass of toilet paper on the table, and then walked away, still without uttering a word.

I was almost beginning to enjoy the grimness of it all, and

then I started to look around me. Too many of the drinkers were staring at me, and I began to get a tingling of paranoia. There's nothing strange in going into a local and finding yourself the object of scrutiny; it's natural, and human, to check out a new face on your home patch. But the young men around me didn't seem to be experiencing that impartial curiosity. There was definitely a house image thing happening. Tight T-shirts, short hair, wispily deluded moustaches, uninteresting tattoos. And white. Chapeltown may have a giddy ethnic mix, but the Rat was as white as the Snow Queen's ermine stole.

I was careful not to catch the eyes focused on me. That was all it would take. I wasn't afraid, but I had business, and fighting some nineteen-year-old berserker didn't fit in with it. But I did have to make sure Jed wasn't in yet. I'd last seen him when he was twenty-two or three, long after Ju and I had drifted apart, so I was confident that I could still recognise him. He was still prowling around the estate on the lookout for things to steal when Ju was away at art school. I think by then he'd forgotten who I was. So I looked about me as surreptitiously as I could.

Not surreptitiously enough.

'What you fuckin' lookin' at?'

My heart sank. That question never leads on to anything good. There isn't a right way to deal with it. Play it meek, and you'll end up humiliated with some guy pissing on your chips. Play it tough and you might end up spanked. But now I did look at my accuser. He was small and wiry and ginger haired and his face was bubbling with red-phase acne. He was as frightening as a lame kitten. He sat with three more, sufficiently like himself to be brothers; they'd grown out of their spots.

I got up slowly, picking my stick up from where it was resting against the vinyl of the bench. I walked towards them, limping a little. Whatever conversation there had been in the pub – and there wasn't much – stopped.

'I'm trying to find someone. Maybe you can help me.'

The kid with the acne looked troubled by this. He glanced at his brothers and forced out a laugh. Whatever he'd been expecting, it hadn't been that I would walk up to him, unthreatening but unafraid. Perhaps he was also curious about who I should be looking for.

'There's no fucking poofs here.'

His brothers (or were they just friends? Sometimes friends can grow to look alike) laughed at this too, but they knew it wasn't exactly taxing repartee.

'I'm looking for Jed Flaherty. Are you saying he's gay?'

The three kids fell silent. I'd guessed that I might be able to use Jed's reputation, at least until he turned up.

'I didn't say Jed was, er, gay,' the first youth said, looking this time not at his mates but at the wider room. I got the feeling he'd never used the word gay before.

'Sorry, pal,' I said, sitting next to him, sitting quite close, close enough to make him instinctively edge away. 'I'm looking for Jed, and you said that there weren't any fucking poofs here. That sounds like you're calling him a fucking poof. Don't worry, he's a good lad, he'll have a laugh with you about it. I'll tell him you were only kidding.' I was smiling, confiding, friendly.

'I dint say he was a poof. I dint fucking say it.' His voice had risen an octave, and crackled like static.

'OK, take it easy, pal, don't have a fucking seizure. I'll say nothing.'

And then I walked back to my seat, reasonably confident

I'd be left in peace for a while. The exercise had been useful, if not entirely consoling. Jed, it seemed, was still able to inspire fear.

I got another drink. The barman, though no more talkative, was less malignant in his silence. The pub had got the message that I was a friend of Jed's.

I kept an eye on the door. People came and went. Newcomers ignored me. It was a phenomenon I'd noticed before. It's only when you first enter a room that you can be recognised as a stranger, as an outsider. If you are there already, even if it is the first time you've set foot in a place, then those who come after you will usually accept you as a fixture. Belonging is a function of priority. And so soon I was invisible, just another white man in a pub full of white men.

And then he was there. I'd been faffing in my pockets, looking for change for the cigarette machine, and missed his entrance, but I knew him. His hair was a wiry fluff, unstylable, yet without suggesting rebellion or even independence. The hair took me back. We were mucking about at the morning break on the all-weather sports pitch, so called because it was equally unsuitable for sport in all weathers. It was made out of something called Redgra, a kind of loose sandy gravel. The lines of various pitches – hockey, football, netball – were marked on it in whitewash. Now there was one thing that the Redgra pitch was good for. You could scoop handfuls of it up and throw it at your mates. The target areas were the arse and groin. It made a good big dusty stain, without really hurting. Particularly prized were the whitewashed sections, which left more dramatic patterns against our black trousers. So, Pete was out for revenge on me. I'd splattered him. He chased me with a handful of white-and-red. He fired. He missed. Jed was behind me. The dust peppered him. Nothing he couldn't have brushed off with a couple of flicks. I didn't know Ju then, but everyone knew his brother. Pete was too scared to run. He just waited meekly for his punishment. Jed walked over, his face blank and loose. He cuffed Pete across the back of the head, and Pete fell down. We hoped that might be it. But then Jed knelt down beside him and took his hair in his hand and rubbed his face into the red grit. Pete was moaning, trying not to cry. Someone said, 'Gi' o'er, Jed,' but Jed didn't gi' o'er. Instead he turned Pete over and told him to 'oppen ya fuckin' mouth', and he poured in a handful of Redgra, and then got up calmly and walked away. I didn't do anything to stop him from hurting my friend. I was only eleven.

Well, now I was all grown up.

Jed was talking to the barman. The barman, surprisingly, was talking back. He nodded in my direction, and Jed turned slowly around. Jed was never a good-looking kid. Beneath the fibrous tuft of hair, his face was remarkably red, almost the colour of a strawberry birthmark. His lips were thick and wide, his nose sprawling, his eyes small and pale. There was something about him which reminded me of a deep ocean fish, one of the ones that has not changed for three hundred million years.

All that was still there: the high colour, the wide mouth and thick lips, the psychotic eyes. But in place of the ugly kid, here was a good-looking man, or at least, as good looking as you can be while still exuding a naked will to power. He left his drink at the bar and walked over to my table.

'I heard you was looking fo' me.'

'I'm really looking for Ju. I thought you might be able to help.'

Jed stared into my face. His eyes were filmy, and didn't quite focus on mine; it made it easier to stare back without flinching.

'What do you want wi' 'im?'

'He's my mate.'

Another scrutinising pause.

'Do I know tha?'

'I went to the Body. Me and Ju were mates there. Went to your house a few times.'

There was no sign of remembrance or recognition in Jed's face.

'What does tha want wi' 'im?' he asked again.

The interview had gone well so far: Jed hadn't smashed my teeth in, or shot me in the guts. I thought about lying, about saying I was just looking up my old friend, but it was a mistake to underestimate Jed's intelligence. Because he was hard, people assumed he was thick. Jed Flaherty wasn't thick. Which isn't to say he had a wide-ranging, cultivated mind. His intelligence wasn't wasted on stuff that didn't matter.

'He's supposed to be making an album. He's fucked off somewhere. The record label have asked me to find him for them. They asked me because they knew that I was his friend.'

'They paying you?'

'Yes.'

'How much?'

'Depends how long it takes me to find him.'

'Don't piss me about.'

'A hundred quid a day.'

I could see the pulsing movement as his jaw defined itself and then sank, defined itself and then sank again. He turned

his back on me and went to the bar to get his drink. I let
out a breath. People around me began to speak again. Jed
came back and sat down.

'How do I know you're not some cunt, out to get our
kid?'

The Northern 'cunt' is a less savage word than the
Southern 'kant'. In some contexts it becomes almost a term
of endearment – daft cunt, silly cunt. But Jed's wasn't a
voice made for endearments.

'Why would anyone want to get him? The label just want
him back in the studio to finish the album. They can't make
him, if he doesn't want to. And they're worried he's in
trouble. Jed, I know he came up here two weeks ago. I know
he saw you. If you can help me find him I'll pay you.'

'How much?'

'A hundred quid.'

'Five hundred.'

'What?'

'You're fucking lyin' about how much they pay you.'

'If you help me I'll give you two hundred quid. Not bad
for a chat. That's all I want.'

'Three hundred.'

'OK.' Expenses. If he'd stuck to five hundred I'd have
paid him.

'Gi' us it.'

'But you haven't told me anything yet.'

'Fuck off, then.'

He waved his hand dismissively. I noticed that his nails
were chewed down to the stump.

I took a sip of my pint. I didn't really want to get my
wallet out in the pub. People were still watching. I was
carrying about nine hundred pounds in a mix of fifties

and twenties. I thought I might be able to work a few notes free without taking the wallet out of my pocket. I put my hand to my inside pocket, but Jed roughly pushed my wrist down.

'Not here, you stupid tit. Go for a piss, I'll follow you in.'

I didn't like it, but I couldn't see an alternative. I left my stick behind me.

Mistake.

The Gents was as bad as you'd expect. Urinals uncleaned since Duchamp; a lidless toilet bowl; the hot stench. I pissed, and washed my hands. The electric dryer didn't work, but I checked my reflection in the distorting chrome of its nozzle as I dried my hands in my hair. I was beginning to recognise myself again, after the months of oblivion, and worse than oblivion.

'All you London poofs have long hair?'

'Most London poofs have short hair. In fact, they look like your mates out there.'

That much was true. The punters in the Rat looked like the typical crowd in any Soho gay pub. Short hair, moustaches, muscles. Jed didn't look quite so gay.

'The fuckin' money.'

I took out my wallet. My eyes went down for a second and Jed was on me. He threw me against the wall, one hand at my throat, the other on the wrist of the hand holding the wallet. He was two inches shorter than me, but he was strong. I was off my feet, unable to breathe. But I had a hand free, and I stretched down for the knuckle-duster in my pocket. I reached it as Jed let me go. He had my wallet. He opened it and took out some cash. He counted off six fifties, and put the rest back in the wallet and handed it back to me.

'What the fuck was that all about?' I asked, straightening my jacket.

'Just getting me money.'

'I was about to give it to you.' I don't know why I bothered saying that. He knew I was going to give him it, but he wanted to take it, wanted to impose himself on me physically.

'What do you want to know, then?'

I looked at the door.

'Don't worry. We shall not be disturbed.'

'What is this – your fucking office, like the Fonz?'

He didn't answer, didn't smile. He had a complaisant look on his face after putting me against the wall. It was a face, almost, of post-coital satisfaction.

'Why did Ju come up here?'

'To see his dear old mam.'

'Yeah?'

'And his brother.'

'Don't fuck about, Jed. Was he in trouble?'

'Depends what you mean.'

'Why did he want to see you, Jed?'

'He wanted some help.'

That was good. He had something to say. He had something to say to me.

'What kind of help?'

'A deal.'

'Drugs?'

Jed sniggered, as if I'd committed some faux pas. Perhaps I'd used the wrong term, or maybe it just wasn't done to talk about these matters so directly.

'Yeah, *drugs.*'

'Tell me the fucking story, Jed.'

And so he did.

'Stupid little poof got himself mixed up in things down South. Tried to earn a bit of cash. Met some bloke said they could do business. Some cunt wanted to get into supplying schmeck . . .'

'What?'

'Schmeck . . . scottie . . . *cocaine*, you wanker . . . to the kind of ponces our Ju mucked about wi'. You know what he were like. You an' all, you poof.'

'So what . . . Ju was his contact with the music business?'

'Nah, Ju bought the stuff off of him on tick, paid him back from the profits, that was the deal to begin wi'. But the bloke were a cunt, and anyway, Ju needed more cash. Thought he could get the gear cheaper up here. Through me. An' he were reet. I fuckin' sorted 'im.'

'So Ju came to Leeds to buy coke from you.'

'No fuckin' flies on you, is there. But wi' cash I saved 'im, he got some shit an all.'

'Dope?'

'Dope! Fuck you. Smack.'

'Jesus, you sold smack to your kid brother. You didn't feel like a cunt?'

Jed laughed. He was enjoying himself.

'Me all over. Bad fuckin' example. An' it weren't for 'im. It were fo' them other cunts, poofs and that. And anyway, he was gonna get it from somewhere. At least he didn't get ripped off. He wasn't that fuckin' smart, you know, whatever he thought. You neither, Moriarty, you poof.'

I hadn't told him my name.

'So. You remember me, then.'

'Yeah, I remember you two always bumming each other, fucking snogging in us room.'

I let it pass for now. I was getting there.

'And when he got the stuff off you . . . . how much, by the way?'

'Kilo of coke, half of smack.'

'What's that worth?'

'Hundred thousand, street, for the coke, maybe thirty thousand for the shit.'

'And he paid you how much?

'None o' your fuckin' business. But I gave 'im a good deal. Blood's thicker than fuckin' water, even if he is a poof.'

'OK, then after he got the stuff he went straight back to London?'

'Don't fuckin' know. Don't give a shit. Why wunt he?'

I remembered something Maureen Flaherty had told me.

'I heard someone else was looking for Ju, asking after him.'

There was the tiniest flicker on Jed's passive features. If I didn't know any better, I'd have called it concern.

'Like who?'

'Don't know, just some bloke.'

'There might have been someone, maybe two. Heard there were some plainclothes following Ju, like fucking plainclothes wear suits. We fuckin' done here?'

'Nearly. Do you know who Ju was dealing with in London, the other guy selling him the gear?'

'No, just that he was some cunt. But Ju had a mate, probably another of his bum chums, someone who was in on it wi' 'im. He helped him sell it. He wont on music side. Summat like that, though. Acting or summat. Called Sebastian or some poof's name like that.'

Sebastian. The name chimed with me, but the fit was not quite right. I fished around, flailing to make a connection. And then I had an inspiration.

'Sebastian? Not . . . Christian?'

'Aye, Christian summat. What kind o' fuckin' name's that? Now, 'ave we done?'

'I've just remembered something else. Did Ju have a bird?'

'Don't make me fuckin' laugh. What are you asking me that fo'? You bummed 'im often enough.'

I'd planned on doing it anyway, but that was the trigger. My hand had been in my pocket throughout our conversation. It came out now. Jed's movements had seemed slow and heavy and ponderous, but that was deceptive: another aspect of his paying attention only to that which was important. He tried to duck the punch, and in his movement you could see the trajectory of the upper cut that would follow it. He ducked so he could stay in close, but he should have swayed back, and come for me once I'd missed. Perhaps he reasoned that he might have to take a glancing blow, but it was only a fist, and I was a poof.

But it wasn't only a fist. The brass of the duster rang on the side of his head. A thug like Jed could probably have taken it on the nose or cheek, and kept on coming at me, but the blow stopped him dead, and I saw his eyes grow clear for a moment, losing their milkiness in surprise. I stepped forward and hit him again in the same place, jagging in a downward arc. He was on his knees. Anyone normal would have been on their back. I grabbed him by the collar, and dragged him into the cubical. The toilet was smeared and streaked with shit. I shoved his head into the bowl, pushed his face into the water. He came up spluttering.

'What fo', what fo'? I told thee.'

'Remember Sandford? Little kid, my year? Remember doing this, you ugly fuck? Remember your little brother?

Remember what you did to him? If something bad's happened to Ju, I'm going to come back and kill you, understand?'

In answer, Jed writhed violently, and nearly twisted out of my grip. I hit him again twice on the back of the head. Not as hard this time – I didn't really want to kill him – but hard enough for him to slump. I took off his belt and tied his hands behind his back, although he was limp now, his red face hanging just above the brown water.

And then, after rinsing the blood from the knuckle-duster, I got out of there. We'd been in there too long for every set of eyes to have stayed on the door, but they came my way now. I got my stick and went straight for the exit. I didn't make it. The red-faced kid was leaning on the bar. He stepped in front of me.

'Where you off?'

'Opera North. They're doing *Rigoletto*.'

'What?' The kid looked around, scoffing.

'I'm late. Move.'

'Get fucked. Where's Jed?'

I tried to brush past him.

'Oi!'

A hand pulled me round by the shoulder. The other two brothers were there. Yes, I decided on brothers. Three unrelated ugly gingers in one pub was too much of a coincidence. I hit the arm that held me with my stick. It made a good, solid clump and changed shape, and one ginger was down on his knees. And then, before I got tangled with the other, a low brown shape came from the side of the pub. I thought I was in trouble, and then a big swinging roundarm punch emerged from the shape and landed in the face of the third brother.

Pillock!

'Better get out,' he said.

We pushed past the spotty kid, who didn't know how to stop us, and then we were out in the street.

'We've got to run,' I said. 'I've just beaten up Jed Flaherty in the bogs. He's going to want to kill somebody.' I felt a surging elation, the oxymoronic joy of righteous violence.

'This way,' Pollock said, and he trundled off in his rocking roly-poly run. We went down one street, across the road, down a narrow passage. I was out of breath, but the adrenalin kept me going. In five minutes we'd reached the main road. We dodged the traffic and reached a bus stop, just as a bus was approaching.

'This'll do,' said Pollock.

We sat upstairs, panting, laughing, exultant.

'What exactly the fuck were you doing there, er, Pillock.'

Simon smiled. I saw that he had a soft, silky little beard. I hadn't even noticed it before.

'You said you were off to the Rat. I know it around here, 'cause of working at Jimmy's. Thought I'd wander in. Had nothing better on. But you weren't there. I was about to go home where I saw you come out of the bogs. And then them lads had a go at you. Couldn't just sit there.'

'Cheers, Pillock. You saved my bacon.' I thought about the loneliness that had brought him out here on the chance of company, and I thanked God for it.

'Why, what were going on? You said you chinned Jed Flaherty. You're mental.'

'Long story. I had to get some information out of Jed. But he kept mithering me. And I remembered some of the things he used to do. So I hit him.'

'He's a hard bastard.'

'Not that hard.'

Simon looked at me with something like awe. 'You dint used to be like that. I always thought you was a bit soft.'

I didn't tell him about the knuckle-duster. I had enough vanity to relish the fact that I would have a reputation as the man who'd chinned Jed Flaherty, and I didn't want to compromise it with the truth. Kids who remembered or half remembered me from school would shake their heads in wonder.

'Where you kipping?'

Stupid, but I hadn't thought about it. I didn't even have a change of clothing. I suppose I'd thought I might be able to get a late train back.

'Hotel, I guess.'

'You can stay at ours, if you like.'

Simon's face was full of hope, but the hope was hopeless. I thought about his grim little bachelor pad. Or perhaps he still lived with his mum.

'Yeah, Simon, that'd be great. But I can't call you Pillock any more.'

'Oh, why not?' Simon's face was now shining with joy.

'It means cock, you know. Elizabethan slang for cock.'

'You always was a brainy get.'

Simon's flat was new and neat and not especially sad, although there was that faint trace of too many takeaway curries. He lived in Seacroft. We had a couple of pints in his local, and talked gently about the old days, and soon I'd remembered more about him. We talked about Ju, and I told Simon about the events leading up to my trip to Leeds. And then I told him about the night I had the lobe of my ear cut off, and about my struggle with the peth. He nodded, but had no glib commentary, and I sensed that he'd had struggles of his own, traumas stoically borne, sturdily suppressed. I slept well that night on his sofa, wrapped in a white sheet, and I dreamed of vanquished ogres.

17

The Truth about Ju

There was a lot to think about on the way back to London the next morning. I was less lucky with the train: there were no seats in the carriages, and I had to balance on one of the pull-down seats by the doors. Simon had lent me a clean T-shirt, but I balked at his offer of underpants, despite the fact that he claimed that they were a new pair of BHS specials, hitherto untouched by human arse.

'Keep counting,' he said, as I left. 'I always wanted you to reach the million.'

I had mixed feelings about the trip. In the grey morning I felt less sanguine about the violence I'd meted out. I'd stooped down to the level of the thugs when I'd beaten up Jed Flaherty. It didn't matter that he'd deserved the beating; it did matter that I'd enjoyed it. There were other drugs besides the white and the brown. And I'd found things out about Ju that I wished I hadn't.

On the other hand, it looked like I'd made real progress. Up to this point I'd felt like the man who wades out into the ocean to get a closer view of the sunset, but now the pieces were falling into place, and the key piece was Christian Holbach. It was becoming clear that Ju and Holbach had teamed up with a London mobster to supply the fashion and music industries. But Ju got greedy and thought he could get a better deal by heading north and using his brother's contacts. He got the stuff, paid his money and then disappeared. Suddenly there was a shape to things, and plenty of reasons for Ju to disappear. He'd got himself involved in drugs, and that meant no end of ways in which things could go belly up. Ju could have got into trouble in Leeds. Even if Jed wouldn't inflict deliberate harm on him – and the jury was still out on that – it didn't mean that someone else at the northern end of the deal wouldn't get ideas. Or the London supplier may have heard about Ju skiing off-piste. I was troubled by the other characters who'd been looking for him – to me they sounded like trouble from London. Neither of these situations boded well for Ju. The best I could hope was that he'd got wind that things were going wrong, and that's why he slipped off the screen. He had no commitments, no one who needed him. Why not take what money he had and head for Acapulco?

But there was a third area of unease. Ever since Charlie had told me about the label's shenanigans, I'd been unable to shake off the idea that something was wrong, fake, about the whole set-up. The label stood to lose more money if he ever finished his record. Potentially a lot more money. They were the ones who had most to gain from getting Ju out of the way. They were the ones who had most to lose by him ever showing up again. And that was why they hired a rank amateur like me. That was why they didn't get the police in. And if I was right in thinking that they didn't want to find Ju, then could it also follow that they had something to do with his disappearance in the first place? Crazy? Yes, it was crazy, but that didn't mean it was beyond a scheming egomaniac like Billy Adams.

None of this touched on the one pure tragedy. The girl. Who was she? Nobody took seriously the thought that Ju had a girlfriend. And what did that tell me about Ju? It was time, I thought, as we trundled southward, to think properly about my friend, Ju Flaherty.

Did I ever think that he was gay, when we were together as kids? Never for a second. It could, of course, have been denial. If my best friend was gay, then did that mean I was? Not a question many fifteen-year-old boys enjoy asking themselves. We used to talk about girls all the time. He was interested in how they looked, in how they talked, in the ways in which they were different to, or the same as, us. We didn't much go into the grosser side of things, in the way I did with my other mates. And Ju was effeminate, at least by the standards of our school and our estate. He wore make-up and painted his nails and fussed over his hair. But that was neatly disguised by the trappings of punk. In his pomp he had seven rings in one ear and five in the other. He was one of the first kids in Leeds to have his eyebrow pierced.

But was he gay?

Of course he was gay. Now it was as clear to me as any other fact about Ju. Of course he was gay, and that meant that the girl wasn't his girlfriend. Unless he'd changed, and people can change.

And then the drugs. Ju had always taken a Nietzschean view of the law: it was for others. He stole whatever he wanted, and that meant records and clothes. He took me with him on raids, showed me how and where. He knew where the store detectives were lazy and where they were slow; he knew where they were keen. He justified it (not that I ever challenged him) by saying that he needed these things more than 'they' needed them, that the huge benefit to him dwarfed the minor loss to the shop.

He thought that there was nothing wrong with lying, if

it helped him get what he wanted. I remember him telling my mum about a sponsored walk for the Catholic Fund for Overseas Development, and with the two pounds she gave him he went and bought cigarettes.

But drugs. And not just the coke, but the side order of heroin. It made me feel sick to my stomach that he should be involved in this. I could hear him explain it (in my mind he still spoke with the high, clear tones of a fifteen-year-old, his voice unbroken): 'Someone would supply it; at least this way the world gets a fucking beautiful record out of it as well. Anyone else would spend it on cars and whores.'

I always went along with Ju's schemes because I thought he was cool, and more than that, I thought he really was going to do great things. I thought we both were. And then came the crossbow, and the dog, and the rainbow. I wanted to talk to Ju about those things, and I also wanted to know why he thought that it was OK for him to sell drugs, and who the dead girl was, lying at the foot of his bed, and why she had died.

18

Jed Meets a Man

I pieced things together later. It must have happened like this, or something like this.

Jed Flaherty knew a rage he had never felt before, and he was a man powered by rage. Not knowing his own father had hurt him more than it had ever wounded Ju, and he had none of Ju's quickness of thought, and so the taunts he endured as a young child went unchallenged. And then, at the age of twelve or thirteen, he found that he was strong. From that moment, he didn't need a nimble tongue: he hit people who got in his way, and once hit by Jed Flaherty, you stayed on the floor. He'd worked his way slowly up the loose criminal infrastructure of North Leeds, making himself useful to the men who thought of themselves as gang lords, but who were really just the local thugs, most of them thick, some of them psychotic. And Jed was lucky. After his stint in borstal, he never again did time, although the local police were well aware of his activities and reputation. Most of Jed's violence was against other criminals, and anything short of murder was filed away back at Milgarth station under the title of 'Let the fuckers kick the shit out of each other'. Besides, there were plenty of petty thieves and hard men like Jed Flaherty, and they just hadn't got round to him yet. But they would.

So Jed had led something of a charmed existence, earning

enough through his work to count as wealthy in his world, without coming close to the point where he could leave it. He'd taken punches, but never serious beatings. And he'd fucked every woman worth having in Chapeltown, and even had a couple of slags working part time for him, bringing in a steady five hundred a week.

But now Jed Flaherty had been put down, and left dangling over a fucking shitter. He was going to find that poof Moriarty, and when he found him he was going to take him apart. He walked along a Chapeltown side street thinking about it. His jaw hurt and his head hurt, but he could take that kind of hurt. It was the other kind he couldn't live with. He'd read about what the Mujahadin had done in Afghanistan when they captured Russian soldiers. They cut a strip of skin from round the waist, and then peeled the skin up and tied it in a knot over the head. You needed to be clever with a knife, but then he was. Although he'd worked only as a porter down at the meat market, he'd picked up a few butchering skills. Of course, it was better in a place like that, with the flies, but even in Leeds – or in London, if that's what it took – it would do nicely. He'd have to put him out, so he could work, but then he could sit back and watch him wake up, wake up into hell.

He told his mates this when he came out into the chaos of the Rat. But there was no doubt that he'd lost a lot of face, and so the rage burned like a sodium flare, bright and hot.

There was one thing that would help. He'd been fucking Shirley Tate for a couple of years. A fat bird, but up for anything. You could fuck her in the slit and then in the arse and then in the mouth. You could slap her. Loved it. Yeah, he'd pay a visit to Shirley. Give her a couple. Thinking about it took away the taste of ashes from his mouth.

'Got a light?'

Jed hadn't noticed the big fucker. Smart suit. London voice. Probably a businessman come up to Leeds for a conference or some shit like that, and now out for a spot of gash in Chapeltown. Jed thought about taking his wallet off him – the place was right, not a soul about, nice and dark. But then he thought again. This bloke looked a bit too big, a bit too much like he could handle himself. And he was still fuzzy from the clip that cunt Moriarty had given him.

'Yeah,' he said, fishing a box of Swan Vestas from his pocket. 'Keep 'em.'

The move was so slick it looked to Jed like something out of a Bruce Lee film. The man took his arm, twisted it behind his back, and Jed was on his knees, and the cold barrel of a gun was pressed into the nape of his neck. Jed was panting like a dog.

'What 'ave I done? I done fucking nowt.'

'Shut the fuck up.'

'I'm sorry, I'm sorry.'

'Too late for that. You thought you could move in where you don't belong. Big mistake. Fucking peasants. Making me come up to this toilet. You all fuck your sisters. Bye-bye.'

But then nothing, not even a click.

Fucker. The Glock had jammed. He should have tested it. Schoolboy mistake. Now he was going to have to do it fucking manually. He put his arms around Jed Flaherty's neck. Jed was whimpering like a puppy when you mash its face in its own shit. He got ready to twist and pull. He'd done the theory in the Paras, but he'd never had the chance to do it for real.

Jed was trembling. He'd wet his pants, and saliva was running down his chin, over the other's hands.

'Fuck this. Fuck this.'

He let go, and Jed dropped to the ground. He was still for a second, and the pavement beneath him was so clear he could make out the tiny cracks in the surface of the tarmac, and then he pulled his eyes away from the ground and half turned his face to see the man. He was looking down at him, and Jed couldn't tell whether it was disgust or pity or boredom in his eyes.

'Fuck this,' the man said again, and began to walk away.

Even now Jed thought about jumping him. Now that the immediate prospect of death had receded, he had his courage back. But he wasn't completely stupid. So he pulled himself up and screamed at the top of his voice: 'Wanker!' And then, stumbling, he ran away, like a dog fleeing from under the wheels of a car.

PART FOUR
Another Girl, Another Planet

19

A Public Relations Disaster

I was in London by midday. My next move was straight-forward enough. Christian Holbach was starting to seem like my last best hope. He was in on the deal with Ju, and if Ju had ever made it back to London with his packages of cocaine and heroin, then Holbach would know about it.

I took a taxi to Kilburn (another blank receipt for my accounts), showered and changed my clothes. I was going to send the T-shirt back to Simon, but then I reconsidered, and sent twenty quid and a note thanking him for saving my neck. I figured he might get a kick out of knowing that I'd kept the T-shirt. And then I beat myself up for patronising him, and then I groaned at my way of over-analysing everything, and then I got down to work.

This time I got through to Holbach on his mobile.

'Christian,' said the voice, like a warm tongue in my ear.

'I'm a friend of Ju Flaherty,' I said hurriedly. For some reason the voice, that single word, had put me in a funk.

Nothing for a moment.

'We're all friends of Ju Flaherty.' The voice was like none I'd ever heard: a clipped drawl, a little camp, a little mesmerising.

'I'm trying to get hold of him.'

Laughter. 'We're all trying to get hold of him.' The voice had the power to make me sleepily alert, and I was drifting, thinking of other things, of days with Ju, of nights lying in a Tunisian desert, watching the universe happening above me. I made myself concentrate.

'I'd very much like to meet you. We've got things to talk about.'

'Really?'

'Really. Soon. Tonight.'

'That simply isn't possible.' There was a smirk in the voice now that made me blink with fury. I'm not the kind of person, he was saying, who can just drop everything to talk to a stranger.

'I think it is. I've just come back from Leeds. I heard some interesting things. Interesting things about Ju; interesting things about you.'

'Hey, I'm an interesting guy.' This time there was something hollow even in his smugness. 'And, by the way, you've told me *what* you are, but not *who* you are, which seems a little inconsiderate.'

'My name's Moriarty.'

'I'm afraid I've never heard of you.'

That was intended as some kind of slight. Perhaps in his world it really was bad news if Christian Holbach hadn't heard of you.

'Look, you dumb shit, I know why Ju went to Leeds, and I know what you two were doing in London. Meet me tonight, or I'm going to the police. They don't even know Ju's missing, and I can't help but think it's time they got involved.'

Holbach tutted, and then sighed, as if I'd subjected him to some minor inconvenience, clipped his wing mirror, perhaps, or asked to borrow his comb.

'I can spare you twenty minutes. The Met Bar. Nine. Call me names again and there will be consequences.'

And he hung up.

After facing down Jed Flaherty, being threatened by a London fashion queen wasn't too unnerving.

At eight I got the Tube down to Green Park and walked to the Met along Piccadilly. This kind of thing was always a reliable gauge of my mental state. There were times when just being out in central London on a Saturday night could fill me with disgust or anger or sadness. These were the nights when all I could see were the desperate strays or the lost and hysterical women or the super-rich at lascivious sport. And there were other times when the glorious teeming riot of energy and colour renewed my faith in humanity and my trust in the possibility that things would work out fine in the end.

Tonight I was closer to the second of those mental states. London looked like a good place, and the night was warm without being oppressive, and an elegant Japanese lady asked me the way to the Royal Academy, and I showed her, and she smiled her thanks so widely that I could have counted all her teeth, including the molars.

It didn't mean I wasn't faintly dreading the Met. I'd been once before when a girl I was seeing got invited to a hen party in one of the hotel rooms, and the girls arranged to meet their partners down in the bar. This was back when it was generally accepted to be the single coolest place in the world, maybe just a week before the soap stars and footballers found out about it. It took me ten minutes to persuade the door people to let me in, and when I finally made it and found the girl and got a drink, I realised that this was hell. In all the frenzied chatter there was no exchange of ideas or intimate contact, just a listing of who you knew, a blitz of severed signifiers, words without meaning. It was the moronic inferno dressed in Prada. The preening and strutting had none of the endearing *please love me, please be my friend* vulnerability that I was used to in the kinds of girl that I went for, where attractiveness is a form of communication, a hand held out, a beginning of a conversation. Everything here was a pure, hard-edged, catwalk narcissism: look at me, the beautiful women and the vacantly handsome men said, look at me, and nothing else.

And I saw the girl I had come to meet in the middle of a happy gang, and there didn't seem to be much in it for either of us, so I walked out of the place, and that was it for me and the girl and the bar.

I expected to have trouble getting in again, but when I said that I was there to meet Christian Holbach I was smiled through like a regular. I'd forgotten quite how small the bar was, but it had had a revamp since my last visit, and looked pretty sweet. And it was emptier than I'd expected, with a smattering of wannabes and hangers-on, without anyone to hang on to. Looked like the movable feast had got up and moved. I sat on a bar stool and ordered a beer. The barman dropped the bottle, but opened it anyway, and so a good half of the beer was lost in spray. He poured it. I looked at him. He looked back at me. Some several seconds passed, then he shrugged and got another bottle.

I found a seat at a table and waited for Holbach. A woman came in, and a little shimmer went through the room, like a breeze agitating lake water. She was wearing a dress made from spider's web and smoke and her lips bulged with collagen. She gave a wide, encompassing smile, taking in everything and no one. There were three people with her – a plain girl in a baby-doll dress, a little muscle-bound boy-man with a deep tan, and a black guy with a weapons-grade Afro, like a penumbra of black light around his head. I couldn't even begin to guess who the woman was, but the Met Bar loved her, bending itself in on her, as though she could warp gravity.

And then a man entered the room from the Gents. His eyes shone with chemical brilliance. He was wearing what at first glance looked like it might be a sober dark suit, but something about its cut and the way it flowed about his form and the glimpse I got of an electric-blue lining made me realise that it was incomprehensibly chic and expensive. And on his feet he wore a pair of pink trainers that looked like they were made from salmon skin. His hair was dark and slicked back, with a parting straight down the middle like Rudolf Valentino. He wore a green tie with a knot as thick and heavy as a mace head.

It had to be Holbach. The man went with the voice the way sugar goes with tooth decay.

He walked up to the new woman, and they kissed on the lips, and held each other at arm's length, and then kissed again. It was like the reunion of siblings separated in child-hood, brought back together for a TV documentary.

But even as he was kissing the woman, I sensed that he had noticed me, and that he knew who I was in the same way that I'd known him. He went to the bar and a drink was waiting for him. He walked over to me, his steps small, almost like a ballerina on points.

'So you're Ju's . . . what . . . *friend*?' 'Friend' was drawn out to give it additional layers of meaning, none of them pleasant to contemplate. I was already on the way to wanting to inflict harm on Christian Holbach.

'Matthew Moriarty.'

I put out my hand. Holbach studied it for a while, the

result being that I felt pretty stupid. Then he took my hand. His fingers were long, his nails perfect. Already I felt like a yokel, like a blundering village idiot.

'Have you made any . . . *progress*?' He relished the word, rolling the 'r's luxuriously, giving it the feel of decadence and delightful corruption. I supposed he was taking the piss. 'I do so hope you find the boy. I'm so annoyed with him. He always was a selfish little *morsel*.'

Although he was clearly a practised performer, there was something very strange about Holbach's manner. It was as if he couldn't quite decide whether he should bother to charm me or not, as if he was unsure about when to commit his reserves.

'Progress? Some, not much. That's why I'm here.'

'I would so like to help you, but you know, as I haven't seen him in . . . ooooh, weeks . . . I don't see how I can. Have you tried his stylish little bachelor's pad in . . . where was it? . . . *Ealing*?'

And then he reached into his pocket and took out a green packet of menthol cigarettes. He put one in his mouth, and then lent forward, inviting me to light it for him. There was a book of matches on the table. I threw it on to his lap.

'Maybe you don't know where he is now, but there are some things you do know. If you tell me those, I'll find Ju. That should make us both happy.'

'Oh, ask away, then,' he said, waving the now pluming cigarette with a limp hand. 'Anything that makes us both happy must be worth pursuing.'

'OK. Who was supplying the cocaine for you and Ju in London?'

Holbach laughed.

'I do so love the direct approach. And now I see what

you were driving at in that brief but pleasant phone call. Nevertheless, and you can't begin to dream how it pains me, I haven't got the faintest fuck of an idea what you're talking about.'

'Look,' I said, trying hard to keep a grip on my anger, 'I honestly don't give a shit about you and what you might have done. My only interest is in finding Ju. Tell me who supplied the coke and I'm out of here, and you'll never see me again, and you have my word on that.'

Holbach now matched my own seriousness. He leaned forward across the table, and beckoned me to join him there. Cautiously I moved to within whispering range. He blew a stream of mentholated smoke in my face.

'Mr Nobody.'

And then I did what I was hoping I wouldn't have to do. I reached over and grabbed Christian Holbach's nose between my forefinger and thumb and then, squeezing it as tightly as I could, gave it a full one-eighty twist. Holbach let out a squeaking bellow and banged the table with the flat of his hand. I sensed movement coming from my left, and I reached into my pocket.

'Customs and Excise,' I shouted, holding out the plastic folder with my old ID card in it. 'Back off.'

The two guys who had come in with the woman in the spider's web dress stopped dead, unsure how to react. Holbach was still squealing and banging on the table. Then the black guy – the first to regain some composure – came forward and said, politely, his voice as plummy as a polo player's, 'Can I check that?' The educated voice gave me a moment's unease. Would he see through the trick, notice that the pass was old and faded, that the hair and clothes were out of date? He touched the card delicately, without taking it from me. And then he shrugged, and opened up his fingers like a fan, and walked away with his friend. He obviously wasn't getting mixed up with Customs just to bail out Holbach. Whose nose, by the way, I was still holding with my other hand. I slipped the ID under his face.

'I was always shit at covert surveillance work,' I said. 'You know, all that slipping about invisibly, blending in.' And then I gave his nose a final squeeze and twist, and pulled my fingers down his nostrils, the way you do to get the last of the slush out of an ice pop. Then I held out my fingers, feigning disgust, and wiped them on a clean tissue. I held the tissue up to Holbach.

'Right here I have a cocktail of substances. I've got some sweat and some mucus. I've got particles of London soot, and diesel deposits. But that's not all the lab boys will find, is it, Christian? Because we both know what you were doing back in the bogs with your pals, don't we? So there's a few grains of stardust there as well. So that means we have your DNA, and hard evidence you've been snorting cocaine. Just using, and that's not necessarily very serious, if it's your first offence. But it also means my colleagues in the Met come round to your place with the junkie dogs, and the financial experts start having a good long look at your bank accounts, to see what's gone in and what's gone out, and then you suddenly find that they've frozen your assets, and if the sniffer guys *do* find anything interesting, well then, that's ten years, and the rest you can fill in for yourself.'

It was difficult to know at first whether Holbach took this pile of ordure in. His eyes were watering, and his nose looked like it had been given a fucking good twist, but still he gazed at me emotionlessly, his handsome, intelligent features betraying nothing. He was, in some ways, an

impressive character. But I guess the nose-squeeze had softened him up a bit because when I met them, his eyes
dropped and he said, meekly, 'OK, OK.'

'Go on, then. From the start. About you and Ju, from
when you first met. And don't bother filtering – let me
decide what's important.'

Holbach sighed heavily, and then lit another menthol cigarette. His hand trembled slightly, and he looked nervously
around, to see who was watching. Nobody was. The woman
in the spider's web and smoke had drawn the Met around
herself and Holbach was already yesterday. The only glance
came from the posh black guy, and he was still letting his
discretion kick valour's arse.

'OK, OK,' Holbach repeated. 'I met Ju back in the early
nineties, when he still looked like he might *be* somebody. I
was just getting up steam in fashion PR then, and I got him
into some of our outfits – Prada, Moschino, Armani. Until
then he still looked like a girl punk getting pissed on cider
on a park bench. And his friends. Jesus. Puddingy boys in
sweaty T-shirts and Dunlop Green Flash, and all they talked
about was amps and reverb. So I took him under my wing,
and he was happy to nestle there, and learn about the way
things worked. You see, it was at the time when fashion and
music started to play together again, after years of sulking.
Remember the models in the Pulp video, *Common People*?
– they were mine. And all that nasty beer he drank then.
Would have given him a little tummy in no time, and even
you can see how silly that would have looked.'

'So you introduced him to cocaine.'

'It was love at first sight. But he wasn't too naughty. He
really was quite *professional* about his music. So he played
all night and worked all day. Shame he never seemed to get

very far. Like one of those toy steam engines you used to see in worthy museums. The wheels spin and pistons pump and the little whistle goes toot-toot, but the poor machine never moves. And those nasty men at the record company were always, ooh, how can I put it? – *on his back*. And finally they made him go and work in some grotty borough with a BNP councillor and a kebab shop on every corner. And we hadn't seen each other for aeons, but I get a phone call, and we have a drink, and he tells me about his idea.'

'His idea, not yours?'

'Oh yes, definitely his. Sweet scheming little mind!'

'What was it?'

'Well, our Ju had met some Kray-lite character with blue-rinse hair and a voice off the Veldt, who thought how nice it would be to move on from selling crack to pregnant Somali teenagers to helping out the creative community with their pharmaceutical needs. Perfectly respectable idea. And Ju had told this character that he had the connections in the fashionable world, which he did, meaning me. And so we sold a little ice, and that helped Ju to pay his bills.'

'But then you thought you could undercut London prices by buying in Leeds.'

'Marginal, really. It was more that Ju had taken against his bouffant bad boy. You know how capricious he could be.'

'His name.'

'Bernardo Mueller. Never met him myself. Sounded like a scream.'

Mueller.

Although the logic of it had already established itself in my mind before Holbach had spoken the name, it still made me reel. Ju was a local celebrity, Mueller was the local don. It was only a matter of time before they met.

'This is important. Did you see Ju when he came back from Leeds?'

'Neither hide nor hair. In fact, for all I know, he's still there. Except, who'd stay in Leeds longer than they had to?'

'Do you think it's possible that Mueller found out what was happening, and did something to stop it?'

'Not beyond the bounds of possibility.'

'And you're not frightened?'

'Frightened? Of you?'

'Of Mueller.'

'He doesn't know anything about me. Ju wanted Mueller to think that all the connections were his.'

'I think you'd be surprised what Mueller can find out. He's a man of some ingenuity. He had his goons up in Leeds asking questions. He's a violent man. Maybe you should be scared.'

'Won't you put him in jail?'

The question had a childlike innocence, and for the first time I stopped hating Holbach's guts.

'Yes, I'll put him in jail for you. Will you tell me something else?'

'Oh, ask anything. You've already ravished me, now I'm your slut.'

'Were you and Ju lovers?'

Holbach spluttered and choked on his cigarette.

'Lovers?' he said, the choking becoming laughter. 'What on earth makes you think I'd be interested in a little tranny like Ju Flaherty?'

'A little what?'

'Oh, you heard. And now, whatever you say, I don't quite believe that this is part of your investigation.'

'Fine,' I said, trying to take in what Christian had said.

'You've been very helpful. But take this as a lesson. You got yourself mixed up in something nasty. By some miracle you might just come out of it without the shit sticking. Next time it's the prison or the morgue. And if I find out you've been bullshitting me, next time becomes this time.'

I got up, and thought about shaking Holbach's hand again, but then I just gave a little wave, which hardly felt like the right way for an ass-kicking Customs investigator to end the encounter. I walked out through the bar, past the crowd around the unknown celebrity, past the passively staring black guy. Outside the Met I finally felt I could breathe properly, and I took in a couple of good lungfuls of petrol fumes and ozone and hydrogen sulphide, and felt much better.

I felt a tap on my shoulder. It was Holbach. I thought for a moment that he had remembered something else to tell me, and then he moved. It was as neat a head-butt as I'd ever seen, or felt. The aim was perfect, but deliberately, I think, he'd held back on the force. As it was, I fell to my knees, with my nose bleeding profusely into my hands.

'Where the fuck did you learn that?' I asked, bubbling through the blood. I suppose I should have been fighting mad, but I felt more surprised than anything.

'Stoke,' said Holbach. His voice was cold and hard with flattened Midlands vowels. Not at all his usual chocolate cake and whipped cream.

'What was it for?'

'You said "if it's your first offence". If you were a real Customs officer, you'd have known. I'm a stupid cunt, sometimes.' His voice was still in Stoke, but I could feel it slipping back down to Soho. 'Bye-bye,' he said, mimicking my own earlier wave.

'Yeah, Christian, I'll see you.'

And I sat on the kerb and waited for the bleeding to stop, playing the interview over again in my mind. So now I knew who Ju's London supplier was. And I knew that Ju had double-crossed him. And I knew what kind of man Mueller was. I felt sick, and excited, and fearful. My next move would have to be reporting back to Hellbent. Then they could take it to the police. Either Ju was hiding from Mueller, or Mueller had found him. Either way, I knew he was out of my reach.

And then I thought about the last thing Holbach had told me. And as I sat by the road, with the traffic thundering by, the truth came on me like an illness. I stood up slowly. There was blood on my shirt, but I'd wiped my face clean on a hanky. I pulled my jacket across to cover the stain, and hailed a taxi.

'Egremont Street,' I said to the cabbie. 'It's off the Edgware Road.'

20

A Mortal Coil

It was ten by the time I reached the house. I didn't bother with the bell, but went straight round to the back, following my earlier route over the fences and dung heaps. The back door was still unlocked. Obviously no one had visited since I was last there. The house was dark and silent, and my breath sounded loud in my ears, stertorous and harsh. Just enough light leaked in from the street lamps for me to find my way. I went to the stairs, and could still make out the shapes of the nightmarish Goya prints, and they now took even more morbid forms in my imagination, and monsters consumed babies and women were gutted and flayed.

I reached the room where I'd seen the body of the girl. There had been no odour before, but now there was a thick sweet stench, and the room hummed faintly with dozing bluebottles and blowflies. I retched, but managed to keep down my guts. It was darker in here, and not much light came in through the small window; I flicked the switch.

Immediately the flies began to circle. I took out my handkerchief and stuffed it to my face, but it didn't help much, and so I put it back in my pocket. I looked down at the body. I thought that even in the few days since I had last seen it, the process of decay had begun to hollow out the humanity, reducing the flesh to bone and air, but that was just imagination. I knelt down. I put my fingers to the chin, below the long fringe of wild curls, and tilted back the head.

There are easy ways to die and there are hard ways. Judging by Ju's face, heroin overdose was an easy way, a good way. There was no sign of pain in his features, no fear, no horror at the coming darkness. He wore lipstick and eyeliner and even, I think, some foundation. Despite the stench, I sat down beside my old friend. I knew that I should not touch the body, but I could not stop myself from taking his hand. I said a prayer for his soul, and I remembered some of the good times we'd had. There was a time when we hitched to Manchester and got into the Hacienda through a fire door to watch the first concert there by the Smiths, and Morrissey threw gladioli into the pit and hard kids fought over the flowers, and afterwards we slept in Whitworth Park and talked all night about the greatest songs, to keep away the fear of being alone in a strange place with long-coated tramps. And I remembered telling Ju about my first girlfriend, and he took the piss so mercilessly that I knew he must approve of her, and that his piss-taking was his love gift to us.

I didn't shed any tears for Ju; in fact I found myself smiling as the memories came back. I thought about the first time I saw him play his bass guitar, running his fingers up and down the frets as if he knew what he was doing, when really he was only trying to look cool. His fingers. The fingers of his right hand on the frets, because he played left-handed. We used to joke that left-handers shouldn't be allowed in bands because they messed up the look – you know, all the guitars pointing the same way. I mean, can you imagine how big the Beatles might have been if Paul had played the right way round?

And then I looked at the syringe still in Ju's left arm.

His left arm.

That meant that he'd injected with his right. Why would he do that? I thought it must be because he couldn't find a vein in his right arm. That happened to junkies, after a while, until they ran out of veins on their arms and had to use their legs or groin or ankles. But then who'd ever said that Ju was a junkie? I pulled back the sleeve on his right arm. It was clean, no sign of bruising or scarring, and I knew that Ju hadn't taken an overdose.

So Mueller had found him. I pictured the scene. The two big thugs holding him down, Mueller astride him, the sexual taunts, the possibility of a sexual assault. And then the fatal syringe, all made to look like an accident. So there was nothing peaceful about Ju's last moments, unless the heroin was able to bring some peace and forgetfulness before the end. And now I had another reason to kill Bernie Mueller. I kissed Ju on the cold, hollow cheek, and swore that I would avenge his death, and then I left him. This time I went straight to the phone downstairs in Ju's living room, and called the police operator. I said that there had been a murder, gave them the address and hung up. And then I got out of there as fast as I could, pursued by Goya's phantoms, and by the feel of Ju's cold flesh on my lips.

Back in my flat the sense of grief and the tragedy began to bear down, like the stone that crushed the Catholic martyrs. Somehow Ju's fall, the fact that he had become involved in something evil before his death, added to rather than subtracted from the pain. I knew that he had once been a good man, that his instincts were to help the weak, to goad the strong, and so he must have been in terrible turmoil to have done what he had done. I knew from bitter experience that sometimes life closes itself off to you, leaving one narrow path, so that your actions take on the force of necessity. And there was the paradox that every choice we make in life reduces our freedom, because once that choice is made the world of opportunity in the path not taken is lost. And that narrowing reaches its culmination at the end of our lives when there is no choice left at all, when all our freedom has been consumed.

And money was always nestling in there at the heart of the corruption. I remember talking once to an officer of the River Police at a joint conference they were attending with Customs. He said that every year a dozen or so men kill themselves by jumping from the bridges, and they invariably do so for the sake of love or money. And by looking at the hands, he told me, you can always tell which, for the fingers of those who died for love are torn and bloodied, from scrambling at pillars as the cold and swirling waters close over them, and the loss of love finds its true perspective; but the fingers of the bankrupt are clean and smooth.

The label had let Ju wither on the vine, cutting off sustenance, because they knew that if he ever released the project, then they stood to lose more than if he never finished it, and it was his desperation in the face of their betrayal which had forced him into the hands of Mueller.

I found a bottle of duty-free gin, bought years ago on a ferry ride to nowhere. There was nothing to drink with it, but I had ice in the freezer. I spent twenty frustrating minutes reconnecting my old turntable to the amp and then I pulled out my records. Most of them I hadn't listened to since coming to London. Most hadn't even gone to Manchester with me for my university years. But I'd always been kind to records, and changed the stylus, and smoothed away the dust from the grooves with a special cloth, and so I knew that they would play true.

First of all I played 'Love Will Tear Us Apart' by Joy Division, and then I played 'Jeane' (once I'd found it on the B-side of 'This Charming Man') and then I played 'Another Girl, Another Planet', and finally the This Mortal Coil version of 'Song to the Siren', and that seemed a good place to end.

21

The Professionals

I later found out that it was during that night, as I played my old records, and wept for the loss of Ju, and for the loss of Ju's innocence, that Bernie Mueller sent Liphook to kill Liss.

It wasn't an easy decision for him to make. Although he liked to think of himself as a top gangster, Mueller didn't have much of a gang. He had Liss and Liphook to do his muscle work, and they were on the payroll. Everyone else was outside the loop. He had an accountant and a solicitor, but only in the way that any businessman might. He had rent collectors, and some of those would do a little low-grade frightening, but they were just freelancers. So losing Liss meant losing half his team, and the good half at that, because there was no denying that Liss had more brains than Liphook. And Mueller was always a bit embarrassed about Liphook, with his thick voice and busted nose. Yes, Liss was definitely prettier; it was just, it turned out, that he had no guts.

But it wasn't just that he felt let down by Liss. He had a bad feeling about him. The feeling that he might not be content to stay where he was in the organisation. And Mueller had seen his fair share of betrayal in his time, and so he knew how rare a commodity loyalty was, how common the *Et tu, and fuck you, Brute.*

Mueller had come to London in 1979. Before that he'd been a junior officer in an élite squad of the South African Defence Force, fighting deep in Mozambique. Their job was simple: atrocities. They'd drive into a government village and kill everyone. Sometimes they'd do the same to the rebels, the Renamo guerrillas, just to keep things active, make sure no one got round to thinking about peace or planting crops. Once in a while they'd get a tip and go on a swoop to capture some of the ANC men and women skulking over the border. Sometimes they'd question them in the field, sometimes they'd bring them in. Mueller enjoyed the work. He was fearless without being reckless, and his comrades appreciated that, although most of them also thought he was a creep.

He still prized his memories of those days: fighting for a cause he knew was right, camping out in the bush, living off the land, the companionship and love of the other soldiers, even the kaffirs in the squad, good boys, most of them. Some bad memories too. That ANC bitch they caught on a raid to the outskirts of Maputo. No one had ever been that far behind enemy lines. Worked on her for three days. They all had a go. Let the kaffirs on her. Burnt her down to nothing, watching the fat run out of her, and then the black turn to grey. Not a fucking word. Her dad was some old communist cunt. They told him that she'd blabbed just to add a bit of disgrace to the family, maybe get them a necklace or two. But not very satisfying.

It was easy to move from the South African security world to London. The SADF had plenty of high-up contacts in UK intelligence. The thinking back then was that South Africa was a bulwark against communism, keeping things tight down there, stopping the Soviet influence from fucking up the whole of Africa. So intelligence was swapped, and interrogation methods copied. It was an accepted perk of loyal service that you could move to the UK and settle down. And that's what he did. It took him a while to find his feet, but there were enough of his old comrades around to keep him from feeling isolated. He tried working as a private security consultant, but there was a lot of competition, and it took him a couple of years to build up a stake. Then he bought his first property, and never looked back. Kilburn, Cricklewood and Willesden were his territories, and he found the perfect way to operate. Buy a slum with tricky tenants – the worse the tenants, the better, as they dragged the price down. Then kick out the tenants, furniture out on the road, bedbugs, fleas, lice, kids, the lot. Usually meant a bit of argy-bargy, but that was part of the fun. Then get in a new lot, too weak to fuss, grateful to have anything. Bangladeshis, Pakis, bog Irish. Squeeze them in. If they squealed, kick them the fuck out too.

And with tenants you had a nice way of riding the property market. When property was cheap, buy it up, get the rent. Values went up, sell on; values drop again, buy big. For the first few years he was a one-man band, collecting the rent himself. And he could be charming, when he wanted, and if a husband was out at work when he called, then he could sometimes be persuaded to give a week's credit in exchange for a blowjob, or a quick fuck, with the woman bent over the draining board, and the cutlery flying all over the kitchen, and cups smashing on the floor. Once a husband came home and caught him, but Mueller shut him up with a few slaps.

For the first ten years, Mueller stayed mainly on the right side of the law, if you didn't count fraud, and threats with violence, and assault and battery. But then he began to see the opportunities that property opened up for you. There was sex. Brothels were cheap to set up, and if they were a hassle to run, then that was a price worth paying. And then drugs. Heroin, then cocaine, more recently crack. Setting up a crack house was a piece of piss. Get in a couple of blacks to run it for you, make sure there was enough distance so that when the police closed it down (in the end they usually did) all you had to do was play the ignorant land-lord, the poor sap who didn't know what was going on, move the set-up down the road, start it all off again. And because he was a businessman, it meant that he could run it all more efficiently than the competition, fucking igno-rant niggers that they were.

Easy money, but not nice money. Let crack-heads into your house and you've got piss and shit all over the shop. See, a crack-head gets the urge to go as soon as he gets to the door of a crack house, before he even smokes a rock. Some kind of physiological reaction. So he goes to shit in the bushes, or in plain sight in the garden, or right on the fucking doorstep. It's how you can tell a crack house: by the shit. Mueller was a civilised white man, and he didn't like that kind of behaviour, people turned to dogs, white women acting like dumb blacks. And that was why he jumped at the chance of moving upmarket, of supplying good clean coke to the fashion and music set. These were more his kind of people. People with a bit of imagination and flair. And with the odd exception, they were nice white people, not the nigger scum of Willesden and Kilburn or the thicko Irish up in Cricklewood.

He'd met Flaherty in the Zip. Mueller was good at seeing what people needed, what they wanted, what they craved.

It didn't take long for him to see that Flaherty needed a father almost as much as he needed money. Someone to tell him what the right thing to do was, someone he could look up to and trust. He'd even come to this apartment more than once, just the two of them, not the rest of the circus. Mueller liked him, liked his quick little feet, his sharp tongue. The kid had played some of his music, the stuff he needed the finance for. Most of it was crap, hardly a tune in there. Just noise. But that didn't mean that the arrangement they had wasn't sound. It was all respectable, civilised, mutually satisfactory. Yes, he'd liked the kid. Felt a special fondness for him. And Flaherty said he'd introduce him to some of the celebrities he knew, said he could get him into some of these clubs you saw in the magazines.

And then the stupid little shit had gone behind his back, made a foray up to the ancestral homelands. Well, Bernie Mueller couldn't stand for that, no matter how fond he was, no matter how his heart might be engaged. And it wasn't just Flaherty he had to take care of, although that had been handled very neatly, oh yes, more than one score had been settled there. But he'd still had to send Liss up to the frozen fucking wastes on an embassy to point out to the shit-eaters the way things were, how the big boys played. And Liss had let them all down.

Liss was ex-Para. Had good stories himself about sorting out the micks in Northern Ireland. The way they'd pick off a couple of joyriders each season, bit of payback for the shit they had to take. Funny he should have gone so soft, unless it was all part of the treachery, part of making Mueller look small, look weak. Liphook was just a psycho, never done any line of work other than inflicting violence. Thick, but reliable. For a psycho. Each thought himself superior in technique and accomplishments, and each wanted to be considered Mueller's right-hand man, but there was a degree of mutual respect between them, the knowledge that even if the other was not his equal, then the two of them together were the hardest fuckers around.

Liphook was pleased when Mueller told him to kill Liss. They were in a high place, with London glowing orange and white below them. Liphook was sunk low in a leather armchair, a beer cradled like a phallus in his hands.

'He's let me down badly,' Mueller said. 'He's let us all down. I sent him to do a job of work, and he botched it. Some little snivelling shit of a Northern cunt. Should have been put out of his misery. Sending a message. Now I look shit soft. Now I look like I don't pay attention to detail. Bad enough the fucking peasants up there think this about me. But news travels. As soon as London hears this, I'm suddenly looking at faces with a smirk all over them, suddenly there's whispering behind my back. Am I clear on this, Mr Liphook?'

'Clear as Evian, Bernie.'

'So I've got to get a little sanity into the situation. There's no need for any artistry. I'm not vindictive on this one. All I want is a bullet in his head, so the world knows I'm straight. Got that?'

'Sure, Bernie.' Liphook was smirking. It didn't mean much with him: his face smirked all by itself.

'You've been to his place?' Mueller had half an eye on the porn channel playing silently in the corner.

'Barbecue a couple of months ago. Chops, sausages, the works. Some sort of spicy yogurt marinade for the chops.'

'Sort of like a chicken tikka?'

'Yeah, but not red, boss, just a kind of creamy colour. And you know, on chops, not chicken.'

'Nice.'

'Yeah. Rained. You want me to do the wife and the kid?'

Mueller paused for a few moments.

'No, no. Like I said, no artistry. Unless they get in the way. Just ring the fucking bell, shoot him.'

'Nuff said.'

'Good boy.'

Liphook drove out to Stoke Newington. He brought his new weapon, a CZ 75 automatic pistol, made in Czechoslovakia. Lovely gun. Much better than that flashy Glock that Liss used. Half the world's police forces went for the CZ. Bought over the Internet as a neutered starting pistol for eighty-five pounds, and then given its balls back by a friend of a friend in Chelsea for fifty quid. Meant he had one of the most reliable and lethal handguns in the world for under a hundred and fifty notes. And it carried a sixteen-round magazine, none of your eight- or ten-round shit. Not that you ever wanted to be in a situation where you were loosing off that many bullets, but you never knew.

Liphook didn't have much faith in plans. It was one way in which he differed from Mueller and, to a lesser extent, Liss. Liss and Mueller were both army trained, where you had guys whose jobs were to make up that shit. That was the point of them. But the real world didn't work by plans. Following a plan meant ignoring the contours, it meant giving theory precedence over practice. Liphook's way was to go straight for what you wanted, but to think on your feet, to react to what was going on around you. So he was well into Mueller's conception of the thing. Like he said, ring Liss's bell. If Liss came to the door, he was going to smile at him, and then shoot him. If the woman came to the door, he was going to ask her if he could see Liss – she knew him, she knew they were partners. She'd get him, and then he'd shoot him. But then, whatever Bernie said, he was going to have to shoot her too. Nice-looking slut. Maybe give her one first. No need to do the kid, unless he got up.

Parking was a cunt. Two o'clock. Everyone tucked up. Liss lived in a house off the Green. A bit open at the front, but he remembered that the back door was nice and quiet. He thought for a moment about breaking in and shooting Liss where he lay. But he guessed that there were probably decent locks and other security measures – fucking lasers, for all he knew. Not *that* thick, Liss. So he rang the bell. He had his hands in his pockets, and the CZ was nestled nicely in his palm, safety off.

He rang again. He expected the lights to go on, expected Liss to open the door in his dressing gown. He looked forward to seeing his face change from irritation to surprise to dread as he saw the CZ come up. He was still smiling at that when the piano wire looped around his neck, and he knew that he was dead. The wire cut deep into his throat, and he couldn't have screamed had he tried. For some reason the pain wasn't sharp but numbing and dull, and it seemed to fill the whole top half of his body. He thought that the wire was going to take his fucking head completely off, and he didn't want that, thought it would make him look stupid, his head and his body not even fucking joined together.

He was going black, as if a sack were being lowered over him. And then the wire loosened, and he felt a hard punch in his kidneys, and he was down on the floor.

Liss was on his back.

'Why?'

He tried to answer, but nothing came out.

'Spit, you fuck.'

He tried to spit. He was very frightened. He knew that Liss was going to kill him, and he didn't want to die.

Finally he managed to whisper: 'You should have killed the cunt in Leeds.'

'There was no need. We'd made our point.'

Liss wished he had killed Jed Flaherty; wished it with all his heart. But it was too late for that now.

'Bernie took it badly.'

'So he sent you to sort it out?'

Liphook was thinking more clearly now. Perhaps there was a chance.

'Nah, mate, just to have a word, just to make sure you were still onside.'

Liss punched him again in the kidney, and Liphook convulsed with the agony. Something hard and cold was pressed against his cheek.

'I took this out of your fucking pocket. You don't take the CZ out just for a stroll. What about my fucking wife and my kid? What was going to happen to them? Were you going to do them too?'

'Jesus, we're mates! Nothing, I swear it. Look, it's true, Bernie said to give you a bit of a scare, a bit of a jostle, just to see if you were still sound. There was going to be no . . .'

And then he swung round hard with his elbow and made good contact with the side of Liss's head. He twisted out and up, and the two men were grappling. Liss still had the gun, but Liphook had his wrist. He hooked his leg around the back of Liss's calf and pushed him over. They fell together, with Liphook on top. He took a gamble, and let go of the gun hand, knowing that it would take a second to cock and fire, and that was all he needed. He landed two hard punches to Liss's chin, and then took the gun back. Liss looked him in the eyes, and spat, feebly. Liphook smiled back and put the barrel under Liss's chin, to absorb some of the sound.

That was when Liss's wife, Louisa, stabbed him in the back with a multi-purpose serrated kitchen knife, as good for slicing tomatoes as bread. Liphook still would have had time to kill them both before he died, but Liss used his surprise to knock away the gun, and then he put one arm around the back of his head and the other to his chin, and broke his neck with a click like a cracking knuckle, wishing all the time that that was what he'd done to that dumb tosser in Leeds.

22

What Wreath for Lamia?

I woke early the next morning. Despite the gin and grief, my mind was clear. Bernie Mueller was going to die if I could find him, and I knew how I could find him.

I put on a clean shirt and a pair of respectable trousers, and set off towards Hampstead. My limp was all but gone now, but I still brought my stick, and it took me only half an hour to reach the church. The service was at 10.30, and it wasn't yet ten, so I went and found my old place on the bench overlooking the ziggurats and towers of the city. The trees were beginning to shed their leaves, and the air was becoming cool, and I shivered a little, and wished that I had brought a coat.

I didn't think about how far I had come since I had last sat in this place, a shaking, jabbering junkie, unshaven, stinking, a tramp in all but name. This was not a time to rejoice in personal growth. I didn't even take in the beauty, the way I used to. I simply leant forward and smoked without pleasure, and thought over and over again of what I had to do, of the things I must say and the actions I must perform. Then bells started pealing, and I stood up, stretched and yawned, and walked towards God.

I found a seat at the back of the church – not in the bums' pew with my old pals, nor with the respectable families, who sat in the middle or at the front. No one stared at me. No one thought I was Jesus. I was just an anonymous lonely churchgoer seeking companionship and shelter from the storm. And there I waited for them to come. I didn't doubt that the woman and her daughter would be in church. The way they had appeared before and the response of those around them made it clear that they were regular and devout.

Music played. I didn't listen. The church was filling, and I became apprehensive. What if I was wrong and they did not come? What if they were out of London, or if some disaster had occurred to keep them away? Without the women I had no thread to lead me to Mueller and my plans would come to nothing. I tried not to fidget, not to jangle the change in my pocket, not to mutter mad incantations under my breath. And then they walked past me down the aisle, the red and the gold, their bodies touching, their feet in step. They appeared sacred and profound to me, and I was ashamed. They sat too far away for me to observe, but I was content that they were here. The service murmured by, and I tried to stand and kneel and sit at the right times to avoid drawing attention. I didn't listen to the readings or the sermon.

At some time in the service I drifted away. I was thinking about my time in North Africa, working as an archaeologist on the remains of Carthaginian towns lost under the sand. Down we would go through the surface, brushing away the centuries, and it would seem that there was nothing but the barren earth, until we would find a dark layer of carbon, marking the burnt end of a civilisation, and the beginning of our true work, and beneath the carbon we'd come across Roman artefacts, and then beneath the Roman, the Punic, my goal. And sometimes the local kids, urchins and orphans with clouded eyes and Gruffalo teeth, would come and watch us work, and laugh at what we were doing, but once I found a tiny terracotta figure of a flute player, and I showed it to the children, and they gathered round and reached out to touch the little boy. And then the Arab foreman shooed them away, and they broke up again, laughing and calling out, their skinny limbs flailing at the blue sky.

The service was over and people were leaving. I waited until my couple had walked by, and then followed them. I imagined for an ecstatic instant that the girl had looked in my direction, that her blue eyes had flickered with recognition, but then I thought that could not have been so, because I had changed so much since the last and only time that she had seen me. Outside the church the sky had turned grey and stormy, and the women of the parish were reaching for umbrellas, and the men were putting on coats. There was happy chatter among the parishioners, content and relieved now that their duty to God had been performed. A quiet priest, not fully at ease with his social obligations, shook my hand, his grip as passive and weightless as a falling leaf, and his eyes, fluid and unstable, slid past me on to the next person.

My women were stopped by other parishioners, who talked excitedly at them, old hands like birds' claws touching them, pulling them. The girl whispered into her mother's ear, and then went with a group along the side of the church. The Lamia paused for a few seconds, watching her daughter disappear, and then walked briskly away in the opposite direction.

Which way should I go? The Lamia, I guessed, would go straight home, and it would be sensible to follow her there. But there were other forces at work, and I found myself tracing the steps of the girl. A path led along the wall of the church, past large and imposing tombs. There was a thin line of people walking this way. We went down stone steps and into a building attached to the back of the church. It was dank and grim, and the line formed at a hatch, where a dusty white woman, and a man toiling in some kind of ancient servitude, were doling out cups of grey coffee and watery tea. There was an old ice-cream tub for donations, its bottom peppered with coppers and five-pence pieces. I put in a pound.

'Oh, thank you,' said the lady, her voice mingling suspicion and elderly delight. 'Biscuits through there, help yourself.'

'Only two each. I thought that was the rule,' said the man, mumbling into his hopeless yellow tank top, and the woman looked at him severely for having spoken, and I thought that things would not go well for him that day. 'It was you who made the rule,' he said finally, with great courage.

I took my plastic cup through to the room indicated by the woman. There were about a dozen people in there already. I noticed the tramp who had saved me from disgrace on my last visit. He was sitting by himself with a pile of pink wafers on his lap.

'Wonderful sermon today.'

Yet another of the ancient ladies was talking to me. She was wearing a man's trilby, and a heavy coat of many colours, most of them brown. Her face was oddly set, as if she were peering into a microscope. As she spoke, parts of her appeared to flake off and drift towards me. I had a vision of her crumbling to nothing.

'Yes, er, very much so,' I replied, trying to think of something religious to say. 'Uplifting.'

By good fortune it happened to be quite the right thing.

'Oh, I'm so glad you thought so too. And here he is, the

gentleman himself. The young man thought you uplifting, Gerald.'

I looked around. Gerald turned out to be the wan priest with the soft hands. His reply was so quiet I failed to pick it up at all.

By now the room was quite full. More elderly women were heading towards me, like Velociraptors after a wounded Triceratops.

'I must just get a biscuit,' I said, airily, and hurried towards a trestle table, laden with stale delights. And then I found that I was next to the strange and beautiful girl, whose long red hair I had first thought oily and lank, but which was now so bright and perfect that it seemed to glow with its own light. She was talking to another young woman, an African laughing loudly, the sound beautiful and incongruous in this place.

'Oh, look,' said the black woman, mischievously, 'another one under ninety.'

In fact there were a few kids running wild, poaching biscuits and hiding under the tables.

The redhead looked around, smiling, and the smile faded slowly from her lips when she saw me. Her eyes were almost at my level, and in the dim light here they seemed not blue but green. Little lines of perplexity formed between them, and her wide mouth began to shape a pout.

'I love you.'

For a second I thought the words might really have slipped out. They filled my consciousness like helium in a balloon.

'Wonderful sermon today,' I said.

'Really? I wasn't listening. I think I remember you. You came to church before.' Her voice was deeper than I'd expected.

253

'Yes, I've been once before. Months ago. But you wouldn't remember me. I was different then.'

I could see the girl trying to bring back an image.

'OK. But I'm pleased to meet you. My name's Emma.'

She put out her hand and I took it.

'And I'm Dorothea,' said the African, standing on tiptoe to look over her shoulder.

'Hello, I'm Matthew. Look, I'd appreciate it if you'd talk to me for a while, so that the Graeae don't get me.'

Dorothea smiled. 'Ah, you mean the Grey Ones? Three old hags who have to share a single tooth and single eye between them? You aren't really very nice, are you? Oh, but look who's just come in. I think I'll go and talk to him.'

I turned and saw that a young priest with public-school floppy hair had come into the room. Suddenly the whole place oriented itself towards him, like a field of sunflowers.

'Everyone loves Francis,' said Emma to me, confidingly. 'Dotty doesn't believe anyone can be holy and gay at the same time, so she still thinks she's in with a chance.' And then Emma glanced at me and blushed. 'Sorry, I shouldn't gossip when I don't even know who you are.'

'I promise not to tell. Do you come every week?'

'When I'm not at college. Whenever I'm home I come with Mummy. But I don't mind.'

'Where is she now?'

'Oh, she hates all this. She never comes into the crypt afterwards.'

'But you like it down here?'

She giggled, and then became grave. 'It's something to do. And sometimes,' she said, leaning towards me, almost whispering, 'they have Bourbon creams.'

'But not today.'

'If there were Bourbon creams every week there'd be no surprise. It's a metaphor for something. Life, I expect.'

'Where do you go to college?'

'I'm up at Cambridge.' She couldn't hide how pleased she was about it. I was pleased for her too.

'What do you study?'

'French and Italian. Why do you have that stick? I mean, you don't seem to need it.'

'Well, you know, like the Chinese say, talk softly, but . . .'

'Carry a big stick. Ha ha. It makes you look old.'

'I am old.'

'Not really.'

She looked at me seriously, and then she put a Rich Tea biscuit in her big mouth, and spun away from me, and found her friend Dorothea in the adoring crowd around the handsome priest.

I had spent long days imagining what this beautiful and strange girl would be like. I was expecting a fatal Pre-Raphaelite model: I'd never guessed that she was just a normal student, frivolous and funny. It would have made me smile if the circumstances had been different. One of the mistakes we always make is to imagine that beauty must bring with it profundity, but beauty can be the shallow water as well as the deep.

A few minutes later I escaped from the crypt, still shuddering with the aftershock from the sepulchral coffee. As I crept away, I saw that Emma watched me from the corner of her eye, and that her chatter stopped, and that she may have been about to come to me. Outside I waited in the shadows of the graveyard. It began to drizzle, and I took shelter under an old yew tree, and the air was dark and spun with spider's webs.

It wasn't long before Emma emerged with her friend, and they walked together out of the churchyard. I followed. At the gates they waved goodbye; Dorothea went along Church Row into Hampstead, and Emma back towards the Finchley Road. I'd had training in surveillance techniques back in my old Customs days, but that was overkill for this job. I stayed well back, and she didn't look behind her, but marched confidently through the fine rain, her strides long, her arms swinging. I just walked fifty yards behind her, making sure I always had her in sight. She disappeared somewhere on Frognal Lane. I hurried to where I last saw her and, as I suspected, saw that there was a gate in a wall. Frognal Lane has plenty of big houses behind high walls. It's a discreet area, the kind of place where those tired of fame live, or those who have other reasons to shun the world. I must have walked past this house a hundred times before: it lay directly on my old route to the graveyard. As a junkie, I vaguely envied the people who lived behind the high walls, thought how sublime it must be to ascend above the squalor.

I jumped to see what was beyond the garden wall. I caught a glimpse of an Arts-and-Crafty kind of house, red brick, leaded glass, high chimneys and low gables. It was a pretty house, and now that my mind was clear again, my envy spat like a cat.

I wasn't sure what to do next. I didn't want to talk to the Lamia with Emma there, and I began to regret not having followed the woman straight to her house. So I decided to sit and wait. It wasn't as if I had a range of other social obligations for the day. I crossed the road and found a sheltered spot where I could watch the gate without being seen. I had Ju's iPod with me, and that helped to pass the time.

It also helped to remind me what I was doing, why I was here. And I needed a reminder, because following the girl had made me feel like scum. But, as I listened, another thought came to me. I was thirty-eight, and I was listening to the same kind of music that I'd relished as a fifteen-year-old. True, the music compiled by Ju included various excursions around the world – Bulgarian choral music, Madagascan pop, Islamic religious wailing – but that was just a holiday, and home was the same old verse/chorus/ middle eight and round again formula. And I suddenly thought that perhaps I was too old for this, that the music was meant for kids who still think rebellion means listening to music that their parents can only hear as noise. And what a harmless way it is for using up the anarchic impulses of the young. It's exactly what the capitalist doctor ordered: a revolution in which you use all your money buying little discs made of plastic.

So why did the music still move me? Nostalgia, a reactionary emotion, not a revolutionary one. Because I haunted my own past; because I loved the things that had gone for ever, hated the present and feared the future. And pop music is a time machine in which, like the old joke about the Italian tank, the only gear is reverse.

The gate was opening. Emma walked boldly out, her arms swinging, her thick hair dancing. I shrank back, but she was happy and innocent, and wasn't watching for lurkers in the shadows. I had the same urge to stretch out to her, to caress her innocence and beauty, drawing some sustenance from it, that I'd felt all that time ago in the church when I was one of the bums. But she was safely away down the street and I quickly crossed back over the road and went through the gate. On the other side of the wall I was in a country-cottage garden a hundred years ago, with roses and lavender and sweet peas, and a bird bath on the lawn. I walked to the front door and knocked. After a few seconds the door opened. The Lamia was smiling, but her smile died when she saw that it was not whoever she'd been expecting. She had taken off her long raincoat and was wearing a white blouse and a black skirt, all wrong for church.

Her name. What did I call her?

'Mrs Mueller, I need to talk to you.'

She looked at me now with a puzzlement that turned gently to horror, and she tried to close the door. I put my stick in the way, and the hard briar splintered the softer wood of the jamb. I pushed my way in.

'Please, I'm sorry to do this, but a friend of mine has been killed, and I need to ask you some questions.'

'Get out, get out,' she screamed, finding her voice at last, and she flung herself on me, slapping and scratching at my face. I tried to hold her off without hurting her. I wasn't comfortable forcing myself into this woman's home, using my strength to overcome her fear, but I needed Mueller, and this was the only way. The woman stopped striking out at me and stood back.

'If you tell me what I need to know, I'll be gone, and you'll never see me again.'

'I remember you,' she said, hatred coiling like a cobra in her voice.

'Can I come in? I only want a minute of your time.'

And then she sprang at me again and clawed at my face, and I felt her nails tear into my cheek. I fought the impulse to strike her, fought against the red rage. She stood back from me, and now she was panting, and there was a feral look in her eye. Perhaps she was surprised at what she had done to my face. I was lost again, hopelessly out of my depth.

On impulse, I knelt on the floor before her, and held out my stick.

'Take this,' I said. 'You could kill me with it easily. I swear I'm not here to hurt you. I'm here because your husband killed my friend. I know that you hate Mueller. Help me find him.'

I dropped the stick at the woman's feet. She flinched away from it, and then stood back against the wall. She was sobbing, but I could not see any tears. Then she turned her back on me and walked out of the hallway and into a room. I hauled myself up and followed her.

I entered a room of calm, old-fashioned elegance. Light gleamed and danced on polished wood. There were flowers everywhere. That was my first impression. And then, after a few moments, I began to see that there were signs of decay: the flowers were dying; there were patches of damp on the walls; a window pane was cracked.

'Take this.'

The woman handed me a cloth, and I pressed it to my face and nodded my thanks. I looked at the cloth. There were three red streaks on it.

She sat down on one of the two sofas that faced one another across a coffee table. She was clutching a packet of cigarettes, and she fumbled one into her mouth, lighting it with a cheap plastic lighter.

'My daughter will be home soon. I don't want you here when she arrives.'

'I'll be quick.'

'And don't call me by that name again. I haven't used it for ten years.'

'Then what should I call you?'

'My name is Miranda Elliot.'

'And you remember . . . who I am . . . what happened between us?'

'Why should you think yourself memorable?'

'You said. . . . Well, *I* remember.'

She looked at me properly for the first time, and I looked back. As with the house, an initial appearance of perfection gradually dissolved. There was something wrong with her make-up – not, I thought, a carelessness: if anything the opposite. As with art and civilisation, it seemed that make-up might undergo the stages of development from early archaic, where simplicity and naïve energy ruled, through the perfection of the high classical period, before the descent into decadence, where over-elaboration, excess and folly drowned out the beauty. Eyes, skin, mouth – all had been subjected to the rigours of her art. Each lash, each puckered millimetre of lip, bore the marks of her attention. But still, the lipstick had run beyond the lips, and the mascara had left a dark dust below her eyes.

'Would you like a drink?'

I had been lost in contemplation, and at first her words were just a sound like the movement of leaves in the tree-tops. I had to blink my way back to the room, to the reality of her presence.

'Yes.'

And with her offer, and my acceptance, I knew that something was going to happen. She returned with two large glasses filled with vodka and tonic and ice and angostura bitters. I swallowed a mouthful. She sat opposite me, her short skirt high on her narrow thighs.

No, not very churchy at all.

'Why did you marry him?' I asked, concentrating on her face; on anything other than the thighs and the skirt.

'Because my parents hated him.' She half smiled through a plume of smoke, and the smile was as bleak as a drizzling sky. 'And because I was alone. I was beautiful once, you know. There was a time when I had London eating from my hand. And Mummy wanted me to marry into one of the great families, because she felt that that was her own birthright, and it had been taken away from her. I was a model, you know.' She paused, and I don't know exactly where Miranda Elliot was right then, but it wasn't in the house on Frognal Lane. 'David Bailey was in love with me, and Snowdon . . . oh, you don't care. But then time passed, and . . . things happened, and I wasn't a young girl any more, but a woman in her thirties. I met Bernie. He seemed so full of life. He had ambitions. He was going to help me to set up an agency. I took him to meet my parents in Sevenoaks. He brought a bottle of hundred-year-old Moët to impress them, but they thought he was so vulgar. And then I was pregnant. I didn't know what he was then. After we were married he . . . did things to me. If I'd known what he was . . .' Her face was ashen. 'You said you had a friend?'

'My friend was called Ju Flaherty. He was a musician. A good one. He got into money trouble. He went into business with Bernie. Then he tried to get out of it. Bernie killed him for it. Or had him killed.'

Miranda Elliot, my Lamia, put her hand to her mouth. 'I'm sorry,' she said. 'There's nothing he won't do. Nothing.'

'There's something else. Something to do with me. The night I wouldn't let him into the Zip Bar. Remember, you asked me? Well, after that, he had me beaten up. Worse than just beaten up.'

'So, you're not just trying to find him for the sake of your friend?'

'No, not just for the sake of my friend.'

'What will you do when you find him?' She had changed again. Now she was alert, almost eager.

'I don't know.'

'Will you . . . kill him?'

'I don't know.'

'Don't lie to spare my feelings. I want him dead. I want to be out of his reach. He still comes here. He still believes he owns me . . . us.'

'What about your daughter?'

'She doesn't know what kind of man her father is.'

'You never told her?'

'I tried to. But it's a difficult thing, when a child loves her father. I don't want her to hate me, and she would if I told her what he is like. And in ways he was good to her. It's his money; this is his house.'

'Why don't you get out of it, leave here?'

She looked at me as if I'd suddenly started speaking in tongues.

'And go where?'

'There's always somewhere else.'

'There's nowhere else for me.'

'I'm sorry, how you arrange your life is none of my business. Will you tell me how I can find him?'

She lit another cigarette and drew deeply into her lungs. She stretched her neck, and the space between her thighs opened another inch.

'Do you know the Wellbank building, in St John's Wood, overlooking the park?'

'Yes. Big modernist apartment block.'

'He has a penthouse at the top. Number eighty-two. What will you do to him? Tell me, please.'

'Bring him to justice.'

She snorted at the pomposity of the phrase.

'How? I want to know exactly what you'll do to him.'

She was leaning towards me. The fingers of her left hand were inside her blouse.

'I'm going to hurt him.'

'How are you going to hurt him?' Her eyes had become huge and black, the pupils dilated and ecstatic.

'I want to do to him what he did to me.'

'What was that? What did he do to you?'

And now her eyes were half closed.

'He beat me until I was unconscious. Him and two others. And then . . . then he would have killed me, but someone disturbed him.'

'So you feel that you have been . . . unmanned.'

'I didn't say . . .'

'He's hurt me too.'

'I know,' I said. 'And I'll hurt him back, for both of us.'

Up until that moment there had been something chilling and inhuman in her manner. She was like an implacable goddess above such human weaknesses as sympathy or love. But now she changed. She seemed to see herself, see what she had become, see that she was aroused by the thought of death. Perhaps she also saw how she had wasted her life in bitterness. Her shoulders narrowed, the fierceness of her melted away and, though her head was bowed, I could see the tears roll down her face.

And I couldn't leave her isolated in her grief, and not just from pity, but because her grief was my grief also, and we were bound together in this. So I moved to her side and put my arm around her. She resisted for a moment, but then pressed her face to my chest, and the tears soaked into my shirt. And then she looked up at me, and she was so helpless and lost that I felt I was the old one, and she opened her mouth, and I kissed her gently.

When I opened my eyes I saw Emma framed in the doorway, the Sunday newspapers in her arms, her fatal hair heavy on her shoulders, her face as empty and beautiful as a pharaoh's.

And then she was gone, and I stood up and rubbed my face with my hands. Miranda looked hurt and lost again, but then I think she began to understand something of what I felt, reading it in my face, and the Lamia reasserted herself, and the fierceness returned.

'Go,' she said. 'Hurt him.'

And I ran from the house like a coward with the witch at my back and demons flying around my head and the keening of loss in my ears.

23

I Skipped over Water

At home I tried to shower away the memories of the day, but I kept seeing Emma, her face blank with shock, and the hard, dry, metallic taste of the Lamia's flesh was in my mouth. But at least I now knew where to find my quarry, and I had no intention of delaying the end of my quest. I did think briefly about telling the police about Mueller and my belief that he was responsible for the murder of Ju Flaherty, but I was pretty sure he was too smart to leave any evidence of his involvement. Anyway, I was after a different kind of satisfaction.

At five o'clock I telephoned Jonah Whale. We hadn't spoken for a long time, a couple of months at least.

'Jonah, I need some help.'

'Well, son, you know I've always said that if there was anything I could do . . .'

'I need a gun.'

'A gun? Why in the name of Christ do you want a gun?'

'I can't tell you, Jonah. You have to trust me.'

'I'm not saying I don't trust you, but it's not easy, not like the old days. It takes some organising. When do you need it?'

'Tonight.'

'Can't be done, Matthew. And even if it could, I'd need to know more. Guns aren't my kind of weapon. Guns give courage to cowards, and when cowards get courage, that's when people start to die.'

'So you won't help me?'

'I can't help you. Not with the gun. But why don't we go out for a drink tonight? You can tell me what you've been . . .'

But I'd had enough, and as soon as was decently possible I said goodbye and put down the phone. A gun would have helped. Jonah was right about guns giving courage to cowards; it was exactly what I needed. I would have to find other props.

I had a black plastic clipboard that I used for lecture notes. I put a couple of sheets of lined paper on it, and scribbled some headings at the top. Then I got a brick from the street outside and put it in an old shoebox, and wrapped the shoebox up in brown paper and tied it with string, and wrote a name on the front, and an address. At six I put on a black jumper, black jeans and a black motorcycle jacket. I'd had the jacket since my student days, and I hadn't worn it for years. It was too tight to zip up, but it still looked OK when I left it open. I decided to walk down to St John's Wood. It took me an hour. Then I went into a pub I'd never been in before and drank two pints of beer. It was one of the islands of old London working-class culture, lost now in the sea of millionaires and celebrities that was St John's Wood. And as in most such islands, the natural gentleness and sympathy of the working man had been ousted by a grumbling sour resentment edged with violence and the threat of violence. Middle-aged men with fading tattoos and the big heads and short stout bodies of mushrooms stared at me with open hostility. Kids in sleeveless T-shirts and tracksuit trousers laughed and gulped lager. The barman held my tenner up to the light, and then passed it under a fluorescent reader, and then scrunched it under his ear, listening as intently as a safe-breaker. I wouldn't have minded, but I guessed that most of the other punters were burglars, car thieves, fences or rapists, so it seemed a touch harsh to pick on me. But sitting in the pub at least gave me the chance to gather myself, to smooth away the jangling nerves, to bury the doubts.

At about eight I got out of there and walked the ten minutes to the Wellbank tower. It took me a while longer to work out how the hell to get into the thing. I noticed that there was a car park in the basement, its opening blocked by a pole, with a keypad on one side, no doubt for the residents to punch in their codes.

When I finally found the lobby I was confronted by an oasis of palms and a pool with a trickling fountain and big goldfish with insane flowing fins like ball gowns. There was a desk, and a man in a cap, his mouth as pursed as a cat's anus.

'Help you?' he said, unhelpfully. He kept one eye on a bank of TV screens to one side.

'I've got a delivery here for a Mr . . .' I looked down at the address I'd written on the package . . . 'what's this? Muller.'

'Mueller?'

I looked again.

'Mueller, that's it. OK if I take it up?'

'You can leave it here.' I could smell his breath like sour milk from across the desk.

'Is he in?'

'He doesn't like to be disturbed.' Well that, at least, seemed to confirm that he was home, allaying my greatest fear.

'It's got to be signed for.'

'I'll sign.'

'Hey, give me a break, they said the recipient had to sign. Maybe you could call up, tell the guy I'm coming?'

'No. I said I'll sign. That's the way we do it.'

I looked at his cat's-arse mouth and his little eyes and his peaked cap of authority, and knew I wasn't going to get anywhere.

'Fine. Here you go.' I handed him the clipboard with the lined paper, and pointed with my finger. The porter made his mark.

I went outside again, aware that the porter was still watching me. I walked away down the street, and then doubled back. I'd checked out the lobby enough to see that near the bank of four lifts there was a door marked 'Emergency Stairs'. I assumed it must lead down to the car park as well as up to the floors above.

I slid under the pole. The car park was full of BMWs and Mercedes, along with a smattering of dinky little roadsters for the wives. There was no one about, but I had to be quick: one of the screens in the lobby covered down here, and if the porter saw me, I was in trouble. I found the door to the emergency stairs and began running up. The tower was at least twenty storeys, so this was going to take some time.

What I didn't know was that I wasn't the first person to take the back-stairs route to number 48, Wellbank Tower, that evening, and the person who had preceded me had a much greater burden than his own weight to carry.

Each floor was marked by a big red number, and I was at fourteen when I heard the sound of footsteps above me. There was no chance to hide, and so I put my head down and plodded on, assuming that the person descending was just some fitness freak who'd read in his copy of *GQ* that taking the stairs gives a better workout than an hour in the gym. I didn't want to meet the eyes of whoever it was, because I didn't want to be remembered, and if you don't see someone's eyes, then they never become more than a shape to you. So, despite the almost overpowering urge to look up, I kept my eyes on the floor as the figure approached, his feet heavy, but also quick on the steps. And then the person must have seen me, because he stopped, and I could hear his breathing, and it sounded too rapid for someone who has just run down the stairs. I plodded on, saying nothing.

I don't know how close I was to death then. Perhaps not close at all. Perhaps a glance away. If I was safe, it was because I did not look at the man, did not see of him anything more than a looming shadow on the wall. I passed him, and I sensed that he was scrutinising me, waiting to see whether I turned to him, waiting for some greeting. But I climbed on, trying not to show my fear, and then I heard him pound down the stairs again, and my heart grew calmer.

At the twenty-second floor the stairs came to an end, as, almost, had I. My legs were jelly, my back was drenched with sweat, my chest heaved and ached. Even my old knee injury flamed into life. I spent five minutes sitting on the stairs, my head in my hands. I knew that I had to be fired up for what I was going to do, and so I thought again about Ju, about our days together, about the sordid misery of his end, and even more than Ju, I thought about my humili-ation in the alleyway, the queasy, sexual horror of it, and my determination renewed itself as the sweat dried on my shirt, and the air came back sweet into my lungs.

I went through the emergency door and into a large,

well-lit space, and I was dazzled after the relative gloom of the stairs. There were two doors: one marked '47', the other '48'.

And then I stopped. I didn't know what to do next. Any competent person would have thought about this moment, the moment before the locked door. In my mind it was always inside the apartment, the desperate fight, the over-coming, the revenge. I would beat Mueller with my stick, take out any of his henchmen who happened to be there. But now here was a door, and in the door a spyhole. If I knocked, he would come and look through the hole, and see that it was me. Even if he could not recall the circum-stances of our last meeting, what made me think that he would open the door to me, smiling?

My alternative was to wait here until he came out. I knew he was in, and at some point he must, surely, emerge. And then I could push him back into the apartment, and finish.

It was nearly nine o'clock. It was Sunday. There was no guarantee that he wouldn't stay in for the night, watching the telly, or doing whatever it was that gangsters did on Sunday evenings.

No, I had to do something. I rang the bell. I checked in the pocket of the leather jacket for the thirtieth time: yes, the knuckle-duster was still there. I gripped the stick halfway down the shaft and smacked the head hard into my palm, partly to reassure myself with its mass, partly to keep myself alert with the pain.

Nothing.

I rang the bell again. And then I knocked with the stick, leaving a mark in the paintwork. My heart sank, and yet I felt a great relief. Bernie Mueller still frightened me. I thought I could overcome him, but there was a chance that he would prevail, and that the things he had done to me, or nearly done, would now be completed.

I waited another minute. I put my eye, pointlessly, to the peephole, and saw only the dark of my own pupil reflected back. And then I turned the handle. The door didn't open, but it rattled loosely: it was on the latch, unlocked. I'd never slipped a lock, but I'd seen it done, and I slid a credit card (expired a year before) into the crack, and turned the handle, and the door swung open before me.

I stood on the threshold, unable to move. Inside, the lights were on. I thought I could hear a TV somewhere, muttering and sniggering. I walked in, my steps as clumsy as those of a reanimated corpse. There were closed doors to my left and right, and ahead of me a line of light from one left ajar. I moved silently ahead. I listened at the door and heard the laughter and polite applause from the TV, but the gap was too narrow for me to see anything. Should I carry on with my silent approach, or should I slam back the door and crash in, my stick at the ready?

I pushed the door, and stood quietly as it opened.

The first thing I noticed was the line of windows, black and enormous with the night. And then I saw the chandelier, a huge crystal sneeze, like something in a Dubai hotel ballroom, and then I saw the big silver TV, and then I saw the black leather sofa, and then I saw the bodies of the two men, one half on the sofa, the other on the white sheepskin rug at its feet.

The man on the rug was lying face down. His right arm was thrown out to one side and there was a knife in his hand: a thick-bladed bowie knife, and the blade was dark. The man on the leather sofa was Bernie Mueller. I walked towards them, holding my stick out like a wand. More laughter from the TV. A dim host was asking questions of a pretty starlet. He was flattering her, pretending that she had conquered Hollywood. She looked familiar. Was it the woman from the Met Bar? But it was the face of Mueller which drew me, not the starlet. There was a bruise over his left eye. He was wearing a yellow silk dressing gown, open to show the thick grey hair on his chest. Except that most of the hair was matted with blood. The blood had spread from a gash going across his belly from side to side, rending the yellow silk.

There was a low table by a chair. There were two clear plastic bags on it, both torn open. One contained brown grains like raw cane sugar; one a white powder. I struggled to take the scene in. It looked as though the two men had been engaged in a fatal struggle. I tried to work out the choreography. The man on the floor must have given Mueller this slash in the guts, and then Mueller had somehow managed to retaliate, to knock him down. Or it was the other way round, and Mueller had mortally wounded the other man who, in his death throes, had managed to knife Mueller.

Either way, they both looked pretty dead. I moved next to the man on the rug. He was huge, square, oddly familiar. The back of his head was a mess, with white bone and grey brain mingled, ground in the mortar of his skull. I looked at the side of his face, and I nudged it with my foot to get a better look. I recognised one of the men who had beaten me in the alleyway. It was the one with the broken nose – what was his name? Liphook. And as I was looking at him, and enjoying the fact of his death, Bernie Mueller groaned, and another burst of laughter came from the TV. My hair stood on end, and I took a step back, stumbling over the body on the floor.

Mueller coughed twice, and then turned his head and vomited, the thin matter splattering his cheek, the sofa, the floor. He opened his eyes and tried to sit up, but slumped back down again with another groan. And then he saw me.

'Ambulance,' he croaked. 'Call an ambulance.'

'No.'

'What? Who are you? Why are you here?' His voice was barely a whisper.

'Don't you remember me?'

He squinted at me, and shook his head, although it might have been to clear his vision.

'Should I?'

'You left me for dead once, in an alleyway. I stopped you from going into a bar, and for that you would have killed me.'

Mueller looked puzzled for a moment, and then began to laugh, but the laughing turned back into coughing. He put his hand to the slit in his stomach. Then he held the hand up before his eyes, trying to understand what had happened to him.

'Oh God, the cunt,' he said. And then he looked back at me. His face showed little of the terror and pain he must be feeling. 'Is that why you're here? To pay me back? You're a little late for that, old son.'

'Not just for that. What happened here?'

'Call me an ambulance. I'll pay you. I'll give you ten thousand pounds.'

'Tell me what happened. This man worked for you. Why did he attack you? The drugs. . . . ?'

Mueller again tried to laugh, again lost it in anguished coughing. He seemed able only to move his head and one arm: the rest of him was immobile. He was breathing heavily, and his face carried a sick film of sweat, but I could see him making calculations, trying to find a way to live.

'Not him, not him. I had two boys. Liphook and Liss. Liss let me down. He was supposed to do a job for me in Leeds. But he chose to go his own way. He had ideas. He was making plans. I had to act. So I sent this one, Liphook, to put things right. But Liss was too good for him. And then he knew that he had to put me out of the picture. He brought the body here. Carried him up the fucking stairs: twenty-two floors with a man on his back. He held the face up to the peephole. I let him in.'

Mueller stopped, exhausted. I waited.

'He staged this to make it look as though we'd killed each other over the drugs. Up the fucking stairs. Strong man. Fucking idiot. Hit me, then did this to my belly when I was out. Didn't think I'd wake up. Thought I'd leak away here. Didn't know that I am strong too. Didn't know someone would come. Call the ambulance. Fifty thousand pounds. All we did was give you a slap, teach you a lesson. Good compensation, eh?' He smiled a ghoulish smile, the saliva thick and white in his mouth.

'If it was just me, that's what I'd do. But it's not just me.'

He didn't seem to understand.

'OK, how much do you want? Say it.'

'How much have you got here?'

'You say how much you want.'

'Your time's running out. How much longer can you live with your guts peeping out like that? Another twenty minutes?'

Mueller looked at me, still appraising, still calculating. And I was still afraid of him.

'There's a safe. In the bedroom. The key's here.' He moved his hand feebly towards his trouser pocket.

I stood beside him, and put my hand in his pocket, and felt the key. And Mueller grabbed my hand, and pulled me close to him. I couldn't believe he still had the strength. I was too startled to struggle. His mouth was an inch away from mine, and his breath burnt like acid.

'You take the money, then you call the ambulance, you hear? Do you hear me?'

'Sure. Let me the fuck go.'

He threw my hand down.

'Where's the bedroom?'

He nodded back into the hallway.

'First left. Safe in the wardrobe.' I could hear that he was tiring, that he was dying.

I found the safe, a small metal cube. Inside it there was a black felt bag with a draw-string. I opened it. There were two wads of notes, one of twenties, one of tens, each four inches thick. I had to put a steadying hand on the wardrobe. There was something else in the safe: a handgun. Some kind of automatic. I put it in my pocket and went back into the room. Mueller was watching the TV.

'How much is here?' I asked, holding up the bag.

'Sixty-eight thousand pounds. Loose change. Ha ha. Now call the ambulance.'

'Not yet.'

'What the fuck not yet?' There was panic in his voice for the first time. I liked it: it made me feel stronger. 'You do this and I'll give you more. The same again.'

'A name: Ju Flaherty.'

Mueller looked at me, his rheumy eyes swimming, his gaze going in and out of focus. His mouth opened and closed, and he licked his lips.

'What he to you?'

'He was my friend.'

'He was a cunt. He cheated me.'

'So you killed him.'

'He was a crook. A thief. Why do you care?'

'I told you: he was my friend.'

Mueller laughed again, the sound like a deflating tyre.

'Do you think he gave a fuck about you? He had no friends. He was scum. He'd have done anything, sold anyone. For his fucking stupid tunes. Couldn't even dance to them. Nursery rhymes. The boy was a fucking pansy. Women's clothes. Pervert. Sick.'

'I don't care. He was my friend.'

'Well, I didn't kill him.' There was a petulant note now.

'You mean you didn't personally. So who did – this one?' I kicked the body on the floor. 'Or the other, the one who sliced you?'

Another almost silent laugh. He was going to tell me. He couldn't stop himself.

'So you were the punk in the alleyway. And who was it who saved your neck? Yes, the big man. Well, the big man's not really so big. He took something that belonged to me that night, and that meant he owed me one in return. And he isn't stupid enough to carry a debt to Bernie Mueller. So I asked him to pay it back. A life for a life. I didn't want my boys getting mixed up with Flaherty, didn't want to leave a trace. So I sent Whale. And Whale did a good job. He took pictures so I'd know he hadn't double-crossed me. Poof wearing a skirt.'

Jonah.

My head was reeling. I felt sick. Jonah couldn't have killed Ju. But of course Jonah had killed Ju. Killed him because he owed Mueller. Owed Mueller because he had saved me.

The blood spread out and touched everyone, linking us together like a family. I hated myself, and I hated Jonah.

'Forget more money,' I said, coldly. 'I don't want more money. I want Jonah. Will he come if you call him, if you tell him?'

'What is this shit?'

'Will he come? If you phone him, I swear I'll get the ambulance. I'll call them straight away, they'll come before Jonah. Make it good. Get him here.'

Mueller was drifting, not thinking clearly.

'Phone,' he said, pointing to the coffee table with the drugs.

There was white powder on the phone. I blew it clean, and dialled. Then I put the phone to Mueller's face. He half raised his hand to take it, but was too weak. And then he was speaking.

'Mr Whale. Yeah, me. No, don't feel so good. Got some money here for you. Fair to pay for the job, keep everything friendly. No, right now. Sick. 'Bye now.'

I took the phone away.

'Call,' he said.

I looked at him, and sat down in a deep, comfortable chair, facing the door. I put the phone on the arm, and the gun next to the phone.

'Call, please,' he said again, so faintly I could barely hear him. I reached over and picked up a magazine from the table. *Country Life.*

'You read this shit? Don't tell me you've got a place in the country. You probably breed racehorses, go fucking fox-hunting.'

Mueller's mouth was opening and closing. I didn't then try to think about what might be going through his mind.

Now I wonder whether he was reliving his past glories, the victories over his enemies, the humiliations and sexual degradation he inflicted. Or was he filled with impotent rage and frustration? So many more things to do. Or perhaps he thought of his mother, and imagined that she was here with him, taking his head in her soft arms, singing him to sleep.

> I had a little nut tree, nothing would it bear,
> but a silver nutmeg and a golden pear.
> The king of Spain's daughter came to visit me,
> all for the sake of my little nut tree.
> I skipped over water, I danced over sea,
> and all the birds in the air couldn't catch me.

I got up and unlocked the front door to the flat, and I left the door into the living room open. Then I went and stood before the big windows. We were high here, and London looked magnificent, as if the Milky Way had fallen to earth, and folded itself into the contours of the land, like a sleeping cat.

'Whatever you want.'

It was just a whisper from Mueller. Whatever I wanted. I looked out over the pattern of light, and I thought about Christ taken to a high place by Satan and offered all the kingdoms of the world, and the glory of them. But I knew that what I wanted from Bernie Mueller he was already giving me.

I went back to the chair. From where I sat I could see both doors, the inner and outer. And there I waited calmly for Mueller to die and for Jonah to come. Every few minutes I'd glance at Mueller, and he would be staring at me, a look of childlike wonder on his face. One time I looked, and the dressing gown had sloughed open, exposing his genitals. I got up and flicked it back across. His eyes caught mine, and he mouthed a word. I think it was 'water'. I sat down again, and read an article about poplar trees, how much less oppressive they were as a windbreak than *Leylandii*, how much better for wildlife. If we wanted the golden oriole to return we must plant more of the poplars in which they nested. There was a photograph of a pair. He was a pure yellow, vibrant as a van Gogh sunflower. She was a pretty green, drab only in comparison to her mate. Yes, I thought, let us plant poplars and encourage these beautiful birds.

'He'll eat you alive.'

I looked up at Mueller. He was completely grey, and at last his eyes were closed, but I could still see his chest rise and fall. And then I turned back to the magazine.

Twenty minutes later I sensed a shadow, and looked up, and Jonah was there, watching me.

'I'm sorry to see you here,' he said.

I picked up the gun and rose slowly to my feet.

'Come in, Jonah.'

Jonah walked into the room. He looked at the corpse of Mueller, and then at the other body.

'What has occurred here?'

'Well, I don't know exactly, but I think Mr Mueller sent this man to kill another man, but the other man killed this man, and then meant to kill Mueller, making it look as though Mueller and this man had killed each other. And he left these drugs lying around so it looked like they'd fought over them. And I think we know where the drugs are from, don't we, Jonah?'

There was only the tiniest of pauses before he said: 'I took them from Flaherty, the musician.'

'When you killed him.'

'Let me explain, Matthew.'

'You don't have to explain. Mueller said you owed him a life. But you know what, you didn't owe him a life. You didn't owe him anything. You killed an innocent person.'

'He wasn't innocent. He was a drug dealer. He was . . . corrupted.'

'He was lost.'

'Perhaps he was lost.'

'Tell me what you did to him.'

'I told him that his time had come. He was calm. I said that there was an easy way. That I could give him an overdose of the heroin. He understood. He accepted.'

'How could he accept his death? He had everything to do . . . everything . . .'

'Because he understood what he had become. Because he had lost himself. It was the word you used. And he put on . . . the clothes, the woman's clothes. It was the thing he wanted. It wasn't a bad way to die. There was nothing more left inside him.'

'You didn't have to do what Mueller told you.'

'You don't understand. It's the way. I would have been dead.'

'You could have left.'

'I have nowhere else. This is all there is. This or death.'

'Death, then, Jonah.' And I raised the gun. Jonah was ten feet away from me. He said that Ju had faced death calmly, and he was calm now. The gun shook in my hands.

'Matthew, if you do this the act will haunt you for ever.'

'Will Ju haunt you?'

'They all haunt me.'

'Well then, this is your release,' I said, and I pulled the trigger.

Nothing happened. I looked at the gun. I didn't know

anything about guns, but I didn't think it was empty. Safety catch. Couldn't see one, wouldn't have known one. Jonah walked over to me and took the gun out of my hand.

'Go away, Matthew,' he said. 'Go away for ever.'

'You said there was nowhere else.'

'Not for me. Perhaps for you.'

We looked at each other. Jonah appeared ancient, immovable, but I held his eyes.

'What will you do?' I asked.

'I want to look around here, make sure there is nothing to link me to these people, to this place.'

'I took the money from the safe,' I said. 'Mueller said he would give it to me if I called an ambulance.'

'Then call one in half an hour, earn your money.'

I picked up the bag.

'You killed my friend. I don't care if he was corrupt. It makes you evil.'

Jonah closed his eyes for a second and then opened them again.

'Flaherty told me something. He said that the drugs were not his idea. He said that the man at his record company suggested it, and put him in contact with Mueller.'

'Did he say who?'

'Adam, or Adams, I think.'

I nodded, and stood there for a while, gazing out at the black sky and the starry earth.

'I need this,' I said, more to myself than to Jonah, and I picked up a packet of heroin along with the money and left the apartment.

It was after twelve. I thought about getting a night bus, but then decided to walk. There was a place where I used sometimes to lie and smoke at night – a grassy bank outside a petrol station. I went there now. I lay back and gazed again into the cloudy night. I was still experiencing the cold numbness that had filled me since I entered Mueller's flat, but by tiny increments feeling returned. It wasn't nice. I had enough philosophy to understand that I'd killed Mueller. I could have called the ambulance and saved him, but I hadn't. And the act was premeditated: I'd gone there to kill him, I'd just chosen a cowardly way to do it.

And then I'd aimed and, in intention if not in fact, fired a gun at Jonah Whale's head.

I hated Jonah for killing Ju, but he'd done it only because he owed Mueller for saving my life. Oh Jesus, the world was fucked up. I was fucked up.

Well, there was someone else who needed to be fucked up too.

24

Hellbent

At ten o'clock the next morning, a grey, chill Monday, I walked into the Hellbent offices in Holland Park. The cute girl on reception had changed her ponytails to plaits, and her nails were purple rather than black, but she was still cute. She looked at me, trying to remember where she'd seen me. I said a bright 'good morning', and went straight up to the turnstile. I tapped in the number of the beast and I was through. The girl was still looking at me, trying to work out what she should do, but in the end she did nothing. I was probably the new geek come to install a firewall. Or something.

I took the cool lift all the way up to the third floor and punched in 666 again to get into the room. A couple of heads turned when I entered, but it was Monday morning and they all looked red eyed and zonked from their weekend of clubbing or self-abuse. I marched down the middle of the room between the tear-shaped desks to Adams' office. I went straight in without knocking.

He was sitting back with his feet on the table, talking into a phone held in the crook of his neck. His eyes opened wide when he saw me. I stood in front of him and put my rucksack on the desk, pushing his feet aside to make space.

'Hey, look,' he said, 'I'll get back to you in a minute . . . yeah, you too.'

He was in the act of putting the phone back in its cradle when I opened the rucksack, stuck in my hand and pulled out a fist full of pale brown powder.

'What the f . . .' was all Adams managed before I grabbed his hair and ground the powder into his face. I rubbed it into his eyes, into his nose, and into his mouth. It spilled over the desk and the floor. I grabbed another handful of the smack and did it again. He was screaming by now, and he tried to get up, so I punched him twice on the side of the head.

The door opened behind me. I turned round to see Coen and Thurber. Coen stood in the doorway with his mouth hanging open. It was Thurber who shouted: 'What's going on?'

I held Adams's head up. His eyes had swollen shut and he was sobbing.

'Tell 'em, Billy. Tell them what you made Ju do to finance his album. Tell them what the brown stuff is, Bill. What . . . no? Can't speak? Or do they already know? OK, Mr Thurber. This is heroin. He's probably ingested enough to kill him, so you'd better call an ambulance. And I'd stick my fingers down his throat, if I were you, to make sure he isn't dead before it gets here. And if you want to call the police, that's cool too; I've a great story for them.'

Then Coen ran towards me, shouting something, I don't know what. I knocked him down, but that meant letting go of Adams. He sprawled on the floor and vomited.

'Why don't you calm down and tell me what this is about?' said Thurber. The doorway behind him was full of wondering faces, as the whole office had gathered to see the fun.

'Don't act the fucking fool, Thurber. I'm guessing you're

not part of this, but you just might be. Adams knew that Ju's record was only ever going to lose you money, and he never planned to release it. He didn't even want Ju spending money in the studio, so he starved him out and ground him down, and then suggested he help himself to a little drug money.' I bent down and dragged Adams up by his collar and threw him into his chair. 'That right, Billy?' When he didn't answer I slapped his face. 'I said, *is that right, Billy?*'

'Yeah,' he slurred. And then, 'I need help.'

'Soon enough. More than Ju ever got. Because Ju got in over his head, didn't he, Bill? He had to mix with people who do that shit for a living. He didn't understand the game. They killed him, Bill. And tell me, Billy, why did you hire me?'

I knew the answer, but I wanted to hear it from him. But it was Thurber who answered.

'Because you're a two-bit loser, a waste of fucking space. You were never going to find anyone. But at least it made it look like they were trying.'

I pulled my fist back, and I would have punched Adams again, but Thurber stepped up and caught my arm.

'Enough,' he said. I shook him loose, but I didn't hit Adams.

'Hey, Coen,' I said, the rage beginning to ebb, 'you knew it was Ju back at his flat, didn't you? You knew. So why didn't you tell the police? You told me you were going to tell the police.'

Coen was wiping his bloody nose, but it was Thurber who spoke again.

'I think I know the answer to that one too. Adams was about to sell the rest of his stake in Hellbent to Matsushika. A screw-up like this, one of his artists . . . well, Billy, maybe even the suits at Matsushika would notice something like that, maybe call it off, maybe think again about value.' He shook his head. 'Someone call an ambulance,' he shouted over his shoulder. 'OK, Moriarty, what do you plan to do about this?'

'I've just done it. And here's my bill.' I handed him a typed note and a stash of receipts. 'Comes to eight thousand pounds. I'll take a cheque.'

25

I Danced over Sea

Hellbent, now fully owned by Matsushika, hushed up the drugs, but the stink of it hung like a cloud over Adams. Billy had the money from the sale of his share of the company, but he was out in the cold, and that was tough for a limelight junkie like him. The last thing I heard he was managing some shitty band lucky to get a gig in a Camden pub. Coen went back to the States, where doubtless he's still kissing arses for a living. Hellbent released the *Nut Tree* album, trying to go for a John Lennon/Jim Morrison death-cult thing. They left the loose ends and the sparse production. The critics liked it, and enough old fans bought it to make the venture worthwhile, but Ju never burst out of his cult status. Maybe another generation will discover him, and he'll be the Nick Drake of the 2020s.

His funeral was in Leeds. His brother was there, in a black suit a size too small for his bulk, supporting his mother. I gave my condolences to Mrs Flaherty and she said, 'God bless you, Matthew,' and Jed looked at me blankly, though I suppose he was contemplating murder. But not yet. Mrs Flaherty looked sober, but I guessed she was going to be drinking the rest of her life away. Ju's royalties, modest as they were, would help her. The church held a smattering of fans, and a few music-business types, session musicians and roadies. Charlie Mercer was there, smelling like a field of burning ganja. Some of our old school friends were there as well. Some I recognised; some recognised me. I was spending the night with Simon in Seacroft, and the rest of the gang joined us there, and we played Ju's music through the night, and there was more joy than misery.

The local papers back in London were full of the Mueller killing. Forensics saw through the charade, and the police were soon looking for the third man. They finally found Liss, holed up in Kent. He told the story straight, and that helped me to fill in the gaps. His plea of self-defence worked on the Liphook murder charge, but not with Mueller. He got life, and his wife wept in court.

And me? Well, I was a wealthy man. I had Mueller's blood money, and I had the eight thousand pounds I'd earned from Hellbent for tracking down Ju. I didn't have much else. I wanted to find Emma, to tell her about myself, about what I had done, about how I had become the person I was; to tell her about her father. But I didn't have the courage or boldness to face her, and most of all I was terrified of meeting the Lamia again. So I filed Emma away as another lost love, lost without being found, lost without her ever knowing that she had been loved.

I knew that I needed some serious redemption, and there was a lesson for me in the corruption of the medieval church: I was going to buy my way out of hell.

Not many of us can name and date our own personal original sin. I could. Years before, when I had been working as an archaeologist in Tunisia, I had slept with a girl who may not have been able to give her consent. It was an act that I repented daily, an act that drove me to my knees. It was too late now to do anything about that act of desecration, but there were other ways in which I could atone, and even if they could never truly assuage my personal guilt, they could at least add some counterbalancing good to the world's evil.

Two days after Ju's funeral I flew to Tunis, bringing only hand luggage. I had Mueller's money stuffed into my pockets. I walked through security at Heathrow, and again at Tunis, sweating and cringeing, but nobody stopped me, and all that happened was a brief bag search at Tunis. From Tunis I took a bus down the coast to Sousse. I stayed the night in a hostel, sleeping in my clothes, paranoia racking my body like malaria. The next morning I caught another bus for Sfax.

Tunisia is a beautiful country but I took none of it in: my journeys were internal, my path dark and obscure. Some of the locals talked to me, and when they asked what I was doing, I told them something close to the truth, and they became silent, and smiled at each other.

I arrived at the busy bus station in Sfax in the burning heat of the afternoon. I asked the way of a couple of kids, and soon I had a train of laughing helpers, who took me to the convent. Years before, the leader of the dig I was working on, a professor with an Old Testament beard, and baggy shorts, organised various trips to take in the local culture. It was all part of ingratiating ourselves with the Tunisians, which helped get the permit to carry on our work. One trip was to the Convent of St Theresa in Sfax. The French nuns ran an orphanage for handicapped kids. Tunisia is progressive and enlightened by North African standards, but children born limbless, or with Down's syndrome, or those lost in solitary madness, don't fare well. The dozen or so nuns kept them clean and fed them, and there was a palpable sense of love, but that was about all they could do. They needed money. On that trip we chipped in a hundred Tunisian dinar, maybe fifty pounds. The nuns were ecstatic, and promised to pray for us.

We reached the convent. It was the same concrete box as before, baking in the heat, cold at night. Perhaps more run down. I gave my guides some coins, and waited in an office, where a silent nun fingered her rosary in front of an ancient acoustic typewriter. After half an hour I was shown in to the Mother Superior, Sr Carmel. She was tiny and hunched, and her chin sprouted grey hairs. We spoke in French, and she smiled at my articulation, which was rusty and old fashioned.

'I have come with a donation from England.'

'We are always delighted to receive gifts.'

I took the money out of my pockets, and put it on her desk in an untidy pile.

Sr Carmel looked at me gravely.

'This is so much money. I am uneasy.'

'It was donated by the people of London for you, for the children.'

Still the nun looked at me, her face showing more concern than pleasure. And then she sighed.

'I will give you a receipt.'

'That's not necessary.'

'It is required.'

She took out a pad from a drawer and laid it on the desk. She then began counting the money. I looked around the room: at the crucifix on the wall, at the lurid picture of the Sacred Heart of Jesus. There was an old calendar, kept, I thought, for the sake of the picture of a laughing African boy drinking milk.

When she was satisfied that she had tallied the amount

correctly, Sr Carmel began to write out my receipt. From somewhere I heard a disconsolate wailing, and then the sound of running feet, and then the wailing ebbed into sobs, and the sobs into sighs. She handed me the receipt, and I made as if to stand, but I could not.

'Sister, I would like to stay here, if I can. For a time.'

The words were a surprise to me, until they came out. And then I knew them, and what they signified.

'Stay?'

'Sister, to help.'

'There are many ways to do God's work. Is this just ostentation?'

I could not look into her face.

'Sister, it is for my soul.'

Finally I looked up, and saw that she was smiling.

Acknowledgements

My thanks to Alex Bonham at Hodder & Stoughton for all her help and encouragement. Thanks also to Jamison Stoltz at William Morris.